Praise for David Kyle's previous epic
THE DRAGON LENSMAN.

A. E. Van Vogt:
"An amazing literary achievement. Kyle pervades the vast universe created by the late, greatest SF writer. I recommend it without reservation to all who read and enjoyed the stories of E. E. Smith, Ph.D."

Richard Lupoff, *San Francisco Chronicle:*
"Any devoted fan who has read and reread Smith's Lensman books will find THE DRAGON LENSMAN a labor of love, the closest approach in spirit and style to Smith's efforts."

Baird Searles, *Isaac Asimov's SF:*
"It's great fun, and Kyle has caught the charming quality of Smith's prose. If you haven't read the old ones, let this one lead you into them."

LENSMAN
FROM
RIGEL

David A. Kyle

**Based on the characters
created by E.E. "Doc" Smith**

BANTAM BOOKS
TORONTO · NEW YORK · LONDON · SYDNEY

In memoriam to
"Doc"
The First Historian
and
Ron Ellik
The Second Historian

Dedicated to
Van and Hal
and always
The Galactic Roamers

LENSMAN FROM RIGEL
A Bantam Book / October 1982

ISBN 0-553-20499-8

Published simultaneously in the United States and Canada

Bantam Books are published by Bantam Books, Inc. Its trade-
mark, consisting of the words "Bantam Books" and the por-
trayal of a rooster, is Registered in U.S. Patent and Trademark
Office and in other countries. Marca Registrada. Bantam
Books, Inc., 666 Fifth Avenue, New York, New York 10103.

PRINTED IN THE UNITED STATES OF AMERICA

0 9 8 7 6 5 4 3 2 1

Contents

Foreword

The exploits of Tregonsee of Rigel IV have hardly been documented by the historical research department of the Galactic Patrol. This book is the first to give proper recognition to the extraordinary contributions to the progress of Civilization by the Lensman from Rigel.

Until the beginning of the new series of adventures in the universe of the Lens of Arisia, the official chronicler had been exclusively E.E. "Doc" Smith. Then came the first book, *The Dragon Lensman*, which was about Worsel, the Second Stage Lensman from Velantia, written by the new head of the Patrol's historical section. Previously, the half-dozen books by Doc Smith explained the coming of Civilization and its powerful champion, the Galactic Patrol, with the great Tellurian, Kimball Kinnison, in the central role. The time had come to pay proper tribute to other Lensmen of other alien races and Worsel was the first. This time it is Tregonsee who is honored.

The time of our story falls within the early part of the twenty-year period marked by the marriage of Kinnison to the Red Lensman, Clarrissa, and the maturity of their very special children of the Lens. The conspiracy of evil represented by Boskonia, a mysterious network of criminals, had been smashed by Kinnison leading the Grand Fleet of the Galactic Patrol into a titanic battle near the planet Klovia in Lundmark's Nebula, the Second Galaxy. In the mightiest clash of arms ever in the history of space, sending thousands upon thousands of warships into conflict against each other, the enemy had been defeated. The two galaxies were safe and the Patrol then began its new task of dismantling the remains of old Boskonia.

What at first seemed a simple task, however, was not. From the shattered confederation of hundreds of thousands of solar systems which was Boskonia, there grew a new threat. Like the severed parts of a beast which refused to die, but which, instead, instinctively fused together to re-form a creature and thus renew its malignant ways, the parts of the conspiracy came together as another challenge to Civilization. This was the Spawn of the Boskone.

The trouble with the Spawn came in the Second Galaxy, newly conquered and, under the direction of the Galactic Council, now governed by Kimball Kinnison himself.

The Second Galaxy was the twin of our own native Milky Way galaxy. Billions of years ago that lenticular spiral galaxy had, through the miracle of chance, run headlong into the starry disk that was the Milky Way and the two of them had for an unimaginably long period of time passed one through the other. Billions of planets had been formed and on them life, seeded by the spores of the ancient race of Arisia, had begun to evolve. Civilization thus was born. And the dark counterforce, too, was also born to dispute its future.

Arisia, from which the life forms of goodness and morality came, was the home of an unimaginably ancient race in the young Milky Way, existing before the Coalescence of the galaxies. The Arisians had advanced almost to the ultimate in evolution when the new planets were forming. By force of mind alone, they were the benevolent masters of their section of the universe. On a planet much like Earth, almost alone as a habitable world in a planetless galaxy, they had prospered. Now they looked forward to the time in the incredibly distant future when their seed would populate the billions of new worlds and rise to far greater glory than their own.

There was, however, a serpent in paradise, ready to lead the children of Arisia into evil, chaos, and an eternal living death. This monstrous malevolence from an alien plenum was the race of Eddorians who had stumbled from universe to universe into the Coalescing galaxies and discovered virgin worlds which they could corrupt and rule as masters over slaves for the pure pleasure of total power.

The ablest thinkers of Arisia, however, recognized the threat and instituted their plan to foil the Eddorians and to give Civilization its chance for liberty, freedom, and its destiny of goodness. The Arisians were almost, but not quite, omnipotent. They could not alone destroy the Eddorians. Their means for ultimate success lay in the creation of the Galactic Patrol by one of four Civilized planets, Earth, also known as Tellus or Terra. With the Tellurians joining with the other three centers of intelligent races, Rigel IV, Velantia III and Palain VII, the Patrol grew in strength. Unfortunately, at the same time, Eddorians infiltrated these planets and thousands more lesser ones and stimulated irrational thought and criminal activities in order to destroy the positive forces of Civilization.

The Eddorians through milleniums were the destroyers while the Arisians were the builders. In their fundamental clash, Civilization rose and fell and rose again.

With the development of intelligent and responsible races, the Arisians watched over them. A four-ply mentality of four of the greatest Arisians fused together to form Mentor of Arisia. Every Lensmen knew about Mentor and Arisia, despite the fact that under ordinary circumstances Arisia, a strange planet with unique properties, was absolutely unapproachable except by invitation. Every Lensman knew about Mentor and Arisia because from them came the fantastic Lens of Arisia which each specially-chosen Patrolman wore.

The Lens was a living disc of some million crystalloids worn on the flesh, sometimes like a spectacularly glowing wristwatch, sometimes like an inset jewel on an entity's brain case. Whoever had it had been singled out by Mentor for this Lens which matched the individual's life force, multiplying strength and developing latent talents, and providing astounding communicative powers. It was also a symbol of the best of all Civilized life, for those who wore it were the finest guardians, protectors, and champions of Civilization.

Lensmen were in the forefront of the cosmic struggle of Arisian against Eddorian, of goodness against evilness. The expanding cultures of the many races of two galaxies teetered in the balance between good and bad as the lives and souls of all kinds of intelligent life forms were pushed and pulled this way and that. Lensmen knew that goodness was Arisian;

they knew that badness was Boskonian. They did not know what the Arisians knew, that the ultimate enemy, the terrible leaders at the very top, were the horrible, most vile aliens of any time and space—the Eddorians.

Tregonsee had been one of a relatively small number of Rigellians who had broken with their indifferent racial attitudes toward galactic cooperation. He had joined the Patrol, taken Lensman training, and had risen to be one of the four greatest Lensmen ever, a Gray Lensman of free and unattached status, and then, finally, a Second Stage Lensman personally developed and trained by Mentor itself. Tregonsee had helped defeat Boskonia. Now it was time to help defeat its Spawn.

Doc Smith knew Tregonsee intimately, for he first encountered him as a Lensman on the weird planet of Trenco, where the insidious drug thionite originated. Tregonsee has served the Patrol well and Doc would have told his story with the great affection he had for this rather grotesque but brilliant intellect. Your present historian has tried to capture the personality of this strange alien who is so cool in a crisis, so philosophic about the eternal struggle, and so capable of human understanding of a race from which he is so different. Once again, this historian pledges to be faithful to the spirit of the worlds of the Lens.

DAVID A. KYLE

Tellus

Prologue

~ꝍꝍꝍꝍꝍꝍꝍꝍꝍꝍꝍꝍꝍꝍꝍꝍꝍꝍꝍꝍꝍ~

It was hot. Unbearably hot. Even in his refrigerated plainclothes with their special energy absorbing lining, the human Lensman was very uncomfortable. However, it wasn't just the heat or the cacophony of the city which afflicted the secret agent. He was most affected by the impending confrontation with Tregonsee's "triplet" brother.

The sky was whitely incandescent under the radiations from Rigel, the blue giant sun, and the heat waves shimmered over the aerial bridges and windowless towers of Rigelston, metropolis of Rigel IV. Blinding light shone in kaleidoscopic patterns from the steel streets and steel columns and steel buildings, spraying flashes of colors from the speeding traffic which choked ground and air.

As inflaming as the sunlight was to the Tellurian's eyes, mechanical noises were maddening to his ears. Only his sunshield and his ear plugs made his exposure to the city life tolerable. It seemed inconceivable that Rigel IV, physically comparable to Tellus in so many ways, could be dominated by a sun that was nearly two hundred times farther away than Sol was from Earth.

The Lensman stood in a public square which, with its trellised steel posts and arches of girders, looked more like an unfinished parking garage. A thousand square yards of closely packed two-wheeled torpedo-shaped vehicles surrounded him. The nearest one was directly in front of him, slightly larger than the average, its one round entrance door opened in its windowless side. The doorway was momentarily filled with the quadruplex bulk of a Rigellian as he stepped out ponderously

1

on his four squat feet, like an ambulatory barrel on thick tree stumps.

The Rigellian stopped, slightly swiveling his eyeless domed head, and waved all four of his many-fingered tentacles in a typical cooling gesture. Those steel cars, tightly sealed and unair-conditioned, got too warm in the summertime even for Rigellians.

The Lensman dipped his head a bit, not as an unneeded bodily greeting, but in order to tilt his silver-and-white insulated helmet. The smoky lead glass sunshield curving from his forehead to his chin still let too much visible radiation through at times. The new angle to his helmet's brim put a better shadow across his eyes without adjustment by his hands. They remained drawn up in his oversized sleeves, protected from the burning sun, coming out only from time to time to rub the itching from the drying streaks of sweat on his cheeks.

Into the human's mind came the answers which he had awaited:

"I have come from my other unit to give you our formal request." The Rigellian's tiny, multiple, boneless fingers produced a metallic scroll and held it out. The Lensman slipped his bare, browned hands out of his sleeves and took the scroll, glanced at the embossed printing, which was a distinctively local type of Braille, and put the slender roll in his pocket. "Thank you," he Lensed. "I will Lens my office on Klovia this request and then dispatch it by courier."

"You are a secret agent, then, of Tregonsee's Special Missions Forces?" the Rigellian asked bluntly.

By habit, conscious of the need for secrecy and guarding his tongue and mind, the Lensman nodded ever so slightly in answer to the question. He did so by habit, knowing that few if any sightless Rigellians recognized body language, so he also telepathed, "Yes," and couldn't resist adding a slight chastisement, "You are not supposed to know, and should not mention it."

The human was used to the nonchalant attitude of these enormously intelligent entities, with their unconcern for what they considered the rather silly games that humanoids and the Galactic Patrol liked to play. Rigellians were singularly placid and untroubled about the problems of the other worlds of Civilization. Nevertheless, the cavalier attitude toward S.M.F. and the indifference to any hush-hush security which ought to be shown were disconcerting to the secret agent. How Tregonsee, coming as he did from Rigelston on Rigel IV, had ever become a Second Stage Lensman, not to mention the fantastic fact that he headed the Patrol's Military Intelligence Services and the Secret Intelligence Services *and* created the ultra mysterious S.M.F., was truly remarkable.

"I know your concern," the Rigellian said. "I will not look into your mind, even if you let me. I will not use your name. And do not fear, no Rigellian would be so impolite as to intrude on us. You really did not have to choose this ridiculous place to meet."

The Lensman was not insulted. Rigellians, intensely individualistic, spoke frankly when at home, and very few ever left their planet, for interplanetary travel and trade were of little value to them. Their joint interest and pursuit was now alien anthropology conducted remotely by mental contacts. It wasn't easy finding sufficient numbers of Rigellians who had the desire or the feeling of galactic altruism, although all of them had the wit and wisdom, the exceptional mind control and the sense of perception which so effortlessly penetrated solid matter. No, no one could really take offense at the Rigellians' frankness, knowing that they could never be insolent and were absolutely incorruptible.

"As you are a secret agent," the Rigellian said, "and a Lensman, you should have direct contact with Tregonsee if you desire it. Tell me now, to what degree is Tregonsee dead?"

"I cannot answer that."

"Cannot or will not?"

"Sir, I will file your request for this information, that is all I can say."

"Then I must tell you that we have already sent a message to the Galactic Coordinator of the Second Galaxy saying that we must know the facts within a matter of hours or we will be forced to make this situation public to all Rigellians throughout our galaxy, your galaxy, and the known universe. Death of a Rigellian is a serious matter, sir. We take into account the turmoil still uncontrolled in your galaxy and the unusual nature of your Special Missions Forces, which is unique to your troubles and your foes. But that does not allow us to neglect our own responsibilities to ourselves. We have indisputable proof that someone calling himself Tregonsee has been violently killed by our enemies, the Boskonians."

What the Rigellian said sent a rippling wave of horror through the Lensman. He involuntarily shuddered, despite the terrible heat. Rigellians were infallible when it came to these things. It was not the message directly to Kimball Kinnison tearing away the veil of secrecy imposed by the S.I.S. which so disturbed him. It was the sense of truth, of rumor turning into fact, that was so ghastly. Was Tregonsee, his heroic boss, perhaps the greatest Lensman among the millions of Lensmen, really dead?

For the first time, he began to believe that the secret report of Tregonsee's assassination was true.

What had happened in the city of Rohyl on the planet of Preeko, far away in the Second Galaxy...?

1

Death from the Tube

A dark figure clung to the side of the stone wall of the castle, three hundred yards above the dry moat. Two hands and a foot pressed into the mortared joints of the gray-brown, petrified-wood bricks as the other foot scraped upward in search of the next foothold. From wrists and ankles hung a camouflaged gossamer cloak of mottled gray and brown.

The Vegian catman was almost invisible in the night glow of the castle lights below. On the tip of his counterbalancing curved tail was strapped a small but deadly electric gun, its triggering wires embedded in a neural connection under shaved skin.

Two more yards upward was the edge of the polished sill of a huge window. First one, then the other set of his unsheathed talons hooked over the sill. The lithe Vegian froze there, half hanging, watching the seconds and minutes blink away on the chronometer under his left wrist inches away from his round golden eyes. It would be an easy few seconds for him to swing a leg, then his body, onto the ledge. The projecting joints of the folding shutters, like those of the windows he had passed on his strenuous climb, indicated that there should be no bar to his quickly slipping into the room that was his target. Meanwhile, he had to wait. Soon, but not yet, the time would come for the synchronized attack.

Mando, the intruder, glanced downward. The empty moat was ablaze with floodlights, and the palace guards seemed grotesque gold and silver blobs of metal and cloth moving mechanically to and fro. He looked out beyond the imperial palace grounds, across the squat, dark skyline of the sleeping capital city of Rohyl, toward the curved horizon of the planet Preeko. There, in the distant shimmering haze, the tiny moon was rising in a purple field of stars. He could see the haze glowing now; the lightening sky warned that the largest of the three moons would soon appear and eat away the intense blackness needed for his stealthy climb.

A fan of pale blue light sprang from the ground at the edge of the city. Then another, then another, until arcs of pale blue light stood like a transparent wall between urban center and countryside. Defense barrier, Mando realized. Unexpected. Strange. He was aware now of the tickle on his face and hands as his fine yellow fur, raised in instinctive apprehension, was ruffled by the light breeze of the coming dawn.

He stared upward, straining to see the slightest movement in the upper air. No doubt about it, tiny dots were now intensively on patrol where none had been an hour before. They could have nothing to do with him. The frequent, crisscrossing aerial patrols circling the palace at his level had not increased. He would soon be inside and safe from discovery by them.

The Vegian brought his attention back to the small red numbers marking the time. The moment was nineteen, eighteen, seventeen seconds away.

He swung his feline body up on the sill, his tail arched over his lowered head, gun leveled, ready for a quick, silent, lethal burst against the guards.

The window opening was unobstructed, ornate shutters folded tightly at right and left, the slotted security bars also folded out of the way. As quickly as the torch slicingtool had materialized in Mando's hand, it disappeared, unneeded, back in its pouch. He was now ten seconds ahead of schedule. He glided into the room on his soft, naked footpads. With a few sharp movements of his body, the cloak fell away from his wrists and ankles, leaving him almost stripped.

On his chest was taped a translucent disc of integrated chips and crystals, encased in a transparent purple plastic polyhedron. Deep within it, as from another dimension, angry sparks glowed. He tore the gadget off himself, unmindful of the pain as a bit of downy breast fur came with it, and pushed it gently flat against the floor between his knees. With a screwing motion, he buried it into the heavy nap of the carpet. He did not expect it to be kicked away in a possible scuffle, but such chance was reduced. His escape depended on it there, in the center of the room.

His nocturnal eyes swiftly saw that the room was empty of guards or anyone else. Archways led left and right. The one on the right, he knew from his briefing, should be where Tregonsee would be in the sleep period. At best, the Rigellian would be completely retracted, as immobile as a hibernating turtle, balanced in the center of the room like a huge gray egg—defenseless. At worst, he would be fully awake in a portable security box, or in a closet or bathroom temporarily turned into a security room, in which case, Mando would have to chance a messy area-destruction instead of a single DeLameter shot.

The Vegian catman held tightly to his mind shield with physically painful concentration. Tregonsee, Second Stage Lensman, one of the handful of super-beings in the Galactic Patrol, was capable of a phenomenal sense of perception. Even in a state of sleep-rest he still perceived—to assassinate him without his taking some sort of countermeasure would be impossible. Asleep or awake, to assassinate him would be incredibly difficult. But asleep or awake, it would be done. The killing would happen now within seconds; even Tregonsee would not be able to react quickly enough to save himself.

Mando glanced at his chronometer. Thirteen and seven-tenths seconds to the next phase. He shifted his glance to the thick but featherweight electronic gadget encasing his right wrist. The modified spy-ray, personalized into a Tregonsee-detector, placed his target, by the pattern of cross-hatched green lines, within thirty yards. Intersecting red lines indicated another life form at closer range.

Twelve and two-tenths seconds, then one quick shot—Tregonsee would be vaporized and Mando would be snatched to safety by the instantaneous appearance of the pre-arranged tube.

The room was dark, but not pitch-black. Over the hallway door was a security telecamera and spy-ray pointing in his direction. It was operating, but it was not a factor with only seconds remaining before he revealed himself anyway. On each side of the camera was an electric clock, one for local time, the other for GP time. They were both thirty-two seconds slow. In fact, they were both stopped. Strange! And the dual emergency exit lights, one visual, the other ultraviolet, were both lit. Very strange! The abnormalities bothered him, though not greatly—he was used to the unpredictable.

He was nine and five-tenths seconds ahead of schedule.

Mando would kill. And escape. All during his climb the assassination plot had obsessed him. He had never tried assassination before, but he had killed in the course of his trade. He had become a legendary burglar among the greatest thieves of old Boskonia. From being pursued by countless galactic governments for punishment, he became sought out by them for clandestine service. Now he was a legendary secret agent, a robber who changed the course of history and the lives of trillions of people among countless stellar systems. He was rich. He was infamous. He was unstoppable. He was the scourge of S.I.S., the Secret Intelligence Services of the Galactic Patrol. He had only one ambition now, greater than fame and wealth—to be more powerful than a Galactic Coordinator, more feared than a Lensman. He believed he had achieved that goal. But it would be the incredible destruction of Tregonsee—that unique super-being, the most prominent non-humanoid alien of all Civilization, the head of the nerve center of the omnipotent Patrol—it would be his murder that would prove Mando to be the most powerful man of the known universe.

At the moment he entered the window he was psychologically at his peak, fiercely keen—intoxicated by his vision and the conviction of his own invulnerability.

Time dragged. He was still seconds ahead of schedule. In four and four-tenths seconds the tube would appear, precisely on its mark, even as Tregonsee died.

There would be exciting political repercussions. Preeko, this tyrannical, puritanical, self-righteous planet which all outlaws hated, would be discredited and condemned. Preeko's honor would be forever smeared by the killing of its honored official guest, Tregonsee, the personal representative of Galactic Coordinator Kimball Kinnison, on a mission of highest importance and utmost security. The Patrol might be stirred to overreact. Terrorism, revolution, even war could result. This uneasy part of the Second Galaxy, the whole Withered Arm sector, could degenerate into chaos. The program of Civilization and the Kinnison regime for pacification of the Second Galaxy could crumble with the death of the head of the S.I.S. With the Galactic Patrol disgraced, Boskone would revive. Mando would be the feared hero, unchallenged— provided he killed once more, soon and secretly, his unsuspecting victim his old teacher and sole rival, Eramista. Mando alone would be raised to the heights of immortality.

One and eight-tenths seconds to go. Right on time.

The unclothed, furry body of Mando had squirmed across the carpeted floor, below the invisible sentinel beams spraying across the room, probably with booby traps set to trip gunfire as well as alarms. He crowded against the corner of floor and wall, head and hands within the sleep-room archway, indiscernibly blending into the thick carpeting. In his left hand was a Sub-Delta-ray projector, in his right was a DeLameter one-shot, both still rubber-chained to his hip-hugging equipment belt.

Nine-tenths of a second to go.

Mando did not have to check the red line read-out on his detector—directly in front of him, moving out of the sleep room at fantastic speed in a crouch, was a Preekoan Lensman. Mando blinked and formed a frozen, intricately detailed picture of the Lensman in his mind. He made an instantaneous examination and evaluation. The Preekoan was the size and shape of a large Tellurian, but with the distinctly elongated brown hairless head, Lens banded to the tall forehead, armored from toes to chin.

The Lensman did not see him. The Preekoan went to the hall door and pressed a communications button which did not work. He uttered a soft oath and turned around, still moving at high speed, and saw the Vegian.

The gun on Mando's tail splattered its energy against the coruscant Lens, momentarily neutralizing it and blinding the Lensman.

One surgical pencil-beam dart from the Sub-Delta-ray went in under the Preekoan's chin, through his brain behind his Lens, and out the top of his head. As the body was falling, lifeless, Mando swiveled his head back toward the sleep room and saw his victim, the bulky Rigellian, shuffling ponderously toward him.

At that moment there was a brilliant flare of light from the window, which lit the room, flooded immediately by an enormous explosive noise. The building shook. The Rigellian stopped, recoiled; he noticeably shrank in size, his cylindrical torso shortening, bulging. Mando, too, was startled by the explosion, but did not flinch; his mind shield stayed firm, not slipping for the tiniest revealing instant. Nevertheless, he knew he had been noticed—not from the glare before the eyeless Lensman, but by the atmospheric distortion, a catman figure silhouetted in a bath of vibrations.

Mando's muscular response to the first appearance of the Rigellian continued smoothly even as the explosion rocked the room. Reflexes trained for the ultimate in swiftness brought tail gun and Sub-Delta into action—they cross-fired even as the outside noise rumbled through windows and walls.

Tregonsee was transfixed. His body, in a paralytic daze, had a dancing blue aura.

Mando's finger, on the DeLameter button, half squeezed it, holding at the very edge of discharging the fatal shot, but he could not finish the action. His finger was locked in place by a low, wavering hum from the crystal on the floor. The hyperspacial tube was materializing at that crucial moment!

Mando spat out a long, loud, cursing hiss. "Tlazz!" He had to hold his fire for several seconds or his shot could ignite a wild vortex, a churning fireball of stellar power. He couldn't see the tube materializing, but he could feel it. There was the sickening vertigo of its field, the writhing of space around him, the twisting distortion of the infinitesimal strands of his being. Only perfect preparatory planning had spontaneously stopped his finger at the delicate moment of sub-materialization.

Then the danger was gone. A tiny space-dimensional whirlpool of subatomic particles existed one meter to his right. It was the genesis of the tube, forming, as had been so carefully calculated, at optimum proximity.

Disaster came at Mando from a different direction before he could make another attempt. Another Preekoan Lensman had come from the archway on the other side of the room, taking in the situation at a glance and, with a hurried shot, sliced off the Vegian's tail. Mando's transfixing crossfire was disrupted and Tregonsee seemingly disappeared.

The lights came on throughout the apartment and the metal grilles at all three windows rattled into place as though to trap him. Just as unexpectedly, the lights went off and the grilles retracted.

Mando, desperately searching for Tregonsee, did not return the fire from the Lensman, who dodged back behind the archway. A quick glance at his wrist showed an intricate pattern of green lines—other human types were arriving. And a thick red line was still there. Tregonsee was still in front of him. Then, bewilderingly, he saw that the thick red line was really a double red line, like a ghost, as if there had been a split into twins. A decoy image? Clever! Next there would be four, a dozen. He had to move closer.

He crawled toward the spot where Tregonsee had been. He easily broke through the weak mental curtain of invisibility. There was the blue shimmer of the immobilized Rigellian barrel-body. And, to his astonishment, there also was the seething mouth of the hyperspacial tube! Instead of being a yard behind him, it was five yards into the other room! It was actually behind Tregonsee! That was wrong! His situation was perilous—his escape seemed out of reach! Such a shift had to be deliberate, not accidental. What had changed the calculations? Was he about to be betrayed?

Mando did the only possible thing. He disregarded the Lensman behind him, the others arriving, and leapt around the blue body, firing his one DeLameter ball of force point-blank into the head of Tregonsee. The act ordinarily would have been foolhardy. The risk to himself was deadly, for he had no shelter from the concussion which he should have minimized while on his stomach yards away, most of his body behind the wall. There was no other way to reach the mouth of the tube.

There should have been a gigantic burst of energy. Tregonsee should have been destroyed. Mando, a few seconds off schedule, should have been sucked up into safety by the tube.

The ball of energy simply struck Tregonsee and disappeared.

Behind Mando, the second Lensman, instead of firing,

was supervising two Preekoan Patrolmen in spinning a web of force over Mando in an unbelievably rapid and efficient manner.

Mando flung himself past Tregonsee, near enough to the tube to be drawn into it, stunned by the realization that he had failed. The force web, thrown out to catch him, wrapped around him; its tractor was dragging him backward. Not only had he failed, but, to his horror, the Patrol was capturing him alive, not even seriously hurt.

The tube! There was the fact that the misdirected thing could still pull him out of danger. And then, being sucked up, his own hand tractor rod could pull Tregonsee with him for a kidnapping instead of an assassination!

From the circumference of the hyper circle which was the opening of the tube there had grown the murkiness of contact where normal space intersected pseudo-space. The diameter grew rapidly from one inch to several yards. In less than one second a ghostly swirl of warped space floated in the middle of the room, reaching for him and Tregonsee. Within the middle of the haze, phantom figures were assembling.

Mando reversed the polarity of his weapons, momentarily rending the field which bound him, and, his mind blazing with a near burnout of mental power from the quick crushing of the psychotropic capsules stored in his mouth, flung himself toward the tube's mouth.

A black humanoid shape blocked his way by emerging first. Another body crowded behind.

The unexpected help startled Mando. This wasn't in his plan. No one was supposed to come through the tube.

A rainbow beam of light came from the hand of the leading dark figure and struck down one of the Patrolmen, knocking out the others.

Mando said, "There! There!" and pointed at the glowing figure of Tregonsee. "Blast him!"

As Mando gave his command, the bulky Rigellian rotated his glowing body at astonishing speed, flinging his tentacles in a desperate attempt to knock the raiders and the furniture about, spoiling their aim and generating confusion. At first the rainbow beam missed. But other beams sprang out of the hands of other black figures pouring into the room from the tube. Several beams flashed against the cylindrical barrel-body, slicing upward into the eyeless, neckless head.

The Rigellian tipped over heavily, mortally wounded.

Mando banged his quick-release belt buckle, dropping his guns and equipment, ready to dive for the safety of the tube.

The black-masked leader of the raiding party looked away from the silent, unconscious figures of Tregonsee's bodyguards to stare at Mando, who was now shocked to recognize—Eramista!

Time froze as Eramista's thoughts came in a flash, coldly, "Are you surprised, Mando? You shouldn't be. The pupil should not take on the teacher, since the teacher will always keep a few tricks unrevealed. Did I neglect to teach you, Mando, my finest pupil, never to trust anyone?"

Even as Mando saw the dark leader jabbing the thumb of his left hand down in the catman's direction, jerking his head in a quick, silent order to the two companions at his side, their guns flared.

Mando's two arms disappeared under the blasts.

Mando understood. He was being double-crossed first, used as a decoy and sentenced to death. He had been redundant, never the primary assassin. The tube's mouth had been deliberately misaligned to facilitate his death, not his escape.

Mando's face disintegrated into a scorched mass, and his life ended.

The black leader, spine and head stiff with arrogance, exhausted the charge in his gun by a deliberate *coup de grace* for Tregonsee, calmly slicing the Rigellian body into four equal quarters. Then he swept his men back into the tube with a pompous wave of his arm.

The tube vanished.

The apartments of Tregonsee were deathly still.

The violence had lasted less than seven seconds.

One of the Patrolmen on the floor stirred to life. He dragged himself to the bodies of the sundered Rigellian, the dead Lensman, and the mutilated Vegian. He stared at them, almost unable to comprehend the magnitude of the tragedy. He went back to the other Patrolman and the other Lensman.

They were microwave-burned on their bare flesh, blistered around the edges of their clothing, but they could recover.

Within minutes the dead and wounded had all been taken out on stretchers and the main entrance sealed, a Preekoan Patrolman on guard outside.

The door to the security room within the sleeping quarters opened noiselessly. Lensman Frank Garner, Tregonsee's current aide-de-camp, stepped out, his thick face rock-hard with concern. Captain Garner was a Klovian, a heavy man, his mass of muscles swelling out his Patrol uniform like a silver-and-black package of exceptional physical power. His stocky figure seemed a sort of anthropomorphic Rigellian, a hulking human shadow of his superior, sturdy and stoic on the outside. Within his bullet head, however, was a volatile, dynamic mind to rival the best; for one of those rare occasions, he now allowed his emotions to show through.

"Terrible! Terrible!" He looked at the debris on the floor. Severed pieces of Rigellian harness were in a drying purple smear. The discarded Preekoan armor lay in a heap where the medics had piled it. For several long moments Garner's thoughts said farewell to Meppy and Pat. Then, he toed the Vegian belt, its guns still strung to it. "Who was the Vegian, I wonder? Writti? Mando?"

He went to the nearest window. Outside, a Rohyl municipal police copter and a Patrol scout craft hovered in position. He drew the blinds tight, adjusting vision for seeing out but not for seeing in.

"QX, sir!" the Lensman called, as gruff as a dog's bark.

Another Rigellian came out of the security room. To anyone but another Rigellian, he was identical to the slaughtered one. The almost unnoticeable difference was the slightly larger domed head, with the age-rings around his tentacles a bit deeper and darker. All four of his tentacles were coiled in concentration, resting on the strapping around his waist. His four nostrils, in line and equidistant from each other like his mouths, limbs, and legs, snorted air through atrophied vocal cords for his only form of aural communication—on this occasion, a wheezing kind of emotional pain so rarely indulged in by his race. His barrel body moved slowly, the soles of his bare feet propelling it at a crawl across the burned and stained carpet.

His uniform was simple, a sort of gray leather harness belt around his midriff, sectioned into many cases and pockets. In fact, it was more like a set of four flat tires forming bandoliers stuffed with sundry things, pieces of equipment and personal effects, other objects hanging from clips, like his peculiar, flexible sock-slippers.

The leather pieces, hand-tooled and stitched together, formed the stripped-down uniform of a Rigellian Gray Lensman.

Mando's double-red line had registered true.

There had been two.

This was Tregonsee—the real Tregonsee.

2

The Null-Treg Secret

∾∾∾∾∾∾∾∾∾∾∾∾∾∾∾∾∾∾∾∾∾∾∾∾∾∾∾

At the time of the appearance of the tube and the death
of Mando, the Galactic Patrol ship *Dronvire* was directly over
the Preekoan capital city of Rohyl, thirty miles high, in a
battle-red stance. Although *Dronvire* was essentially a ceremonial vessel assigned to the office of the Galactic Coordinator specifically for the official use of Tregonsee, it was nonetheless a warship. Its small crew of two hundred and fifty
officers and men were a highly trained battle force in charge
of an enormously deadly machine. Their efficiency and power
were now, surprisingly, being stiffly tested.

Two black spaceships, each on the order of two hundred
and fifty thousand tons, outgunning *Dronvire* ten to one, had
unexpectedly attacked. They had come in under screens of
blocking electronics, masked by the swarms of Preekoan
pleasure craft, police boats, and planetary guard ships, and
struck the Patrol vessel fore and aft with brilliant bursts of
violet radiance.

At 3:52 Local in the bright dawn light of the upper air,
the *Dronvire* had been hovering in stationary orbit, waiting
patiently to carry the Tregonsee party away. Three Lensmen
and two Patrolmen were down on the planet in support of
Tregonsee on his four-day diplomatic visit—ostensibly diplomatic, that is, for wherever the Rigellian Second Stage Lensman
showed up there was both planned and unplanned intrigue.
Two days of the visit had passed without event. The Preekoans,

from the president-king down to the lowliest citizen, had been enthusiastic in their welcome for the great and legendary Tregonsee, now Gray-Emeritus, On Assignment. If any trouble might develop, it would be on the ground and the five-man Treg staff, with an additional pair of Preekoan Lensmen and a pair of Preekoan Patrolmen, would be sufficient to handle it. Certainly no threat had been expected here in the heart of friendly space. *Dronvire*, however, was never lax nor indifferent in its attitude or duty; the initial blows had easily been fended off.

Commander P. Lzbert, Lensman, of the GP pocket cruiser, happened to be on the bridge when the attack first took place. He had been called there by his second-in-command because the Preekoan picket ships, in deep space, part of the massive security for Tregonsee's visit, had reported strange readings, although no visual sightings. He had observed the pale blue defense barrier winking into life below, ringing and dividing the city into three concentric circles. Directly under his ship the shimmering roof of the barrier had formed, disrupting communications with the message center within Tregonsee's palace apartments.

As the two black privateers darted away at opposing right angles, repulsed by counter fire, all of the *Dronvire* crew tumbled into battle stations. Like a flock of birds startled by an unknown danger, the hundreds of pleasure craft scattered. Those diving for the ground were buffeted and damaged as they blundered into the energy net of the barrier. The police and guard ships, impossibly outmatched, circled helplessly.

"Signal red-brown, repeat red-brown, to HQ-T," Commander Lzbert said. He was a youngish gray-haired Martian hybrid with natural telepathic powers. His mind flashed around the crew, picking up every scrap of data, and then around again giving them the status of the moment. All the control deck dials, particularly those of the warning devices, were scanned by his own eyes, his own perception, and also through the senses of his crew.

"Sir, a nuclear device has exploded in Peace Square in the city center!" The scanner-crewman, face buried in a viewbox, pressed her report on the commander's brain.

"Yes, I've got it on the screens," the Martian said. "Give me the source!"

17

"Negative."

"Locate the enemy ships. They're off the trackers."

"Negative. They're gone."

Commander Lzbert's deduction was quick and straight-forward—the aerial attackers had come and gone, a mere diversion; they hadn't dropped the bomb. One explosion, a small conventional nuclear device; that explosion seemed to indicate a separate ground action. The two actions were unrelated. The bomb was simply another diversion. Two diversions? Any more? The situation must be worse than it appeared to be. Diversions for what purpose?

He sent another message to HQ-T through regular chan-nels and simultaneously Lensed it: "Signal brown-green, repeat brown-green. Diversionary double bird attack. Diver-sionary small A-bomb. No source. No contact. Captain Buyyer, full security measures red alert. Report."

Anxious seconds passed with no Lens-to-Lens contact. The delay was inordinate so the circumstances had to be unusual and serious. Confirmation of this came with the sudden connection with the mind of Lieutenant-Captain Bob Buyyer, chief *Dronvire* liaison officer assigned to the Treg staff. Tregonsee's apartments had been bounced. Raider dead. Patrol casualties. Headquarters-Treg untouched and safe. Some details being withheld.

"Being withheld?" the commander said, not quite sure he had felt the thought correctly. "Being withheld from me? Don't you mean being withheld from non-cleared personnel?"

"Commander!" The scanner-crewman, mind crackling with mental anguish, telepathically broke into his narrow projection. "Commander, sir! Tregonsee is dead!"

The commander felt Buyyer disconnect while the fantas-tic claim reverberated in his head. He overwhelmed his crewman's mind, shutting off the idea from anyone else. Tregonsee dead! He didn't believe it for a moment, but others might, and rumors would fly. "What's the evidence, chief?" He appealed directly to Tregonsee and his staff. "Who says so?" He tried to scan HQ-T and Buyyer with both his mind and his machines, but Buyyer as well as all of HQ-T were sealed off absolutely.

"Sir! It's an emergency squad report!"

Lzbert immediately monitored the emergency medical

communications with the palace, which were on-going, at the same time quickly reviewing the recorded messages of the immediate past. The information was there. Tregonsee was dead. Beyond a patch-up job.

He still didn't believe it.

What he did believe was that something bad had happened at HQ-T. Lzbert tried to get through by Lens and radio. And he kept on trying.

At HQ-T, the attempt by Lzbert was being noted.

"Captain Garner, the *Dronvire* is probing us. It's Commander Lzbert himself." Lieutenant-Captain Buyyer, the human Lensman, stuck his head out of the security room to make this report to the aide-de-camp. Then, to Tregonsee, he said directly, "He's asking for details on your death."

ADC Garner didn't seem to hear. He stood near where the Rigellian had fallen, viciously destroyed beyond all medical help, and said, soundlessly but clearly, "Meppy. Meppy gone. Mepauhurrat gone." And then, "Pat. Pat gone. Patrone-Ohhare gone." Their lurid deaths for the moment had crushed his spirit both professionally and personally.

Tregonsee didn't interrupt the captain in his grief. He tossed out his own mental reply to Buyyer, "No contact. Keep our seal tight, even with *Dronvire*." He continued to sweep the room with his sense of perception, seeing more than ordinary, light-frequency eyes could see, seeking information from the hair shed by Mando, the traces of perspiration, the impressions from the vibrations radiating from the discarded belt and equipment. "It's the medical team. And the hospital. Tell them to say nothing more. Let all inquiries come to you.—Get me P'Keen."

Tregonsee touched with the tip of one of his tentacles the spot on the carpet where the purple polyhedron had been shoved into the fibers. A slightly scorched and fused patch was clearly visible. Captain Garner knelt down to examine it more closely.

"Definitely has an Ordovik feel to it, Captain," Tregonsee said. "There's no doubt in my mind now. A hyperspacial tube was in this room. And an Ordovik is involved."

"A tube, sir? How is that possible? I thought that thing couldn't be controlled so precisely. And obviously so small. That small? What a terrible spectre that raises. . . ."

"Interesting questions. There's no problem about Cardynge's Limit—a tube as small as this seems to be wouldn't be circumscribed by the Limit. Especially considering that the Limit based on the mass of this system's sun could allow such a tube to be formed even a couple of planets nearer the sun. Precise control? It hasn't been perfected, as far as my knowledge goes, except by some dubious Ordovik experiments. So small? Entirely possible, but the problem is one of control. Accuracy, as far as I know, is lost within a diameter of several hundred yards. A terrible spectre? Yes. Emphatically yes. A controlled small tube is a threat to every high security area any place in the galaxies."

Tregonsee picked up Mando's belt with several of his thick jointless fingers near the end of a tapering tentacle, brushing other, finer, hair-like tendrils over the material. He held it ten feet away from his hemiglobular brainpan that sat on the flat plane of his circular upper body. His Lens of Arisia, usually worn on the upper flesh of a limb as a bracelet, now glowed instead between a pair of his noses, higher up, like an oversized scintillating special eye he had stuck on his broad brow to make up for the eyes he didn't have. He held the belt out as though the Lens could read its secrets.

"To answer your question you asked some minutes ago, Captain—Who was the Vegian? There's no doubt about it. It wasn't Writti. It was Mando. Yes, definitely. Mando."

Tregonsee dropped the belt and nudged it with one of his four feet.

"A dangerous man, Mando," he continued. "We knew he was on a high priority project in the Withered Arm Sector. But we never suspected he might be moved around by hyperspacial tube. That makes this a very big conspiracy. He was clever, we knew that. But on his own he was never a threat to the Patrol. I never suspected that his project might be me."

Tregonsee raised his dozens of tentacular parts outward and upward, making himself look like a tree, its many thick and thin branch ends shaking in a non-existent breeze, symmetrically spread out by his four main limbs. It was a gesture an intimate could recognize as expressing unresolved intellectual concerns.

"I need P'Keen now. Right now."

Captain Garner had a rare peep at Tregonsee's incredible mental powers for the merest microsecond: the Rigellian had sought, found and conveyed his command to P'Keen of Ordov even as the captain had understood Tregonsee's wish to call him. The Rigellian's mind had touched the Ordovik's—zing! —and the communication was over. Had P'Keen sensed Tregonsee's call even before Tregonsee had called?

"Yes, captain," Tregonsee said, catching Garner's admiration, "P'Keen is frequently faster than me. We Rigellians get too much credit. The Ordovik sense of perception is as good as or better than any in the known universe. But you already know that; he's teaching you things you'd never learn from me. He's already on his way here. He left the president-king's quarters even before Mepauhurrat's body touched the floor."

Tregonsee's many arms had slowly floated back down to his sides. He turned toward the security room.

"P'Keen agrees with me. Fix this in your minds." Tregonsee was now impressing his thoughts strongly, not only in Captain Garner's head, but just as emphatically into those of the other staff Lensman and the two GP staff patrol officers there in the security room.

"The other Preekoan Lensman and his two Patrolmen are in the hospital—they don't know and won't know the facts. So, from those of us who have been on the scene there are only six who know for certain that I haven't been killed. The wounded probably think I've been assassinated. There may have been some eavesdroppers or a chance Lens tuned in who registered the death of a Rigellian. Certainly the enemy agents must be convinced of my death. Now, let's consider how that might be to our advantage."

"Are you suggesting a news blackout?" Garner said. "Do you think we can smoke out the identity of the assassins?"

"It's worth the trouble, I think," Tregonsee said. "No news about my death will be disturbing to them. First, they themselves want to know if they were successful. They'll take risks to find out if we say nothing. Second, they'll want the news spread throughout the galaxies to demoralize and weaken our secret organizations."

"News of your death, sir," Garner said, "will certainly be demoralizing to all of Civilization, not just to our own secret service men. You won't have much time after the rumors start before you'll have to reveal the truth."

"I know. But we can try it for a while without any risk. We'll act as if the worst is true. Just among ourselves. No elaboration, just stick to no comment. Not even Lensman's Seal. Mepauhurrat can continue to play his role as my stand-in. Meppy's corpse can be taken for mine for weeks if precautions are taken. I'll stay dead while we watch the developments. We'll tempt the vultures into betraying themselves."

Tregonsee moved into the other room, followed by Garner.

"Send a message to Klovia. I want one of my other stand-ins to show himself to the Coordinator's staff. The rumors will soon get around that Null-Treg is alive and that it must have really been me who was killed here this morning."

"Sir, the staff here has been informed not to mention even an attack against us, let alone an assassination attempt against you," the ADC said, watching Buyyer send off the message to Klovia. Garner waved the transcript from the hospital which already had come through. "The victims have been deceptively identified as having been killed in that terrorist's bomb blast in Peace Square. Their racial classification hasn't been revealed." He clipped the report to his new case file folder. "No one will know a Rigellian is dead except the staff."

"Wrong, Captain Garner," Tregonsee said. "The Patrol will soon know. Not the general public, mind you, but the Patrol. The information will get out because our enemies will see to it that it gets out. My death will be galactic knowledge within the speed of the fastest transmissions. It's probably halfway to the other side of the galaxy already. The other Null-Treg's appearance even limited to the Coordinator's office will simply confirm the apparent fact despite all security."

"Despite all security, sir?" his aide-de-camp growled, more than a little disturbed. He was a loyal, devoted officer in not just the Secret Intelligence Services but the ultra-secret S.M.F., the Special Missions Forces. The idea that secrets could not be kept within the S.I.S., not to mention the Galactic Coordinator's office, was terribly irritating, utterly frustrating. He answered his own question with a disgusted grunt, "Yeah." Another grunt. "Yeah—I know, sir. But that doesn't mean that Meppy was no secret, does it? Won't the fact that Mepauhurrat was here with us be made known, too? Who else now knows about Meppy being here?"

"Only us," Tregonsee replied. "Only one Rigellian came to Preeko. Me. Only me. The existence of a Null-Treg is common knowledge, even outside the Patrol—a Null-Treg is obvious mystification and misdirection. Standard cloak-and-dagger stuff. But it's assumed there is only *one* Null-Treg. And he is back on Klovia. Only we know about Mepauhurrat being here. Eventually, logically, the truth will come out about Meppy. But not from us. Any secret among the six of us is inviolable."

"Message sent and acknowledged, T," Buyyer said. "The *Dronvire* is getting insistent."

"Let Commander Lzbert through. Keep the beam narrow. No Lens. I'm dead. Remember. I'm destroyed." Tregonsee sat down on the floor by withdrawing his legs upward into his cylindrical torso. The bony, padded circle of his base rested on the matting. The soft tips of his tentacles sorted through the punched cards of the situation report as he listened.

"Lieutenant-Captain Buyyer!" It was Commander Lzbert being formal in oral transmission. "Let's go Lens-to-Lens."

Buyyer turned to look quizzically at Tregonsee, who couldn't see the facial gesture in the same way that Captain Garner could, but who understood the implicit question through his perception. The Rigellian moved a tentacle in a thoroughly human gesture of denial.

"Sorry, sir." Buyyer could imagine the surprise at the other end. "Lens-to-Lens is ruled out."

"By whom?" the commander said. And then, after the merest pause, "By Captain Garner? Let me speak to him."

"Garner here, sir."

"Let's go Lens-to-Lens, Captain."

"Sorry, sir. We can't."

"Why not?" The commander's voice was calm, but his tone was cold.

The captain was slightly flustered by not having a reasonable excuse. "Standing orders, sir."

"Whose standing orders, Captain? A live T? Or a dead T?" The commander was no fool. He was a Lensman. All Lensmen were superior Patrolmen. And he was a superior

Lensman. Everyone in that security room knew that Commander Lzbert could not be deceived by indirection. Only a Lensman's lie could trick him.

"We are under top security, Commander," the hoarse-voiced Garner said. "I have my standing orders."

Commander Lzbert tried a different tack. "A message has been intercepted by me signed by Buyyer by order of Tregonsee. Null-Treg has been ordered to show himself on Klovia. Buyyer, who really gave that order?"

"Standing order, sir," said Lieutenant-Captain Buyyer.

"Not bloody well likely, Buyyer! Let me speak to Captain Garner again.... Captain! Let's go Lens-to-Lens! That's an order!"

"Sorry, Commander," the Klovian said, "it's—"

"I know, I know," Lzbert interrupted. "It's a standing order. Is it a standing order that you don't take orders from your senior officer?"

"No, sir."

"Well, then are you still under T's orders, or are you under mine, as ranking officer?"

There was no way out to avoid the showdown, they all could see that; Tregonsee jabbed a narrow thought into Garner's head. "You're my ranking officer, sir, of course," Garner lied, repeating Tregonsee's instructions. "But we have full security here. May I respectfully request that you come down for a conference?"

"Me go there?" The commander was a bit disturbed by the idea. "Shouldn't you come here? Shouldn't you all come on up to the ship? It seems to me you've confirmed a calamitous situation. I have a hospital report that a Rigellian has been fatally wounded. If immediate steps are taken by us all, if *Dronvire* leaves as soon as possible with the Rigellian, there may be a chance at a Phillips recovery. Reconstruction or regeneration. I certainly don't want to waste the time." The commander tried to sound reasonable and not sarcastic. "Is this all covered by your standing orders, Captain Garner?"

"Yes, sir," Garner said, knowing that his answer was an impossible lie.

The commander tried for a final time to get a hint. "I'll send an honor guard immediately to take custody of the remains. Under plus-plus security blackout, of course. Am I to understand that such an honor guard is proper?"

"Yes, sir, of course, sir."

For the first time since contact, Commander Lzbert's voice sounded strained. "I now accept the incredible! There's no time to waste! Get your butts the hell up here as fast as possible!"

"No, Commander. We'll wrap it up here."

"Garner! Buyyer! Such action sounds inappropriate! In fact, it's preposterous! But I'm on my way! Don't do another damn thing until I arrive to take over! Your standing orders better make more sense than you do!"

"Yes, sir, come as fast as possible," the lieutenant-captain said and broke the connection. "I feel as though I've kicked the commander in the shins."

"Don't be disconcerted," Tregonsee said. "Commander Lzbert is properly upset, but we'll straighten him out. He'll have to know the real situation. Let's get to work—we've got to have our action plan ready for him when he gets here."

They were, indeed, completely prepared, packed and ready to go when Commander Lzbert arrived. It was an angry ship's captain who entered the apartments, practically humiliated by the junior officers. They forced him to squeeze through a partially opened door, denying his executive officer admittance, and clamped a mind-block on the seething Martian to prevent the slightest chance of a telepathic leak when Lzbert first found Tregonsee alive.

"How the purple fires of hell...?" the commander finally burst out when unrestrained. "How the purple fires of hell could another Rigellian get on this planet without me knowing it?"

"I regret you've been deceived, Bert. And for most of the past year," Tregonsee apologized. "It's happened on every planet we've ever visited."

The four on Tregonsee's staff were being amused by the revelation, but it took an effort for Lzbert to be good-humored. He awaited the explanation rather grimly.

"Remember, Bert, what great care we take with my armored atmospheric suit which we cart around with us wherever I go? We treat that suit as if my life depends on it.

And it does. Somebody else's life depended on careful treatment of it, too."

"I did always wonder about it," Lzbert said. "It weighed twice what it should have weighed, but it never got examined through its radiation shield because of diplomatic immunity."

"It was always presumed to be empty. Oh, I know you had your suspicions, Bert—that it might have been stuffed, at the worst, with contraband goods."

"As I say, sir, I did wonder about it."

"But no one knew, except my central staff, that it carried another stand-in, another Null-Treg with me."

"So! A secret that was really a secret!"

"No one could have suspected the truth. Least of all you, Commander, who would normally have been entrusted with the deception. No one except six of us knew that there was another Rigellian here on Preeko this day." Tregonsee's telepathic thought had that dry humor which his association with Tellurians had cultivated in him. "He was male, of course. My wife would have insisted on that."

They all smiled, except for Tregonsee who couldn't and Lieutenant-Captain Buyyer who had just completed receiving a signal on the special S.I.S. channel.

"Gentlemen," Buyyer said, his youthful face gray, always a certain indication of extra bad news, "GP-Klovia-HQ reports five other hyperspacial tube attacks on five of our greatest scientists. The objective was different from the one against us. Not murder. Kidnapping!"

3

Riddle of the Datadrones

D. D. Cloudd wrapped the thick fingers of his heavy gauntlets around the grips of the handle bars and slammed his boot down on the accelerator. The rocket sled jumped forward under him. His knees, clamping around the engine's combustion chamber, barely kept his rump from sliding up over the curved back of the metal saddle. The heat from the plume of fire at his back could be felt through his light armor, but there was no thunderous roar from the shredded matter disintegrating into billions of ergs in the void of space. Only the familiar caressing quiver of the machine between his legs gave him the sense of accelerating power. The stars hung unmoving in the velvet blackness as the curved bowl of the edge of the Second Galaxy stretched in front of him.

With a twist of his left wrist, the engine gimbaled and the trail of fire flickered into his view to the rear of his left side. The incandescent tips of the snapping flames threw blue-white light into the corner of the globe which was his glass-steel helmet. His black eyes, nearly invisible behind his semi-opaque radiation goggles, were weirdly changed into reddish-golden discs with tiny, contracted pupils.

"Charge!" D. D. Cloudd shouted into the small, hollow bulge in front of his nose and mouth. Through his ear pads he could faintly hear himself, his voice true and natural with no electronic enhancement, and it made him feel physically close to himself, unfettered and free. It was once more one of

27

those rare times when his mind was cleared of its shadows, when his mood was elevated, when his soul was at peace. His machine, *The Spirit*, nourished him, sustained him. *The Spirit* was, indeed, for that moment, *her* spirit, fittingly memorializing the spirit of the one he mourned, Lucille.

An invisible hand suddenly grabbed them, man and machine, abruptly slowing them despite the raging, flaming power, bringing them to a complete stop.

"QX, Dee Dee!" a voice said in his ear. "The fun's over! We've got a scope-sighting at three-three-oh degrees right on our axis!"

Cloudd lifted his boot off the accelerator pedal even as he felt the grasp of the tractor beam, and jerked the machine around with some stabs of retro fire. The GP comm-con ship swung into view, a speck of light a thousand miles away from him now, although he had, on his joy ride, left it only seconds before. The boys at the tractor beam controls had been riding herd on him in their usual precise manner. When he went out for one of his pleasure jaunts, they knew what he expected of them—that they would pinpoint his every movement and be ready to yank him back where he belonged. It wasn't just to protect him from the usual natural troubles and the threats of ambushing, bushwacking Boskonians or inquisitive, short-circuiting datadrones—it was also to protect him from himself. Every so often he had rocketed out too far, in danger of becoming lost in the immensity of the void of deep space, and raising the scare of an expensive, time-consuming search by one or more ships before being found. Or maybe never found. D. D. Cloudd, everyone knew it and allowed for it, was sometimes a wild man caused by, the gossip held, some deep torment of grief.

"Thanks, guys! Three-three-oh, right on!"

There it was, the identified floating object, a datadrone barely on a trace reading on the tiny diode printout visible inside his helmet near the corner of his right eye. He couldn't yet judge its size or shape. He would have to rely on the comm-con scope.

"Fill me in, guys."

He got a torrent of audio and visual information which indicated one main fact: the datadrone was a 2X2, a small double satellite probe, cylindrically shaped and not much more than four feet long. This type of probe had been observed as large as twelve feet long, actually six separate ones joined. It was typically black, obviously a color chosen to make it as unobtrusive as possible, studded with lensed apertures in various sizes. It had no fins or rocket tubes, evidently propelled by magnetomotive or electrogravitonic forces. It bore no marks of any manufacturer. It seemed a one-piece casting rather than an assembly. Examined by three-dimensional perception penetration by various expert Lensmen from time to time, there was no indication of who or what made them, not the slightest suggestion of their source. It had become a fast-growing enigma of space.

The only thing which mental-wave examination had determined so far was that these machines were information collectors, probes from some mysterious intelligence, drones remotely controlled by some as yet undetermined radio frequency undetectable because its medium was hyperspace. When they had first begun to appear, only within the past half year, a descriptive term had seemed to spring spontaneously into use in the lingua franca of space, to be picked up by the Patrol. The term which stuck was "datadrone."

Cloudd, however, had no doubts as to their source: Boskonia.

He had observed three types of probes since his first observation of a cylinder five months before. This small cylindrical kind was the most common. The next largest, 18 feet long and torpedo-shaped, with long, open bays in its sides, had been seen a score of times, but only once by him. The largest had been seen only one time, at a great distance, by extremely sensitive instruments; its size had been judged to be fifty yards in length, very thick, with much superstructure covering it. In no case had any life form been observed. Type-50, the largest, had disappeared even as it was spotted. Type-8, the long torpedo shape, had been scanned by several Rigellians and Posenians before each machine had dashed away to disappear at hyperlight speed. Type-2X6, its smallest unit being 2X1, had, however, been captured a half-dozen times, three times by D. D. Cloudd himself. The first time made him a minor celebrity, and the third time made him an official datadrone investigator for the Patrol.

Cloudd was an enthusiastic hunter of them not only

because he believed that the drones were Boskonian-Spawn generated, but also because he was dedicated to wiping out every man and machine belonging to the scum of the spaceways known as the Spawn of the Boskone.

"Let's get at it," Cloudd told himself, talking to oneself being a habit lonely workers in space quickly cultivated. "Let's punch in my backup." His gloved fingers danced across the bank of over-sized buttons, the blinking red numbers rapidly changing as he fed the data into his onboard computer. Comm-con would be picking up the same information, showing the same displays, ready to operate him remotely, but only in an emergency. "Now, *Spirit*, baby, let's work together."

He manually fingered, elbowed, and toed his primary and secondary thrusters into forming a parabolic course. His first objective was to get himself between comm-con and the drone, to mask his steady approach.

He soon straightened out into a direct advance. The drone was invisible to his eye, and with neither a sense of perception nor a Lens, he had to rely on his own self-generated information or what was being fed from his mother ship. A quick glance at a dial, a peek at his interior printout, reassured him that the tractor boys still had a feather-light touch on him. He would need that if he could lasso the drone.

The thing hung steady in his viewing plate, although they were now matched with intrinsic velocities of several miles per second. The time had come to make his move. He snapped on his targeting device and slammed down on his foot accelerator, relaxing his grip on his rotatable handles so as not to interfere with the tiny retro corrections of the automatic targeting. His machine leapt forward at an almost unbelievable rate of acceleration. Because he was now locked in an empathetic inertia field with the machine, he suffered only a jolting snap, rather than being left unsaddled and alone in empty space with a riderless machine tearing off into infinity.

At the moment of his charge, Cloudd triggered a tractor beam directly forward in his line of flight. He was picking up speed so fast within milliseconds that the beam itself was barely moving faster than his machine. So quickly that he couldn't see it or even catch a reading, but sensed by his mind from past experience, the drone took evasive action. It was now heading off almost at right angles to his course. The tractor beam, however, had scored its hit. Cloudd preferred to draw an analogy with the old time American West: he had roped his ferocious steer. In actuality, however, it was much more like hooking a fish with an elastic line. The drone moved this way and that, stretching the tractor beam, but always, after a brief surge, losing distance.

Then the drone did the trick of a desperate fish. It headed back like an arrow toward *The Spirit*. If it didn't snap the beam, Cloudd knew it would be more than happy to collide with him, pulverizing them both at such high speeds. Now it was his turn, manually with all his skill and nudged on by his tactically prepared, thoroughly programmed computer, to dodge and squirm for his own life without letting go. He enjoyed the dangerous game. Nowadays these were the moments when he really felt most alive, when he was so close to death. Two assistants had lost the deadly game within the past month. They had been vaporized into a cloud of smashed molecules. He had had no more volunteers, so now he had this fun all to himself.

Another quick jab of his finger, anticipating his computer by another millisecond, and Cloudd had blanketed the drone with an electromagnetic field, and killed its power. The mysterious force which drove it simply ceased to be, kicking back no side effects. There was no dial flickering before or after. That it was an outside force, beamed into the drone or possibly sucked into it, was easily demonstrated by the way it was suffocated and subdued.

He tethered the four-foot long, dull black cylinder to his machine and then looked around. The comm-con ship, of course, was not in sight, nor was it registering on any of his instruments. How far the quick but violent conflict had carried them couldn't be judged. He could pick the information out of his computer, probably, and because his friends knew he was out here, in effect lost, they would be actively searching for him, too. It wouldn't be like the time he had joyously ridden so far away, without being monitored, that he had nearly run out of oxygen before he had been found. Now he had a powerful radio for emergencies, but it was really limited to extreme, severe situations, because it was also an invitation for a Boskonian, outlaw or otherwise, to get to him first. He hoped never to use it; it would be an invitation to ignominious death—or worse. Even with that radio, he was no longer foolish. He was always tracked now, especially when he was just out skylarking.

He waited patiently for seven or eight minutes, but then could no longer patiently bear the suspense. He put a tractor beam hook on the drone, with a several-frequencies beacon attached, and left it, to begin a wide, 50,000 mile sweep.

Unexpectedly, one chance in a million, perhaps, his instruments picked up another sighting. It was another Type-2X. The readout indicated a 2X4, perhaps the missing section to be linked up with the captured 2X2.

This time Cloudd had no comm-con backup. It was up to him on his own to trap this one. He made his decision within a split second of spotting it, and once more, but without circling, clamped down on his accelerator and headed straight for it. At the same time he broke his self-imposed communications silence by dispatching a pre-taped message: "Drone two by four. In pursuit." It wasn't a call for help. It was actually meant to be a message for the record—possibly from beyond the grave.

Cloudd came barreling in on his machine like an old-fashioned kamikaze pilot. If his judgment was right, if his reaction time was perfect, he would just miss it and net it in a blanket of force and tractor beams. If he didn't, well, he would be joining Lucille and so it wouldn't be all that bad.

The drone was up to the challenge. It took off like a frightened rabbit pursued by a bloodthirsty hound. At first it zigged and zagged without shaking its pursuer. Then it went into an undeviating line at maximum acceleration, beginning to draw away from the helpless Cloudd, who was pounding the sides of his machine with his knees and urging it on as if it were a living thing.

"By Klono's Curse!" Cloudd yelled to himself at what he suddenly saw. "I've pierced the veil!"

Registering on his target viewplate was the background symbol of a spaceship. It was unmistakably Boskonian! The drone was heading for it like a terrorized rabbit for its hole in the ground. And there were more of the little cylinders in the vicinity.

"Drones *are* Spawn!" he growled. "I knew it! I knew it!"

Behind his mental turmoil and the passion of his feelings, D. D. Cloudd's remarkable mind was ticking over faster than his computer. He would follow the drone in, hoping to mask his own tiny mass with the alarms sent up by the probe's own movements. Then he'd call for a duodec bomb to be torpedoed out at him from comm-con, and he'd deftly steer it into the Boskone's tubes and outrace the cataclysmic explosion.

Barely one-half minute had passed from the moment he had observed the ship, made his decision, and attempted to ride in under the cover of the drone. In barely one-half minute, the ship's lookout or its periphery screen or both had spotted him. They must have been exceptionally effective, although perhaps they had been on the alert for another reason, maybe the drone itself. Anyhow, he had been observed. There were missiles coming up at him, his own plates showed. A set of ten blazing balls in a line came out of the forward turret, another set followed from the rear turret.

A rapid run-down by his computer didn't identify the weapon. They were photon-encased warheads, and the brilliant white lights radiating from the series of them were now searing his sight. They were moving much slower than the speed of light. Now his computer identified the bullets: radiant energy on the outside, capable of burning out standard circuitry, with an interior of Sonic-P radiation, capable of paralyzing the respiratory system of a human. A souped-up P-gun! He was startled, not because P-weaponry had been outlawed, though Boskonians still used it, but because he had been identified as a human being. The time had been fantastically short for the enemy to have observed him, classified him as a life form, and identified him as human. They must have thought him to be an easy victim and his strange machine worth capturing undamaged.

Without a moment's hesitation, Cloudd broke off his tracking action on the drone. He turned tail and ran.

Was it that moment's hesitation so many years ago, when he should have turned tail and run, which caused the tragedy

33

then? Was it his foolhardy bravery or just plain obstinacy that had caused Lucille's death?

He looked at his screens. The pirate ship was following him, but slowly. They obviously were tracking him, curious as to where he had come from and where he was going, appearing such a pathetically tiny figure on a tiny machine in the middle of nowhere. Well, they were in for a shocking surprise. When the comm-con ship dropped its cloak of invisibility, the cat that was trailing the mouse would come face to face with an unfriendly dog.

No, he wasn't being cowardly now. His instant decision was based on attack, not retreat. He could lead the Boskonian and its brood of drones to destruction. God Klono, how he hated Boskone and its Spawn!

That day when Lucille died—if he hadn't turned to snap at the pirate's heels, she would still be alive. Probably, that is. When the liner had been attacked she had been lacerated by the blast, burned within her lungs by the inhaled radiation, partially paralyzed by the Vee-Two gas. Vee-Two gas! On innocent civilians—women and children. The swine! The damned swine!

He had swung the lifeboat around to impress in his mind the shape and markings of that Boskonian murder-ship. He had wanted to remember it well, in the greatest detail. If he hadn't turned back, even for those brief seconds, they would never have rayed his craft and left them for dead. He had been lucky. A month floating in space and then rescue, the sole survivor. Lucky? Not really, when it was his whole future life in her that he watched draining away—death coming within days of salvation. Poor Lucille. The wife that would never be, always to remain just his betrothed.

Damn the Boskonians! Deucalion lived and Pyrrha died! And he would exist only to be her avenging angel.

D. D. Cloudd was filled with hatred, but it did not blind him to his task. The Boskonian ship was keeping its distance, so he casually detoured to pick up the drone he had staked out. As he did so he formulated a trap.

He broke radio silence. "Pull me in. Stay cloaked. I've got quarry to harvest." Would they understand?

They did understand, those marvelous guys on the tractor beam controls. He was whipped inside the single entry port, dragging the captive 2X2 drone behind him. "Tell the captain, steady as she goes," Cloudd tossed over his shoulder as he dashed into the munitions room, helmet under his arm, white scarf flying. He took an oversized duodec grenade off a rack, armed it, and stuck it inside his sleeve bag. If he jogged the pin loose, that section of the ship would be atomized when the rest of the munitions went. Along with him, the tractor beam boys would go, too. What the hell, they were his friends so they would all go together.

"The devil . . . ?" said one of the crew, seeing what he had done with the small bomb.

"I'm gonna get that rat out there," Cloudd said. "Tell the captain to stay clear. Until the obvious."

Cloudd was back on his sled and out the port before anyone could issue any restraining orders.

There was the Boskonian still there, sitting like a cat before a mousehole, ready to pounce. There could be no doubt in their intelligence section that inside the warped spot in space before them sat a Galactic Patrol ship waiting to strike a counterblow. But they wouldn't be expecting him.

As he hurtled back out toward the pirate, he took the bomb and fixed it to one of his tractor hooks. The hook, with its tracking device, was designed to follow any evasive action of a drone, attach itself, and be a marking beacon and an easy "hook" for a slender tractor coupling. With the bomb and the tracker interlocked, Cloudd placed it back in the release rack.

He could now eyeball the enemy ship. He also spotted the drone he had been chasing, floating end-over-end with no other movement, stationary in relation to the ship. Then, as he approached it, it turned at right angles and shot away, off his screens, and out of register. The acceleration must have been tremendous. He had a preposterous idea that it was propelled by a mini-Bergenholm engine.

Real heavy, dangerous stuff was now coming up at him. As the rays passed through the protective shield they made the field luminescent. Real heavy stuff. But they weren't aimed at him! They were ten degrees to starboard. That couldn't be bad marksmanship. It had to mean something else.

35

Puzzled, Cloudd adjusted his viewing plate at full magnification along the trajectory, searching for a target at which they might be firing. He found it.

"By all the purple fires!" Cloudd told himself, "I'm hitting the jackpot."

Whirling crazily around, as if out of control from a malfunctioning gyrostabilizer, was a Type-50 datadrone. Type-50! Spidery, complex, cryptic! He could not spot it visually, but his electronics all identified it and displayed it under three simultaneous magnifications. It was the first one he, personally, had observed, and the graphic recordings his equipment was now making of it would be better than anything the Patrol possessed.

He turned on his transmitter and opened up his radio channel. No need for secrecy now, and comm-con should know as much as possible about what was happening.

Comm-con was automatically getting everything, practically as it was developing, but he felt the need to talk anyway. "I've uncovered the nest. It's a Spawn ship. Type-50 nearby. Drop your screen and move in. I'll do my best to keep them occupied." Planting his bomb could come later, as a last resort.

He turned on a visual signal in addition to his radio transmission, to protect himself from being unobserved and thus to be caught in his own side's fire. He had to take the chance that the Spawn ship, in the excitement, wouldn't notice his signal and use it to zero in on him for an annihilating blast.

Nowhere, in every direction near the spinning Type-50 drone, could he find what was threatening it. The potent enemy beams were certainly not after him, weaving all around the drone, as though defending it. But from what?

Cloudd felt his space scooter lurch. His instruments confirmed that he was in the grip of a tractor beam which was fast drawing him—as well as the drone—closer to the pirate ship. If he were the pirate captain, he'd clamp a number of tractors on both himself and the drone, and whisk them away to another empty sector of space and force the Patrol ship into a cat and mouse game. By now they certainly knew of the Patrol's presence and strength and, although the Boskonians had the power to fight a more-or-less equally matched engagement, they wouldn't. They fought principally for loot, not because of fundamental rivalry.

The Patrol ship's tactical action could be only seconds away, so Cloudd seized the initiative. With only fair luck he would delay the enemy and its satellite long enough to permit their capture.

Cloudd jabbed on the power and dove straight down the tractor beam. Halfway to the ship, he launched a tractor hook at it, swerved, bending the pirate's tractor beam dangerously close to the probing destructive rays stabbing toward the drone. The pirate snapped off the tractor beam, fearful of the feedback of the two incompatible forces if they touched. Cloudd then pulled up close to the large drone, between it and the mother ship, synchronizing his own movements as nearly as possible with the erratic dancing of the drone. Any shots taken at him now would have to be delicately plotted, due to his size, if they didn't want to simply wide-spray him and thus destroy their own drone. Come on, Patrol! Hurry up!

The Boskonian captain knew what he wanted to do. The gunners widened the beam and nearly got Cloudd and *The Spirit*. It did clip one end of the drone in a shower of sparkling colored balls.

Out of the damaged drone came a Type-8, and then from it, like seeds puffed from a seed pod or a covey of quail flushed from a thicket, came a score of 2X1 types, scattering in all directions. There was a multitude of muzzle flashes from the ship and almost continuously, one by one, the 2X1s turned into lines of flaming Chinese firecrackers! As a climax, the Type-8 vaporized in a purplish flash!

Cloudd did a quick re-think. The drones couldn't be Boskonian after all. Now he began to see the truth. Datadrones belonged to some unknown third party. Not Boskonian, not of the Patrol. The pirates hadn't been protecting the drone, they had been trying to disable it. They weren't a mother ship attempting recovery of a wounded child, they had been trying to disable it to capture it, just as he was. And they probably thought that it was some new kind of Patrol technology. He would have to reconsider his entire datadrone program, develop an entire new approach—and he would have to isolate, if not drastically modify, his personal vendetta against the Spawn.

He launched his duodec bomb, speeding it toward contact with the hook he had already planted on the enemy ship.

One of the lethal beams barely slipped past Cloudd and struck the Type-50 as a searing white horizontal line almost centered between stem and stern, missing the painted ZZ symbol on its side. Cloudd recognized that usual, customary identification: it was proportionately larger, compared to the ones on the little 2X1s, a double Z, but with softly curving angles like a reversed set of double S's. The mark of the drones.

The searing line became a cut, and the blade of the beam went through, slicing the Type-50 into two parts, the larger section exploding in a blossoming field of released molecular particles. It was somehow strange, like nothing he had ever seen. No doubt now. The datadrone was considered unfriendly by the Boskonian. Cloudd's deduction was confirmed.

The blast should have pulverized Cloudd, too, but he was lucky. At the moment of the explosion, a tractor beam from the attacking Patrol ship enveloped him, cushioned him from the blast, and snapped him to safety, right out of the yawning jaws of a fiery hell.

The various forces knocked him into a blackout.

Some time later, when he had recovered, he found himself on the cot by the interior airlock of his own ship. The Officer of the Deck was standing over him.

"Did we get the S.O.B.?" Cloudd said, trying to push himself upright.

"The Boskone? It took off under full Bergenholm drive."

"I tried to put a tractor hook on it. Didn't it stick?"

"Yes, we spotted the hook and latched on to it. We had a tug of war for a few split seconds, but they cut away with their shears. They're gone. But I'll bet they had a real scare."

Cloudd was on his stockinged feet, right hand pressing a pad against his nose to keep the bleeding stopped, staggering toward the control deck. The ship's captain met him in the doorway. The suppressed anger marking the captain's stern face softened a bit, but Cloudd felt an unaccustomed sense of guilt for his unsanctioned recklessness. As a sort of conciliatory gesture, Cloudd threw the captain a weak but sincere salute with his left hand. Two fingers, the last two, were half missing, the result of not this but some past foolishness.

"You're a lucky barst'd, Cloudd," the captain chided him in his thick, old English accent. "'Twas a foolhardy move you made." He clapped him on the shoulder. "But a brave one, mate. We almost had ourselves a live Boskonian and one of its drones."

"My theory's wrong, cap'n," Cloudd said, ignoring the compliment. "The drones aren't Boskonian. Consider this: Judging by the size of the pirate ship, they would be as updated on activities in this remote sector of the galaxy as we are. They smashed the little drones and tried to capture the larger one, as if they thought we were controlling them."

"Bloody hell!" said the captain. "Do I surmise we have an unknown alien power in the fish stew?"

"I wish the Type-50 hadn't been destroyed," Cloudd said wistfully.

"Tell yer, Dee Dee, m'boy, things aren't as bad as you think. We've got part of it stowed aboard. And it's mor'n just a wee piece!"

Cloudd just let a big grin slowly split his face.

"Pardon me, captain," said a messenger who had just come up behind them. "Readings show something like a nova in the general direction of that Boskonian. A brilliant flare of a rather insignificant energy reading."

"About the sort of thing made by a certain exploding Boskonian ship?" the captain commented, with a wry smile. "It could be a decoy flare, off enough degrees to mislead us, if we were chasing. But then on the other hand, it could have something to do with that duodec bomb you planted, Cloudd!"

D. D. Cloudd, Patrol Technician Class Triple-A, made his smile even broader and it didn't even waver when the captain added, "About that bomb, Cloudd, I haven't made up my mind whether it's a medal for you—or a court-martial!"

"Pardon, captain, but there's also another message. It came in just before the enemy broke off the engagement. F-I-O, for information only, signed Kinnison."

"Just prior to the disengagement? The message came in the clear?"

"No, sir. Simple code."

"Well, son, I'll come up and study it."

"It's not that long, sir. It's very simple. The enemy could have decoded it before disengaging, if that's what you implied, sir. It just says, 'Hyperspacial tube attacks have been reported against individual personnel. Report any abnormal instrumental or personal readings.'"

"My staff has been so informed?"

"Yes, sir. One more thing, sir. The drone is awaiting examination by Technician Cloudd. But there has been a tragedy. One of our new technicians, a man of little experience, opened it without authorization and was killed, possibly by a burst of anti-matter. We have left everything untouched for Technician Cloudd's attention. Scanning indicates that the drone contains an Ordovik crystal."

4

Shell Game

ᘒᘒᘒᘒᘒᘒᘒᘒᘒᘒᘒᘒᘒᘒᘒᘒᘒᘒᘒᘒᘒᘒ

Three abnormally large coffins sat in the center of the room. Standing at the five corners of the pentagonal lounge of the *Dronvire,* in formal stance but at ease, were the honor guards. On the right upper arms of their silver dress tunics were wide mourning bands of black.

Captain Frank Garner, in the ritual role of Officer of Honor, sat on a high, wheeled war room stool at the head of the oval containers. The curved sides of the plain, handcrafted metal chests were polished to a mirror finish, banners of the Galactic Patrol covering the closed lids, draped halfway from head to foot. He sat relaxed. The situation had been stabilized, the mock death of Tregonsee was now under way to provoke some revealing reaction from the hired assassins or their bosses, and the *Dronvire* was about ready to leave for Klovia and home. Best of all, every one of the five scientists had been recovered unharmed, released within an average of an hour or so of captivity. The reports weren't clear, but evidently all five tubes had remained in place the entire time. Perhaps the tubes had misfired, thwarting even one successful kidnapping, or perhaps they had held the men under hypnotic interrogation for days or weeks, using stretched-out multi-dimensional time. In the temporary mental absence of Tregonsee, Garner had ordered an extensive S.I.S. inquiry with a recommendation for questioning at a high level.

Standing in front of the Klovian Lensman was a skeletal

figure in immaculate Patrol ceremonial uniform. The same kind of black band was on his arm, and the same distinctive over-the-shoulder braid identifying him as one of the staff of Tregonsee hung from his narrow shoulder. This was P'Keen, the Ordovik Lensman with the unique touch of aristocratic Manarkan blood. His breeding had given him startlingly all-white, but not albino, eyes so that the constant expanding and contracting of his black pupils against the pure whiteness made his gaze hypnotic and piercing. His stick figure was further emphasized by the vertical folds of his eyes and mouth and the vertical vents of his nostrils and ears. He was odd-looking, but he was not unhandsome. In contrast to the huge bulk of the Klovian Garner, the Ordovik P'Keen seemed a ridiculously skinny and delicate porcelain caricature of a decrepit human being. Actually, with his agility and coiled-steel-spring strength, Garner knew that the apparent fragility disguised a physical strength almost as great as his own, within the limitations of weight and mass.

"Sir," P'Keen said silently to Garner, "Commander Lzbert want to know if there are any changes to the news releases which we have prepared concerning the deaths." P'Keen, as a natural, highly gifted telepath, rarely talked aloud if he could help it. "Already one newsman is outside, waiting."

Both of them knew what that cover story was, for they had, with Tregonsee, prepared it. The three coffins supposedly contained the bodies of three Patrolmen, one of them a Lensman, who had been killed by a Boskonian bomb in Peace Square. The three were being returned home.

"QX to the commander, P'Keen," Garner said. "Now that you're here, check on the stowage of Tregonsee's atmosuit. Dronvire is ready to depart."

Garner, unable to make his own inspection, was very uneasy about that suit, the Ordovik could sense. For good reason! Meppy was in one of the coffins, while Tregonsee was being smuggled out of the palace in the suit. Once locked inside, Tregonsee was virtually helpless, so his aides had absolute responsibility for his safety.

P'Keen, in the constraining presence of the coffins, formally saluted and stiffly marched away.

When he looked, a few moments later, the locker where Tregonsee's atmosuit should have been was empty.

Empty! There was no suit!

P'Keen found the idea unbelievable, impossible. With growing anxiety, he searched through the storage room, through the adjoining storage rooms, through the whole deck area. As he made his search, he gathered around him more and more crew members, until a score or more of persons were looking.

Garner caught the sense of panic, followed by the details. This was no accident, no oversight. Tregonsee had been kidnapped. Perhaps this time he really was dead.

Desperate as the situation was, Garner could not abandon the plan and leave his post. Too many spy-rays, watchers, and perceivers would be avidly watching this tableau.

When P'Keen, summoned by Garner, arrived, a complete spy-ray defense and thought screen was thrown around the room to allow their minds to freely exchange thoughts. Garner ordered the doors closed and each of the honor guard to station himself on the other side, to permit no one to enter, and then he had thrown his mind frantically at P'Keen's, seeking every bit of information.

The intensity of their concern and concentration caused them to overlook what was happening.

The ranking officer of the guard, the last to leave, had closed the last door—from the inside. Alone with the two Lensmen, he whirled and stalked back toward them.

They looked up in astonishment at him.

He had drawn his DeLameter and was aiming it unwaveringly at them!

"Gentlemen," the officer said, "you will now proceed to open the Rigellian's coffin."

When he received no response, he waved his weapon threateningly. "I can shoot you both and open it myself, if that's your wish. Now do it!"

Garner and P'Keen, instantaneously reading each other's mind, together threw a powerful, crushing bolt of mental power against the renegade Patrolman. The resistance which nullified their effort flabbergasted them.

"I am a Lensman, too," said the officer. "Now open the

coffin!" They obeyed, wondering what strange plot was afoot. Was someone else looking for Tregonsee?"

When the lid went up, the officer immediately said, "That's not Tregonsee! Open the other two coffins!"

They did and each time the officer became more disturbed. Now he was enraged. Instead of talking, he was hitting their minds with his thought. "That Rigellian is not Tregonsee! What have you done with Tregonsee?"

As both P'Keen and Garner floundered around mentally, trying to throw the stranger out of their heads, fighting to keep their mental shields intact, searching themselves for the proper response, a new twist took place. At one of the doors, there was much noise, and a different shift of honor guards marched in. At the rear of the file of five there shuffled, ponderously, a Rigellian!

P'Keen and Garner were bewildered. Was this one of the Rigellians on the crew? Impossible. This Rigellian was a fantastic apparition, the likes of which the Klovian and the Ordovik had never seen before. Perhaps it was the newsman?

The barrel body was nearly hidden by yards and yards of soft black fabric, many ends trailing on the floor. The guards were Patrolmen whom they had likewise never seen before.

"Taylu!" the Rigellian projected sharply at the renegade officer. "Congratulations! You've found me!"

"Tregonsee!" said Taylu, flustered by having his question answered before he had asked it. "Yes, I'm looking—was looking—for you! I feared that you—that is—well . . ."

"Good work," said Tregonsee—and his two staff officers now suddenly recognized him; Rigellians to humanoids nearly always looked alike—"Obviously, our S.I.S. contingency alert plans for a missing V.I.P. must work." It came to P'Keen then that Tregonsee was dressed in a gossamer gown of mourning. How had he managed that?

"Excuse me, sirs," P'Keen said in his soft voice, his skinny fingers spread wide in a pleading gesture. "Excuse me, sirs," he repeated mentally. "Do you mind—?" He now was pointing at all the guns. The Patrolman called Taylu still had his DeLameter's muzzle near their midsections, and the guards all had their guns trained on the three of them.

With a thought from Tregonsee, they all holstered their weapons.

"Thanks for the concern, Taylu," said Tregonsee. "These are Garner and P'Keen. You've no doubt heard of them." Taylu opened his mind briefly to introduce himself.

To them, as high level S.I.S. administrators, they were only mildly surprised to have it revealed that Taylu was an operator within the ultra-secret Special Missions Forces.

He was Preekoan, an undercover agent high in the Preekoan royal councils, who, being informed by secret S.I.S. channels that "T" was in extraordinary danger, had evoked the authority of a "danger priority" standing order and acted on his own initiative. The mystery at the hospital had prompted him to board *Dronvire* with his legitimate credentials. Acting with other S.M.F. agents already on board, he had managed to be posted on the honor guard. Once in the chamber, he planned to open all the coffins to confirm the death or uncover an abduction, then to report it to GP-Klovia-HQ-T.

P'Keen and Garner, at the centers of power though they were, marveled at the foresight of Tregonsee and the ingenuity, independence and initiative of the men in the field like Taylu.

"As for these other Patrolmen," Tregonsee said, "they also are some of my secret agents in transit," making quick introductions on a first-name basis.

The two Tregonsee aides found this revelation even more disconcerting. Tregonsee, with his prodigious mind, had apparatuses paralleling apparatuses within his secret organizations, secrets being kept from those who keep the secrets. Even they didn't know all the intricate planning and safeguards instituted by Tregonsee, nor about the complicated security arrangements in case of his disappearance, disability or death. S.I.S. cells were scattered around wherever Tregonsee trod—backup forces, reserves of power, unidentified but all-pervasive. Everybody in the room at that moment was part of his far-flung forces. Agents all!

"Everyone, it seems," the huge Rigellian said, "has been trying to expose our deception or rescue me. All our anonymous agents on board in the process of routine transfers have gotten into the act. Some have acted independently, not aware of the others. Some actually are working secretly on behalf of my own HQ out of Klovia. Hiding in my atmosuit, my mind anesthetized, really shook them up. It was a clever

45

deduction which led them to steal the atmosuit, drag it into the radiation-shielded engine room, find me, and then revive me. So, here I am, out earlier than you planned. The S.I.S. response has been outstanding, so it's time now to move to the next act of our scenario."

"Where did you get the mourning clothes?" Garner asked, no longer able to contain his curiosity. "Was it from that Rigellian news reporter for the joint galactic news services who flitted in from the nearby space liner? I thought I had barred him from this ship."

"No, I improvised them. However, that news reporter is aboard the *Dronvire*. I overruled you. He's actually the S.M.F. sector coordinator, traveling on S.I.S. orders from Klovia, worried like the rest. He made a narrow-Lensed contact with me and I decided he could be useful. He is genuinely a newsman. And, incidentally, he's Taylu's boss, which makes him due for a big surprise when he sees you, Taylu."

"Can you tell us now what the next step is which you've planned around your death deception?" P'Keen asked.

"I'm going to stay conscious, project my ego into Meppy's dead brain cells, and convince all illegal monitors that I'm barely alive, though mortally wounded, being rushed back to Klovia, which ought to make my unit-cluster happy. If the enemy can still use a hyperspatial tube after our new countermeasures, they'll attempt to get to me in my helpless state. If they really want me, that is. They might even be foolish enough to ambush the *Dronvire*."

"Aren't all sorts of alarming reports reaching Kinnison and the Galactic Council?" Garner asked seriously. "From Taylu and others? Are you sure you want to continue all this chicanery?"

"The highest levels, including Kinnison, are aware, of course, of the true situation," Tregonsee said. "The trouble seems worse than it is. I'm playing a hunch that we are involved in a gargantuan, outrageous conspiracy. My deception is certain to bring at least one halfway-decent inkling. I need only one solid hint. Now let's all get back to doing our routine things and let me get on with acting no longer dead, but dying. I'm proud of you, Taylu, and the rest of you and the whole S.I.S."

After Tregonsee, his "mourning" escort, and Taylu and

the other Patrolmen of the "rescue" party had gone from the room, Garner and P'Keen prepared for the visit of the newsman, the undercover Rigellian S.M.F. chief. His judicious appearance would give an authentic ring of truth to their cover story. When Garner had climbed back on his stool, P'Keen in position at his side, Commander Lzbert walked in to give them some confidential reports.

"We are scheduled," the commander said, "to rendezvous with Coordinator Kinnison aboard the *Dauntless* this evening. He's presently en route, picking up the five kidnap victims and others at various points along the way. Even with these pickups, breaking his inertialess flight, a meeting is slated for 1055 hours."

Garner told him of Tregonsee's revival and altered plan, but did not mention the appearances or activities of the secret agents which seemed to infest his ship.

"That may explain the sudden new order from Tregonsee," Lzbert said. "P'Keen, you're relieved as Buyyer's assistant and are no longer on my staff. Incidentally, the ship has been undergoing extensive scanning from every imaginable place and from every imaginable source in the Second Galaxy. I'm not certain we can keep our screens from being badly punctured without our knowing it." Lzbert cocked his head at P'Keen. "I'm talking to you, P'Keen, as one of my ex-officers— you've got greater natural powers than either of us, so you're not only better protected, you're also more vulnerable. Don't disappoint ol' Lzbert."

"Yes, sir. Not a chance of that, sir!"

"Next then," the commander continued, "there's this thing about Project 2-5-2-6. Tregonsee is urgently requested to act on 2-5-2-6. I'm supposed to transmit his reply to a list of Patrol sections. What do I do?"

"That can wait, commander," Garner said. Both he and P'Keen knew about that project. It concerned the Boskonian planet of Tanse. S.M.F. communications had traced a priority call for assistance from one of a pair of its best operators who had infiltrated Tanse officialdom. Tansers were reported as celebrating Tregonsee's death! The death plot, in this case, seemed to be bearing fruit. "Notify all sections that Tregonsee will send them a message at 1130 hours." That should be shortly after their meeting with Kinnison was under way.

"What's my job, commander?" P'Keen asked. "Am I now Captain Garner's assistant?"

"Something like that, P'Keen." Garner was the one who replied, giving a throaty laugh and a smile so large that his meaty face grew deep wrinkles and his eyes were half obscured by his round, upraised cheeks. "Only it's practially the other way round. You're my replacement. You're Tregonsee's new aide-de-camp—whenever I'm absent."

P'Keen registered his shock and pleasure along with his wonderment about the change.

He could feel Lzbert's sincere good wishes and congratulations flooding in on him.

"When you get to the *Dauntless*, P'Keen, Treg will brief you on your duties. In the absence of Treg's executive officer back at Ultra Prime, whom we're not to contact for a day or two or even a week, you'll also be acting exec."

The Ordovik was unruffled and showed no emotion, except that his pupils grew as large as an owl's in darkness so that almost no whiteness showed. "I'm honored, men. But I don't understand why me."

"I've got to stay with the coffins," Garner explained. "I may have to take that one all the way to Rigel IV. You see, I'll still be seen as Treg's aide-de-camp. I'll be part of the decoy. However, there's an even better reason—you're an Ordovik, and you can sense hyperspatial tubes. That makes you eye tee, it, my skinny friend. You're *it*."

Garner shook the thin hand. "Now for the shell game. Treg's the elusive pea. Shell number one is the coffin. Shell number two is the atmosuit. When the coffin was moved out of the palace, Treg was in shell one, simulating death. That seemed right. Treg went into the suit then, shell number two. Meppy, sewn up, cosmetically looking like Treg, went into one. We've made the switch twice so far, just to block any interference from the other plane of existence, on the advice of Worsel and Lalla Kallatra. We've got a deep-space radiation shield around the suit now. Maybe Treg won't be able to give off his after-image aura out of Meppy's coffin. In which case we'll be moving the pea around again. Anyhow, the shell game continues one way or another until Treg is able to emerge safely in the *Dauntless*. If anyone can keep in touch with Treg through all these different barriers, it ought to be you, P'Keen."

"One thing I'd like Commander Lzbert to do..." P'Keen hesitated. "Am I now sharing responsibilities with you? Can I give orders?"

"You are and you can," Garner said. "Go ahead. Make your suggestions and give your orders. Just check with me while I'm still around."

"I want you, commander," P'Keen said, "to ask that the Chaplain General immediately join Kinnison. Then inform everyone, absolutely everyone who could conceivably be interested, that we are awaiting instructions from the Chaplain General before making any religious preparations. I have a terrible, terrible feeling that something is about to go terribly, terribly wrong. Get *Dronvire* into space immediately. And send those messages immediately. Can you?—Immediately?"

"Immediately," Commander Lzbert said, and true to his word, actually ran out of the room, away from the mental screens, to instruct his pilot house and his signals room.

"What do you feel?" Garner asked, anxiously.

"I don't know. Let me see if Treg can link up with me."

P'Keen knelt by the middle coffin, over Meppy, his head bowed and resting on the polished curved edge. Captain Garner, still playing the part of ADC, sat quietly on the high stool watching. The Ordovik seemed like a spectral figure of death in the uniform of the Patrol, his bony, white fingers pressed against his thin, white face.

P'Keen concentrated on reaching Tregonsee. He reached with all his power, but near as he was to his subject, as close as they were in harmony, as prepared as they were for mental touching, he could not. He did feel, though, a vague and mystic power of the Lens. He recognized, then, the strangeness of his feelings—there was a sense of decay and death—it was Meppy's Lens disintegrating. Somehow its life had continued far longer on its inevitable time track to disintegration and death. No Lens could live after its owner had died, that was the inescapable fact of the living Lens of Arisia. Yet sometimes, for reasons not completely understood, a Lens might be like the last ember of a dead fire, the final throes of life still stirring in the ashes.

The strangeness came from the interaction with the Lens of Tregonsee. That was the reason for the creeping death of

Meppy's Lens, perhaps. They were there together, lying side by side in an inner pocket of the suit. The host of one, still living; the host of the other, dead. That was where Meppy's Lens had been placed, untouched by any hands because of the certain knowledge of its power to kill anyone but its own, individual, attuned wearer. And that was where Tregonsee's unworn Lens had been placed, hidden from prying rays and senses, so that none should know that because it lived, then so did Tregonsee. A vibrant Lens would be a dead giveaway, he thought, with macabre humor.

What was the sense of foreboding that he, P'Keen, had? What dreadful calamity was his sensitive soul expecting?

Hour after hour passed with the throbbing of the great ship's engines, driving at ever-multiplying speeds of light at an unutterably fantastic velocity which destroyed all time and space.

When the *Dronvire* dropped from inertialess flight to its standard intrinsic, P'Keen, for hours in almost a trance, almost hearing Tregonsee, but never quite, was told. It took a strong bolt of thought from Garner to break through to him.

"We're here, P'Keen!" The mental wave was quivering with concern. "We're alone! *Dauntless* is not here!"

When Kinnison said he would be some place at a certain time, then he would be there, no matter what hell stood in the way. Something had gone wrong.

"Lower the spy-blocks and the mind screens," P'Keen said, his unconsciousness demanding that he give the order. P'Keen knew, with unshakable conviction, that he must always obey his intuition.

A great pressure passed away from his mind. He felt that Tregonsee was silently near him, watching what he was doing.

Then, over thousands and thousands and thousands of light years of distance, as the thought of an S.I.S. agent was reflected back and forth across the galaxies in a millisecond of time, searching on the confidential personal frequency of the S.I.S. head, came the Lensed thought from Rigel IV:

The Federal Government of Rigel IV was about to declare Tregonsee dead by an assassin's bullet. The Rigellian government, a small and simple collection of parttime volunteer public servants, understood that such news would throw the whole peace-keeping process into turmoil and stimulate a revival of Boskonian assaults on Civilization. The Rigellian bureaucracy and citizenry didn't really care, but nevertheless they were meeting their responsibilities and were keeping their decision top secret, and requesting the Galactic Coordinator to confirm the death and to release the facts in the best way to minimize the terrible repercussions. To meet religious dogma, the funeral arrangements had to be announced within the next twelve hours.

"Lensman!" This was Tregonsee's own powerful thought radiating out in answer. "Can you stop this? Can you at least delay such a declaration for two days?"

"No, sir," came the faint answer back without pause. "Twelve hours is the limit. Maybe even less."

"What is the source?" Tregonsee asked. "What part of Boskonia is responsible?"

"It is not Boskone, nor is it the Spawn, nor any scoundrel who causes this, sir."

"Who, then? Do you know who does cause this?"

"It is your own unit-cluster, Tregonsee. Both of them made a formal request here on Rigel."

"My unit-cluster? But I am not dead!"

"Their request for clarification was examined, as it must be, under law. When the government looked, it found much rumor. The notice-of-death has been provisionally requested from the Patrol."

Unit-cluster!

Both P'Keen and Garner—who had been drawn into the exchange—were shocked. They had overlooked the unit-cluster! The faked death had even fooled the remaining duo-egos of the three-fold Rigellian id. The dynamics of Rigellian sociology was never fully appreciated by humanoids.

Once in a while I get surprised, came Tregonsee's thought. *But never this enormously! Efficiency by Rigel IV bureaucracy! How ironic, that this should happen to me! Mepauhurrat I carefully covered, but not myself, who really didn't need it!*

The complicated situation now unveiled could be easily understood when simplistically explained:

Two-thirds of Tregonsee's empathetic soul was now claiming one-third of itself!

5

The Three-Unit Cluster

∽∾∽∾∽∾∽∾∽∾∽∾∽∾∽∾∽∾∽∾∽∾∽∾∽∾∽∾∽∾∽∾

The big pea in the shell game had now been shifted.
Tregonsee was back in the coffin in a drug-induced self-
hypnotic trance of death-brink. This death-brink was the
condition of life-release on the threshold of the next plane of
existence, when the soul hovered undecided between true
life and true death. This was no mere faking of death, a
momentary suspension of the self or a temporary withdrawal
of the life-essence into a secret place, alive but hiding. It was
Tregonsee's attempt to call the spirits of his other cluster-
units in rapport with his—and thus to reassure them and to
forestall the problems they were unleashing. He would try
this until the *Dauntless* arrived. Neither P'Keen nor Garner
would monitor him, for it was much too tricky and dangerous.

Right after the Lensed message from the contact from
Rigel, when Tregonsee had made his decision and had briefed
them about Rigellian cluster culture, given them advice, and
then had returned to the coffin, P'Keen and Garner had gone
to Commander Lzbert's private quarters. There they scruti-
nized the latest of the many dispatches and confidential
reports which increasingly were flowing into *Dronvire's* signals room. The two Lensmen also were explaining to Lzbert
as much as he could be permitted to know of the latest
development.

"By all the icy hells of Onlon!" Garner was exclaiming,
torturing himself again by recalling all details. "Treg knew,

but we didn't, so we didn't help!" As for P'Keen, his continued reaction to the discovered flaw in the plan was the constant pressing of his fingers against the pulse beating rapidly at his bony temples.

"The three-unit clusters, commander," Garner said, savagely shaking his head. "That's a detail which can be our undoing. We may have as much a disaster on our hands as though Treg had really been assassinated, if Tregonsee allows his fearlessness to push him too far."

"Three-unit cluster," Commander Lzbert said, puzzling over the phrase. "I've heard of that. Isn't it some sort of religious secret which humanoids are not supposed to know about?"

"It's not delicate to mention it, that's all," Garner said. "It's an intimate detail in the life of a Rigellian."

"Ah, yes. Something about *mélange-ou-ménage à trois?*"

"Not the way you think. Sex doesn't have much to do with it. Rigellians grow up as units of three. When Tregonsee was raised on Rigel IV his culture made him a part of a companionship with two other Rigellians of identical ages. The three of them were raised together. They were a very closely knit unit, known as a three-unit societal cluster. Sometimes there may be five-unit clusters, but that's another story. When they each reached the equivalent stage of adolescence, they were analyzed for their personalities and were given sexes. Two became male and one female. The third possibility is as a neuter. For the rest of their lives the units of the cluster keep close spiritual touch with each other. They do this even though they may never closely associate with each other again or develop anything in common except their foster relationship. Great sickness or death brings them back into psychic relationship. See what's happened?"

"I think I do," Commander Lzbert said, having absorbed all this information and more in a split second. "The report of Tregonsee's death, followed by his simulated death, drew the other two together."

"Yes, that's it," Garner continued. "The male was a retired, should one say a 'worn out'?, nuclear radiologist; the female was a Rigel culture coordinator. Under law they have the right to be present at his deathbed, to sort of make complete the cluster once more, so it is said. Under their religion it is essential, a clear duty. The two units even have the right to claim his coffin."

"If Boskone has a finger in the pie," said P'Keen, "then steps have already been taken to do just that."

Commander Lzbert held up his hand for silence. The scores of squeals and squeaks and whistles which had been softly permeating the cabin, constantly telling the ship's captain what was always happening in and around his closed world, were changing their tunes and tempos.

"There's a ship coming through the barrier," the Martian said. "It sounds like the *Dauntless*." He jumped up and beckoned the others to follow him into the pilot house.

He was right. The *Dauntless*—that magnificent odd cross-breed of rugged warship and sleek private cruiser, studded with the bulbous pods of a research vessel and staffed by over two thousand Patrolmen—swung slowly in synchronous turning with the *Dronvire*.

"Darn if I didn't miss the maneuver," he complained to everyone around the con, slapping both his thighs. "Breaking through and then matching intrinsics with us, I wanted to see their perfect performance. I saw it once before. They're experts. Beautiful! There are only two ships in the entire Patrol that *Dronvire* can't outshine: the *Dauntless*, there, and the *Directrix*, which is something else again. Oh, well, I'll see it on replay—save that recording!—but it won't be the same thing as the moment it happens." He saw P'Keen's quizzical look. "Everything *Dronvire* does is tro-taped every second, but most of it is discarded sooner or later."

A voiced message was coming in over all systems. The speaker was Kimball Kinnison himself. It was his custom, as a courtesy to all, never to use the Lens when it wasn't needed. The Lens, he felt, was much like whispering—if possible, it was always to be used politely.

"Sorry I'm late. There's been a rash of rumors about Tregonsee's death and I've been plagued with questions." Kinnison knew that Tregonsee had organized his own Patrol ship, *Dronvire*, almost as an extension of himself. The crew was considered as part of Tregonsee's family. In the light of what was going on with Tregonsee's real "family," such a thought was, to P'Keen and Garner, exceedingly ironic.

"Greetings to all you men of the Patrol. I expect to speak

to each and every one of you before we part. Now, if you'll excuse me, there's work to be done. I'd like to go Lens-to-Lens with Captain Garner."

Garner made the narrow-band connection and informed him that it was P'Keen who was taking over as aide-de-camp and that, at the moment, they were both serving as ADCs and acting execs.

"We're in trouble, mates," Kinnison said. "No doubt you already know and have formulated your plans. But I'm not sure myself what's going on. I have reason to believe that Tregonsee isn't dead. I keep hoping against hope. But whatever game you boys are playing, I'll not queer it. That's why I think we're in trouble. Somebody seems to have overlooked Tregonsee's three-unit cluster. Know what I mean?"

Thank Klono for that alert Lensman on Rigel, P'Keen thought to himself. What a terrible embarrassment the intelligence services would have now had without prior knowledge.

"Yes, sir," P'Keen said. "That detail had been overlooked. But we are aware of it and expect to handle the problem." Should he tell Kinnison the whole truth? Galactic Coordinator though he was, he didn't need to know. He probably suspected the truth. Yet, after all, he was the great Kimball Kinnison, the legend. P'Keen had never met him as intimately as this before, so he felt somewhat nonplussed. "How have they contacted you, Kinnison, sir?" The Ordovik felt self-conscious about not using a title for the Galactic Coordinator, but the feeling was clear that Kinnison disliked titles and preferred to be like one of the boys.

"The Rigellian who this month is sort of the Minister of Culture contacted a Lensman on my local staff there and he's now in contact with me. That is, he's standing by for my answer. They want to know, is Tregonsee dead or mortally wounded? Is there any chance for recovery? Can they come to see him? In fact, they must come to see him or else have us send the body to Rigel for proper funeral arrangements. The Lensman has made it quite clear that they feel Tregonsee is not dead, but is being held captive. On the other hand, they also are making a discrepant claim that Tregonsee in disguise as a Lensman called Mepauhurrat is actually dead. I said I'd find out. But do what you must do. You're autonomous. Don't tell me anything you don't want me to know."

"Well, sir," P'Keen said. "You should know now, since we've come together safely. Tregonsee isn't dead. You'll be seeing him soon at the scheduled S.I.S. meeting at eleven hundred. Tell Rigel it will be another few hours before you know what is happening. Tell them the truth, that you haven't received a report from your staff yet. QX?"

"QX, P'Keen. I never doubted his indestructibility. But it sounds like you've got a humdinger of a deception going. See you at the meeting later this evening. Anything else? No? QX. Oh, incidentally, Worsel and Nadreck will both be here, no later than midnight. Kinnison out."

When Kinnison signed off, P'Keen and Garner exchanged knowing glances, without radiating any revealing thoughts. There was a problem they immediately recognized concerning the Rigellian three-unit cluster. Tregonsee's cluster was not a difficult problem to solve—Treg himself had told them what to do and how to handle it. It was Meppy's cluster, his two bereaved Rigellian units about to make their presence felt, who could crack the security and reveal the hoax.

To make good his promises, P'Keen tried immediately to contact his "highest authority"—Tregonsee. He took every precaution to make certain that he did not send Tregonsee unwittingly to his real death. Working as Garner's assistant, P'Keen checked out all security precautions, opened the coffin, and raised a right and left tentacle to expose the soft, flexible shell at the torso's joints. There, as directed earlier by Treg, he applied the drugs. Then, cautiously using insulated gloves to avoid a fatal touch, he took Treg's Lens, which had been recovered from the atmosuit, and disengaged it from the snap-around armlet into which it had been returned. The empty armlet he replaced on Treg's thick upper tentacle. The Lens he placed on Treg's forehead where it glued itself to the leathery shell by natural coadunation. While Garner applied the antidotes and restoratives and closely watched the various monitors, P'Keen began telepathic stimulation, both naturally and by Lens.

Tregonsee recovered slowly. His tentacles slid along the edge of padded sides and he tried to pull himself erect. Until he was strong enough to get out of the box under his own power, he would be trapped there, for it would have taken many more than two humanoids to lift the great bulk of the Rigellian.

P'Keen's mind managed to poke through the thick fog of disorientation.

"Tregonsee, sir! We're now aboard the *Dauntless*. Wake up!"

Despite the great intellect and powerful brain of the Rigellian, it took many minutes before he became coherent.

At first Tregonsee came upright by rocking himself up on the rim of his base with two tentacles pulling, two tentacles pushing. Then he rolled himself out of his bed box and planted his feet on the deck. "I have calmed my cluster," was his first projection. The Lens in his forehead was pulsating with surges of mental power, sending out questions and receiving quick answers. The new problem was quickly grasped and a solution offered.

"Have the *Dauntless*'s communications officer—the Rigellian's name is Cyclo, I believe—contact Meppy's cluster. He'll know how to do it, especially as they'll be expecting some kind of notification. Have him arrange for GP transportation for them to join Meppy. Have him warn them to keep utmost secrecy, which won't be difficult because the other units of a cluster have some understanding of the work their comrade does. Have him notify the Chaplain General and tell the general about an important Rigellian's funeral, standard procedure to be followed. I have just visualized a plan, in every detail, which I will tell you about before Meppy's survivors get here."

Very neat, thought P'Keen. The easy touch of a master thinker. P'Keen knew himself to be smart, knew he could cogitate along with the best brains around without faring too badly, but Tregonsee never ceased to amaze him, even in minor matters like this. The solemn, imperturbable placidity the Second Stage Lensman constanty exhibited, too infrequently punctuated by emotional responses with which his association with human types had corrupted him, was deceptive. Tregonsee was a hidden volcano of dynamic vitality. There was no doubt in P'Keen's very personal evaluation that Tregonsee, Lensman from Rigel IV, was considerably smarter than Kimball Kinnison, the boss himself, or even Worsel, the dragon Lensman.

"Don't worry about the cluster complications, friends,"
Tregonsee said, not reading their masked thoughts under
their strict orders of restricted communication, but intuitively
sensing their concern. "Anyone familiar with the Rigellian
culture will expect these muddles. They're natural. What
stirs up trouble is the fact that Rigellians are so long-lived.
Death, more often than not, is not peaceful. It's usually
violence, such as an accident, not old age, which ends a life.
So the cluster units are understandably agitated at times of
death, and want the facts about their foster relative. It's good
for our society. And it's also very good for our various secret
Patrol operations. Killing a Rigellian, especially one in the
S.I.S., is generally avoided by our enemies." Tregonsee tried
a few faltering steps. "There's another situation that must be
checked. What's the condition of my wife?"

P'Keen's face remained frozen in its smooth, white
calmness. He didn't know the answer to that question. In
fact, he didn't know there was a "condition" to worry about.
Garner replied almost immediately. "She's been given the
password by direct Lens. She won't take her life, although
she's been reported as having already done so. That's a rumor
no one will really accept until proved. That's just a standard
reaction. She's being looked after, secretly hidden, by one of
the boys." Then quickly in explanation to P'Keen: "That
wasn't on your admin briefing tapes. Rigellian spouses usually
commit suicide shortly after their mate's death, if the death is
not a natural one. Tregonsee's mating took place untold years
ago. The lifetime relationship that's formed at the time is
extremely close for many years. But after fifty years or so, a
wedded pair work their separate ways into their own personal
patterns, no longer dependent on the other. Over several
centuries there may be several such matings, forming a group
of spouses, always for life and with friendship between all
parties for ever—well, almost always. Sometimes after fifty
years or so the sex may be changed or neutered. There's
nothing like it in the cultures we were raised in." He paused
as they both thought about the Rigellian mores.

Tregonsee projected a feeling of admiration to Garner.
"I've never heard it expressed so clearly and so succinctly.
But then, I don't hear it discussed. Nor do I ordinarily let it
be discussed. This ship's sealed off. Therefore we can talk

freely of many things. Let us get back to the subject of my faked death. I am satisfied at the way things have been stirred up. Let's get up to Kinnison's cabin and have a conference of war."

P'Keen's immediate impression of Kimball Kinnison, the Galactic Coordinator, was overpowering. As their hands clasped in a handshake, with that peculiar twist which signalled the special, fraternal recognition of one Lensman for another, P'Keen was reduced to an inferiority he had never felt in associating with Tregonsee. Perhaps he didn't remember the past accurately, but more likely it was that Kinnison was everything P'Keen would have liked to be: highest in intelligence, analytically outstanding, perfect in physique. Kinnison was, indeed, the larger-than-life epitome of the pre-eminent race of the Tellurians from the third planet in the solar system of Sol. He was the super-heroic representative, without question, of the species of Homo sapiens, pre-eminent descendents from the Arisian life spores. Kinnison was of modest height, about six feet tall, not as tall as P'Keen himself, but his vitality seemed to add inches on that height. His movements had the flowing grace of a wild animal, and his eyes had the sparkle of a man completely in touch with every part of every living moment, and enjoying it. It was a rugged and handsome head, the Ordovik thought, and exceptionally massive. Behind the warmth and friendliness of his features was the hard foundation of a savage and a repressed killer—hunter and warrior. P'Keen felt himself immediately fall under his personal spell. Tregonsee would always command P'Keen's highest loyalty and respect, but from now on Kimball Kinnison would be his ideal Lensman.

"It's the mysteriousness of the attacks which bother me," Kinnison was saying. "Pow! They come. Zip! They go. We don't know they've arrived until all hell breaks loose. And the dark invaders aren't even scratched before pulling back, Trig."

Kinnison's use of the nickname "Trig" instead of "Treg" was an idiosyncrasy, P'Keen immediately realized, much more noticeable and distinctive to P'Keen now that he was for the first time actually in the presence of Kimball Kinnison.

"Why'd they do the hit-and-run attacks?" Kinnison continued. "They took great efforts to have a dozen or so of our very best scientists caught in five sneaky hyperspatial tube attacks, certain kidnap victims, and they seem to have simply dumped the whole project. Did they fail, or did they actually succeed? How were the attacks engineered? How can hyperspacial tubes be focused so accurately, right through all our defensive measures?"

Tregonsee was in front of Kinnison's large, notorious desk, the green-felted one which looked like a poker table. He couldn't sit in a chair like his two assistants, nor on the edge of the desk like Kinnison, and ordinarily he had no need to rest. But he was still shaky from his trance, so he wrapped a couple of tentacles around the bolted-down resting pole which was there for Worsel to drape his snake-like body around. And there Tregonsee half hung on.

"I think I can answer those questions. In my case they failed; in the other cases they won their unknown objectives. On Rohyl the operation was quick and slick, after sabotage had weakened our electronic defenses. An Ordovik crystal, pre-tuned and probably augmented, was brought into my room by Mando the Vegian cat burglar as a tube pathfinder. When they believed me dead, Mando was callously silenced and the crystal recovered to hide the method. The raiders were a highly specialized, well-trained team, no inside help indicated. Like Mando, the Manarkan leader was probably a renegade, most likely a notorious rival happy to eliminate his accomplice Mando.

"Our defensive measures weren't at fault—only a spectacular, stealthy operation such as that undertaken by Mando, using a new device to focus a tube, could have succeeded. Maybe the device isn't even new. Ordovik crystals are known to attract hyperspatial tubes, but there's always been an Ordovik or someone of similar powers around to detect a screeching-hot crystal. In confined spaces no noisy Orodovik crystal pulling in the end of a hyperspatial tube can ordinarily expect to avoid countermeasures. P'Keen's absence from my room represents meticulous planning of their timetable, and the odd silence of the crystal used exploited the chink in our armor. From now on, crystal-detectors will be mandatory for all high-security areas. And I've made P'Keen of Ordov my personal ADC."

Tregonsee's body rose eighteen inches into the air as his

four elephantine feet thrust downward out of his barrel body. He was feeling much better.

"What the whole story is," Tregonsee continued, "we, of course, don't know. We have no clues, no names, no physical evidence. There is only one unexpected, fortuitous chance given to us—to exploit my assumed death by first concealing then revealing it, for the greatest confusion."

"Let me butt in here, Trig," Kinnison said. "Seems to me all this pretense about your death may be more than it's worth. It may be getting out of hand, with little troubles popping up all over the galaxy and growing bigger all the time. I know you're looking for talk linking you with assassination, but that's a mighty flimsy reason to bring unwarranted discredit on your staff. This all makes the S.I.S. look confused, disorganized and weak." Kinnison suddenly stopped. "Trig, you sly old bulging bag of leather, I'll be damned if that isn't precisely what you want! Right?"

"Yes, Kim. You know how I utilize jiujitsu tactics."

"And I admire your cleverness, Trig. I appreciate that the S.I.S. could come out of this with new strength and great profit. But what about you? Should you risk your life or mind on such dangerous experiments with phony death?"

"There is no undue risk, Kim. I thank you for your concern. My personal plans are well defined in my focus on the name of Mando, our one solid clue. If the Mando attack seems a success and our opponents mention his name—by praising him or by making him a martyr to cover up their brutal betrayal of him, or by villifying him for botching his job—then Mando's name will be heard. When the rumors are traced, I will be led directly to the conspirators."

Kinnison was nodding now in agreement.

"However, this is more than speculation," Tregonsee continued. "Mando's name has been heard on a Kalonian planet called Krish-kree and deified on an unexplored planet called Tanse. This is a lead which I personally plan to investigate with your personal help and that of my staff. In fact, there is such a unique situation which threatens Civilization, I am fast concluding, that I have deliberately drawn my own unit-cluster into it, as though by inadvertence, as potential backup help."

"How unusual! You must expect to confront some extraordinary, stupendous mental forces! I'm impressed!"

"I have three immediate questions to answer. *Who* tried to do this to me and to the scientists? *Why* did they try? *What* new method are they using? My deepest thoughts on *who* lead inevitably to the faceless Boskone. The *why* seems an attempt at the disruption of our intelligence services to protect their secret, probably an utterly new and different assault on Civilization. The *what* is the method or tool of the assault itself.

"Consider the *why*. The S.I.S., or more likely the S.M.F., knows or is about to know something they wish to conceal. They can't destroy our organizations, but they certainly can slow them down with my death. As for the scientists, they have the most advanced knowledge about their specialties of hyperspace, vortices and black holes. Either the enemy wants that knowledge for themselves or they wanted to destroy our ability to defend ourselves against some use of such knowledge. I believe all the prominent scientists present on the attack scenes are vital pieces in the puzzle. They must be assembled as soon as possible at Ultra Prime—if they're not there already under examination."

Tregonsee pulled up his legs and hunkered down.

"In addition, Kim," the Rigellian projected firmly, to show that it was no whim, "I want a conference of the Council of Scientists called there on Klovia at the same time."

Kinnison sat up ramrod straight.

A groan came from his mouth before he silently spoke. "You've really got a death wish, Trig. And now you want me to be part of it. I know things are serious. But are they really *this* serious? But for you, Trig, I'll do it. I'll convene that madhouse and attend, but I'd rather be locked naked in a cage of frenzied, blood-excited cateagles!"

6

Will-o'-the-Wisp Warships

When life seems pointless and personal safety is held in
contempt, a space vagabond usually ends up dying in some
remote corner of the universe, unhonored and forgotten. If
that fundamentally desolate person, however, manages to
retain a sense of humor, even though much distorted by a
cynical sense of the ridiculous, and is additionally fortunate
enough to be a member of the Galactic Patrol, the chances
are that he may end up with significant recognition and
honors. Chances are that he will also be quite equally dead in
some remote corner of the universe.

D. D. Cloudd was certainly headed in that direction. He
had all the prerequisites for being a dead hero of the Patrol,
not really understood by his casual friends but bound to be
vividly remembered. What he was doing in the auxiliary
engine room of the comm-con Patrol ship, and about to do
outside its hull, was putting him just one short step from
immortality.

He was dressed in a massive radiation suit, surrounded
by four movable walls of dureum. As he moved, the thick,
silvery fabric folded grotesquely at his joints and waist.
Buried in the top of the bloated shoulders was a round bump
which contained his head. He was twisted awkwardly to his
right in order to face that way because the suit had no neck
on which his head could pivot. He was staring under a raised
flap through a shielded transparent slit into a mirror he held.

63

The images in the mirror were the objects on a high bench, in front of his left hip. He was using the reflection to keep his gaze from directly meeting the radiation of the objects he was studying. Having determined his next actions, he pushed down the flap and turned back, temporarily blind, to let his gloved hands feel, tap and twist the things. He screwed one Type-2X1 into another Type-2X1 to mate them into a Type-2X2. The double cylinder was now once more the Type-2X2 drone which he had captured.

Next to it, glittering in the light of the auxiliary engine room, where they were, was an Ordovik crystal. It sat in a shallow padded box, throwing brilliant little specks and larger rainbow-hued dots on the interior of the upraised lid.

He drew a heavy metallic cloth over the 2X2 and put down the mirror.

"I have the crystal out, as you can see," Cloudd said into his face transmitter. "And the 2X2 is back together. The radiation lasted only while I had the two sections apart. There is no trace of anti-matter. The radiation readings are now ordinary and normal, but what do the technicians say?"

Cloudd listened as the Rigellian and the Manarkan couple took extrasensory readings and confirmed that the extraordinary radiation had stopped. He had some difficulty hearing them, because their thoughts had been translated into audible sounds for him and broadcast into a room which was full of absorption shields for the ship's engines. This was the only place that he felt he could safely take apart and put back together the 2X2.

"Well, that's done," Cloudd said. "I feel fine. Those funny flashes going off inside my head are gone. I cut the number down when I turned my face away and used the mirror. They weren't so many then. And, you know, having tiny little comets whizzing around behind my eyes with colors I've never really appreciated before was kind of fun."

"QX, Cloudd," said Captain Barnard, faintly in his ear. "You did a good job. You proved your point. The deaths of your two assistants were a matter of technique." Cloudd had always maintained that in the first case a servo, even under the personal control of someone, couldn't be sensitive enough. One death. And in the second case, a person who didn't shield himself from unknown radiation effects, even if his dismantling touch was gentle, was susceptible to induced bumbling. Death number two. The third death, the technician, was completely inexcusable. "Leave the crystal and come out now."

"Not yet, Cap'n. I want to take another look at the other thing."

"Listen, Cloudd. You've been at it for three bleedin' hours. Come out and take a rest."

"After a look, Cap'n. I feel fine."

"QX. Take a look. One look."

Cloudd walked toward the open, flat deck in front of the racks of intricate equipment which were the electronic guts of the ship's engines. There, joined together and stretching out for nearly thirty feet, were many demolition containers, forming one long container. Each section had the stamp of specially structured chain-molecular-dureum representing a fortune in metallurgy. There was virtually no chance that his examination could cause a blast, but the captain was taking no chances on damage to his engines. Those special dureum walls were ample blast protection, backed up by an interior field of force.

Cloudd looked over the side of one of the box walls. There it lay! A thirty-foot section of the elusive Type-50 datadrone! What a shame it held no extra-special secret. Interesting, yes. But disappointingly conventional in its technology. Good work by the captain, though! He had managed to snatch it up while rescuing Cloudd.

Having taken his look, Cloudd moved on to the maintenance airlock door and push-buttoned it into opening.

"No, Cloudd," the captain's voice came faintly again in his earpiece, "I meant a look inside, not outside. Close up that door!" But while the captain was talking, so was Cloudd, much louder, "I'm going to take my look now, Cap'n. I feel fine. The sparks are all gone. There's still some buzzing in my head. I can't hear you too well. In fact, now that I've tuned my monitor to the thing outside, I can't hear you at all." Cloudd kept up a rapid fire of talk, covering the captain's increasingly hot-tempered remarks, such as "Get the bloody hell back inside, Cloudd!" and "Leave it to the servos! That's an order!"

There, in front of Cloudd a hundred feet away floated

the six-foot section of the Type-50 which had been sheared off and left outside the ship as too dangerous to bring aboard. All sorts of warnings about it had been registered by man and machine, and Captain Barnard was a sensible man. He left it outside, isolated by a protective screen off the hull of his ship, and was having it examined by mental probes by capable members of the ship's crew. With what small authority Cloudd had, he had kept the captain from using mechanical servos and devices in fear of doing some unwitting damage.

Cloudd, pushing himself off the rim of the outer lock, said, "I don't want any radio waves or other frequencies out here to touch off something or to disturb my instruments. Mental waves are QX. I want to be monitored by all senses. You espers, do you read me? Well, stay tuned to me." He knew that all members of the crew with more or less powers of telepathy, perception, and ESP would be tuned in to guide him and to alert him to any danger sensed by some appropriate signal.

For the next two hours, seeming to him like only ten or twenty minutes, Cloudd gently caressed and manipulated that alien structure and made it give up its knowable secrets. When he returned to his ship and stepped through the closing airlock door to face a grim Captain Barnard, Cloudd knew that the knowledge he now had about datadrone Type-50 was more than enough to placate the exasperated captain one more time.

"Captain!" Cloudd said immediately upon pulling off the upper section of his radiation suit. "These things are priceless!" He was deliberately breathless to head off the captain's words. "The 2X1s are both intact, not partially burned out like all the others I've seen or heard about. What's left of the Type-50 is a complete Type-8 2X carrier collecting hive and transmitting station."

"Patrolman Cloudd, you magnificently mad, bloody fool," Captain Barnard grumped, "what the hell are you nattering about?"

"The 2Xs," Cloudd hastened to explain, elated over his discoveries and his victory over the captain's discipline, "are probes, as we've thought all along, collecting information and even samples of things. They carry their data and specimens into the bays of the Type-8. The Type-8, in turn, with all the homing devices and docking equipment, cuddles up into Type-50's grandmother's pouch, and lets the 2X6, or its sub-sections, tattle about the galaxy in general and Civilization in particular. All of which is narrowcast off through sub-ether to some unknown listener."

The captain had his arm around a muscular Cloudd, who had stepped out of his pants, virtually nude, and was steering him to his quarters. "Go get this gentlemen his bloody clothes," the captain barked at a crewman, "and a couple of flasks of fayalin out of the freezer and bring them to my cabin."

By the time Cloudd had his clothes on his outside and his fayalin in his insides, he felt extremely euphoric. For one of those rare times when he wasn't out in space thundering around on his rocket sled, he was at peace with himself and glad to be alive. He had told the captain much of what he had learned. He had no explanation for the Ordovik crystal, except that it was unusual enough to be an item the drone could well be interested in. Unusual to a drone, that is, but not to a Patrolman. Ordoviks always carried them because they were considered good-luck pieces; the fact was, however, that the crystals helped Ordoviks with their exceptional parapsychological talents. The fact that it was still intact, not crushed or dissolved into powder, seemed to indicate that although it had been en route to the Type-8 for extensive analysis, the process had not yet taken place at the moment of the 2X2's capture. After a good period of sleep, Cloudd confided to the captain, he would lock up the crystal in a strongbox for shipment to the laboratories at Medon, and then he would label, disassemble, and ship the component parts of the Type-50's sensors, memory-banks, and transmitters to the same place.

Cloudd dragged himself down the passageway leading to his cabin, his feet more and more heavy with fatigue as he drew closer to his soft bed and its promise of sleep.

When he entered his cabin and closed his door, he intuitively sensed an intruder in his room. He recognized his body's signal—there was an itching on the stumps of his two missing fingers. Cloudd had no Lens. He had no extra powers of perception or telepathy. In this lack of gifts, he was a very ordinary man. But he had what many ordinary men did not have: a psychic sensitivity, a strong intuition about people, things and situations.

All Patrolmen normally carried DeLameters strapped to their waist or thigh. Cloudd, however, was not armed at that moment, and he suddenly felt painfully vulnerable.

As a man of action, he did not wait. He ducked across the room and grabbed at his gun, cradled in his holster, hanging at the head of his bed.

A powerful grip around his wrist pulled his hand away, and a voice said, "QX, Cloudd. I'm a friend. I'm a friend. Lock your door and turn on the light."

When the light came on, a very black Tellurian or Klovian stood by his bunk, next to his pistol, hands spread casually over his hip bones. Cloudd recognized him as one of the crew, his uniform insignia marking him as one of the medical personnel.

"Listen to me, Cloudd. I'm an agent for the Secret Intelligence Services. You've made some remarkable discoveries in the past twelve hours. I've been closely watching you for weeks as a man around whom things can expect to happen. I've circumspectly tried to pick your brains, but I don't know everything you've learned. I do know enough to have made a special report on you to my superiors. You will be receiving orders within the hour right from the Galactic Coordinator's office. You're to report to him—and to my S.I.S. boss, Lensman Tregonsee, as soon as possible. You must take absolutely everything with you which, in your judgment alone, seems important toward solving the datadrone mysteries. Your orders give you that power. Take everything of importance. Keep close charge of the drone materials. *This is your personal responsibility.* Watch over them. I've sensed that you have found anti-matter. That's of ultra priority. Get them to your destination *as soon as possible.* No matter what may happen until you get there, *don't be sidetracked. Don't obey any other orders, no matter how authentic they may seem.*"

The black man smiled and stuck out his hand to exchange a powerful grip in greeting and farewell.

"That's it. There's nothing for you to say. There's nothing more for me to say. Forget me. Be careful. And have a good trip." He abruptly strode to the door, unlocked it, turned back to say, "Start packing right now!" and left.

In a whirlwind of activity, Cloudd and the vital parts of the datadrones were off on the comm-con's top-rated shuttle craft to join the Sector Patrol Task Force fourteen light years away. That force was cruising the edge of the charted spaceways bordering the chaotic mass of gases called the Green Parrot Nebula.

When the shuttle craft broke out into normal space to match intrinsics with the flagship, the reception could have been nerve shattering. Cloudd's shuttle, with only two crewmen, was encased in a tractor field and shaken around like a bean in a musicman's gourd. Spy-rays were probing every inch of the craft, sending off all sorts of warning sirens and bells. The cabin and corridor communicators were all blaring, "Patrol orders. Make no aggressive moves. Show your identification. This is the Patrol. You are now under GP control."

D. D. Cloudd was not upset, or even startled, by the raucous reception. As a Patrolman, he knew that any vessel from outside the operating area which was temporarily unidentified was treated as a foe until proved a friend, especially in a state of high alert or on a field of battle. He also felt his mind being tickled by several different probes. He didn't fight the intrusions, though he kept tight security on the confidential knowledge he possessed, and, in recognition of the careful respect with which it was being done, cooperated in the investigation of his motives.

The activities ceased and a voice in his head said, "Three ordinaires now being passed through, QX. Welcome, Patrolmen!" He felt the tractor beams jerk their shuttle craft up and down for an interminably long period of time, as though working them through various force fields and shields surrounding many ships. Finally they came to a bruising halt. He had two emotions: first, he was unreasonably resentful at being called an "ordinaire" just because he was not a perceiver and had no extrasensory powers—he had never considered Lensmen better than he was, just different—and, second, he was surprised at the battle-zone security.

When he was standing before the G-2 intelligence section chief of the task force commander in the active beehive of the G-2 situation room, he understood the precautions.

"Technician Cloudd," the G-2 chief said, "we are approaching a flotilla of pirate ships and are preparing to attack. I don't have much time for you. My commander's orders from S.I.S. are to get you and your shipment as quickly as possible, under guard, to Klovia. We'll take out enough time to record your thoughts concerning your mission and to place it, unexamined, under seal as a safeguard should you lose your life. When that's done, I'll assign three ships— I'll have to check with G-1 about that—so, let's say two ships. I'll assign two ships to escort you to Klovia. They'll be our best. Half our fleet are the latest freedrivers, so you'll travel at least ten to the seventh, if you can comprehend that. You'll be there some time tomorrow our time, covering over eighty-nine hundred light years. That's as quick as possible. You will not be in command, but you will have one of my Lensmen in a mind-lock on you in case you need to communicate under emergency conditions. That's all, Cloudd. Good luck."

The chief turned back to what was obviously a situation tank and fiddled with its curtain, anxious for Cloudd to leave. The screening drapery was there to keep unauthorized persons like Cloudd from seeing things they had no business knowing.

"Sorry, Major," Cloud said, stiffly at attention, being the good Patrolman which he was proud to be if he didn't have to act that way all the time. "I can't have my thoughts transcribed." He didn't like the officious manner of the section chief. The whole reception had set him on edge—the inconsiderate bumpy landing, the "ordinaire" reference, the impersonal interview, the unnecessary reminder of his being "not in command," the idea, good though it was, of having some stranger sitting in his mind. He also felt irritated that the G-2 section chief was a Tellurian woman. Maybe because she was so obviously competent, while at the same time so beautifully feminine.

She heard his words, but didn't react for a split second. Then she said, "QX, Cloudd. I really don't have the authority to order you. I thought it was a good idea. You're dismissed. Good luck, Cloudd." And she turned her back to him. He was nobody, she was busy, but it burned him up. He stalked out of the room and went to his assigned quarters for a fast wash-up and a snack before quickly pushing off.

But he didn't push off quickly. Instead he was summoned back to the G-2 section. She was there and, with a friendly, impersonal nod but without a smile, she silently led him into the adjoining control room. There, sitting in the command chair, was the captain, a young-looking Chickladorian with a mechanical left arm. On his shoulders were the boards of the temporary rank of admiral. Captain he might choose to call himself as a "temp rank," but an Admiral of Task Force he most certainly was to the rest of the fleet.

He turned at their approach and she gave him a smile. She can smile after all, Cloudd thought to himself sardonically, and, embarrassed at the chance of revealing himself, clamped a tight barrier around his mind. In fact, it was a damned attractive smile.

"Hello, Cloudd," the captain-admiral said. "Welcome aboard. I'm afraid you're going to be a bit delayed. Maybe a few minutes, maybe a few hours. We're about to whip a few pirates. The safest place for a V.I.P. like you is here with me. And besides, I think you'll find the action here interesting."

Cloudd glanced around the room. It was much more elaborate, complex, and bewildering than the control rooms of ships like the comm-con he was familiar with. This was a first class ship of the line. There were blinking lights and flickering dials and soft noises of all descriptions filling the machinery-crowded area of sixty-four square feet. In front of the captain was a large screen rapidly flashing different views of space at various magnifications. To Cloudd's unpracticed eye they were a blur of things, with an occasional sharp vision of one or a dozen Patrol ships. There were many slender destroyers, larger bulbous cruisers, a scattering of service ships tucked in behind the larger ones. A large group of Rigellians was spread halfway around the room, semi-squatting before individual panels, big-bodied but uncountable because of the boxes and consoles scattered between the captain and their backs. There were various other races in Patrol uniform, too. The most humanoid types were dressed in complete silver-and-gray tunics, trousers, belts, buttons, and boots. The costuming ranged downward to the Rigellians who, their

71

leathery skin criss-crossed with harnesses, were practically naked. Cloudd looked for the G-2 major, but she was gone.

An aide had pulled a padded wrap-around chair up behind the captain's command chair and indicated to Cloudd to sit. When he did, he found that there were sounds coming out of speakers behind each of his ears, and small visual displays numbering a half-dozen to the right and left of his vision, if he turned his head.

One of the voices, in English, could be understood saying, "Strap down or hook up, everybody. We're moving in." A red light, battle notification, began to blink at the left of his periphery vision. A different voice said, "We are being hailed." Much interfering static crackled everywhere as the modulator was opened wide. And then: "This is Boskone. We demand your surrender."

Ridiculous, Cloudd thought, with a hot wave of indignation. He immediately calmed his rising emotions. Cool it, he told himself, and he did. Obviously, the enemy was a larger force than had been judged. But nobody surrendered in the war between the Patrol and Boskone. Practically nobody. Certainly no ship surrendered—everyone would die first. Positively no fleet would surrender, so the request was stupid. Stupid? No, it was part of the psychology of the pirates to intimidate the enemy; he should know that. The whole thing smelled of Boskone.

A voice in his ear was saying, "Enemy identified as a pirate fleet. Standard Boskonian identification with Spawn changes." Ah, a fleet! That meant it was one of the newer autonomous federations which were springing up like weeds from the recently shattered Boskonian conspiracy.

Cloudd could stare directly ahead at the front wall screens with their changing scenes around the GP task force, but his view was being impeded by the tank, the small, transparent, tri-D projection box which was rising from the floor in front of the captain.

"By the Great Kalastho!" the Chickladorian captain exclaimed. "Check your screen, Hxon!" In his agitation he was pointing his mechanical arm at the fifteen-foot-thick ovoid tank.

Cloudd at first didn't see what the captain was excited about. Tiny colored lights like ghosts of exotic dead fish floated in the three-dimensional depths of the polygonal glassy box which seemed to be filled with a nearly invisible thick fluid, suggestive of an aquarium. The two opposing fleets were clearly marked there, in the minutely cubed model of that section of the galaxy. Although this tank was small in scope, even with its improved miniaturization, the schematic was easily read. A touch of a button or a thought wave would flash quick, glowing labels on objects wherever desired. Red lights for enemy ships, blue lights for the Patrol ships. Yellow lights for stars, purple lights for planets. Some of the yellow and purple lights had halos of blue—planetary systems that were under the jurisdiction of, or at least favorable to, the Patrol. Not very many of those. Like the neighboring sector from which Cloudd had come, this part of the Second Galaxy was no-man's-land, an asylum for pirates and zwilniks, a breeding ground for the Spawn.

Now he saw what the captain had been indicating. When the ovoid battle tank had first appeared, the blue lights far exceeded the red. There had been about fifty blue, or Patrol, ships and only a dozen of the Spawn. When the captain had pointed, there had been a growing number of reds.

The Patrol's formation was pyramidal, with the apex, which was the command ship they were on, somewhat retracted. The enemy at first had appeared as a disc, flat side perpendicular, offering itself like a red target, but now it had curved inward. Its growing strength was turning the disc into a concave shape its diameter almost the size of the base of the Patrol's pyramid.

"See what I mean, Hxon!"

More red lights were appearing at an accelerating rate. The count was up to a dozen dozen now, Cloudd estimated quickly. And growing. One seventy-five. Two hundred. The red formation had become a huge carved soup plate on edge, with flat bottom and curved sides. The sides were visibly growing, reaching out to flank the Patrol while the bottom of the soup plate stretched backward more and more into a cone shape as the enemy heart withdrew before the thrust of the Patrol.

"All ships slow!" the captain ordered. "All ships stop!" The tank had steadily grown in size until it was thirty feet across, nearly filling all the space in the room, its front panels close to the captain's face. Despite its size, the pentagonal box barely contained the growing red disc.

"All ships retreat two parsecs." The tank began to shrink in size. "I'm reducing the control room visual to standard magnification, Hxon. I'll have trouble keeping track of the number of Reds. Keep me updated on your main tank. Where're they all coming from? Give me some Ryerson string-lights."

Cloudd knew about Ryerson string-lights from his Patrol training, but they were sophisticated computations for an advanced battle tank, and he had never seen them used in actual operations before. They marked the course of planets, the paths of fleets, and they could be used to show the source of an enemy's reinforcements.

Some faint amber lines sprang into visibility behind one sector of the enemy fleet, but that was all.

"Sorry, sir," came a voice from one of Cloudd's monitors, probably Hxon's voice. "That's all we register." By its well-modulated and calm timbre, reminding him of that G-2 person, Cloudd was struck by the sense of competency, intelligence and self-control which the whole ship radiated. He knew, with great pride and satisfaction, that he was at the top of the ladder, with the best of the Patrol. How could any Spawn be a match for ships and personnel like these? Even if outnumbering them?

"Damnation!" said the captain. "The enemy force is four times our size now. Its tonnage is beyond what we should logically expect. Its weaponry reads like a blue ribbon unit out of the elite of the old Boskonian Grand Fleet. We are in danger of being enveloped. Even if we start to run for it right now, we'll be outmaneuvered."

"This is situations analysis reporting," said another Hxon-type voice. "Statistically, chances of hurting the enemy more than they hurt us are ten-to-one in their favor. Chances of defeating them are virtually nil."

"Standby for full power retreat," the captain said. He had leaned forward, intently studying the screen and a bewildering series of numbers which he was causing to be projected hodge-podge fashion all over, and at varying depths in, the screen. "All captains! Compute nearest Bosko! Launch long-range missiles! Cover with secondaries!"

Thread-like streaks of luminescence spun away from the blue points of the Patrol ships in the tank, stretching out toward the rim of the soup plate of red lights. Dotted lines of pale green swept out in the same direction. As the lines coverged on the rim of red, the red lights there moved rapidly backward, folding in on their neighboring ranks.

"Fire all primaries, continuous fire!" ordered the captain, half out of his chair now, his whole attitude one of surprise and disbelief. "Hxon! What the Kalathic devil is happening? Our missiles aren't homing. Our beams are weakening into nothing—we haven't even nudged their screens."

"No readings, sir!"

"By all the angels of Kalastho," the captain said, his voice rising with excitement, "we'll push our way out! We'll attack! All captains! Drive eight point five! Double F attack! Eight five! Double F!"

Brilliantly crimson wriggling lines of force, the awful flood of penetrant super rays, appeared in the tank. They were corkscrewing down the red cone to drive the enemy outward, to keep them from contracting and converging on the Patrol, and to intertwine with corkscrewing action into one massive bolt at the weak part of the cone's apex. There was an enormous impact. Frightful and hellish energy boiled into clouds of disintegrating bolts of atomic particles, making the center of the tank look like a peep into a blast furnace. The Patrol firepower was flaming up against the enemy's screens and, judging from the ugly, roiling incandescence, the screens would go down at any moment to allow the annihilation of the center. If the attack failed to break through, Cloudd knew, he and everyone would be doomed.

Then suddenly the tank was almost normal!

Cloudd felt as if he had awakened from a nasty dream.

The Patrol fleet was in place, driving inward, blue lights steadily moving. The yellow stars and purple planets hung steadily in space. A mass of red lights, looking like one large red light, was rapidly fading under full acceleration—to blink out. Gone!

The tank lights went on and off. The tank itself grew larger, smaller, larger. The captain was vigorously manipulating his controls, testing their responses.

"I saw it, but I don't believe it!" the captain said. His normally pale pink face and bare pink forearm had turned bright pink. He turned to look at Cloudd, thin eyebrows arched high, pink eyes wide. "You saw that, my friend, didn't you? The great disappearance?" Cloudd nodded although he knew no answer was expected. "Hxon! Did they just vanish? Nth space? Another dimension? Space warp? What're your readings?"

"Yes, captain," said Hxon's voice, for the first time blurred a bit by emotion, higher in pitch. "Gone. We didn't hurt them a bit. They could have wiped us out. My readings show—all readings show—they simply—pulled out—simply retreated."

The Chickladorian captain, Admiral of Task Force, composed once more, looked thoughtfully at Cloudd.

"You're high priority, Cloudd," he said. "I jeopardized your mission just now. So. You're leaving in the next few minutes for Klovia—and half my force will go along to see you safely through!"

7

Most Secret of Secrets

ㅇ〜ㅇ〜ㅇ〜ㅇ〜ㅇ〜ㅇ〜ㅇ〜ㅇ〜ㅇ〜ㅇ〜ㅇ〜ㅇ〜ㅇ〜ㅇ〜ㅇ〜ㅇ〜ㅇ〜ㅇ

Across the light years, far away on a planet lost among a million million stars in the vastness of space, there came the personal Lens-to-Lens invitation to Worsel, the dragon Lensman.

"No, no!" Worsel remonstrated weakly, already resigned to what Kimball Kinnison had decreed. "Not again? Have you forgotten that the last conference left you just skin and bones? And me a nervous wreck? Kimball Kinnison, the scarecrow—what will your Red Lensman think of that? She'll scold me good and proper if I don't express my qualms!"

"You're off the beam, old snake," Kinnison Lensed. "That was the first time. Sure we had the screaming meamies then. But remember the next time? Aboard the *Dauntless* when we invented the Sunbeam weapon? Wasn't that relatively painless?"

"Well," Worsel said, flickering his thought the way he would flick his tail to show he wasn't happy, "there's a difference. Apples and oranges, as you earthlings like to say. That first conference of scientists dreamed up by you didn't know what its goal was. The second conference had a task for each and every one and you whipped them into it and out of it so fast that they never had a chance to get on each other's backs. Besides, old Cardynge really ran that show. This new conference is going to be as bad as the first one. Not even as bad, simply worse."

Kinnison waited for the agreement which he knew would now follow the complaint.

"On the other hand," Worsel continued. "You're right. We have no choice. It's a good idea. And it should work. Besides, I haven't been in a good internecine humanoid squabble in a long time. And neither have you. Fascinating, isn't it, how the best scientific brains of the known universe are so childish? Pompous, arrogant, egocentric, erratic. Insatiable in their craving for adulation and prominence. And yet not interested in money or power. Geniuses, all—every last entity down to the extreme degree of Z classification!

"Anyhow, it's the results that we'll enjoy. After good friend Kinnison has ground his teeth, torn out his hair, beaten his breast black and blue, bitten his nails down to flesh, and collapsed into a quivering gelatinous mass, he will take a Kinnison vacation—blowing off steam. You'll find the most exciting and most dangerous situation in the entire Second Galaxy and—against your great, good common sense for others but not for yourself—you will personally plunge into the thick of it."

"You make the prospects positively attractive, Worsel! I don't think I could handle it without that peerless tact, those diplomatic skills you possess—and now you promise me a rousing good time as a reward!"

"Excuse me, you two barbarians," interposed the calm thought of Tregonsee, who had been impassively tuned in, privileged to do so, unlike the other two in Kinnison's cabin, P'Keen and Garner. "Before this goes one thought further, stop this ridiculous scheming. I'm officially responsible at this time for Kim's safety. My duty, Worsel, is to keep him out of personal danger."

Worsel recognized Kinnison's half-teasing, if Tregonsee did not, as Kinnison said, "I'll grow worthless behind my desk, Trig, without some hand-to-hand action once in a while. We're big boys and a lot different from you, so stop worrying—I'm afraid it's just a lot of wishful thinking, anyhow. You know, you're beginning to sound an awful lot like Nadreck."

"You'll do what you have to do," Tregonsee said. "Both of you. I know. Forgive me. I guess I'm just picking up that humanoid emotion of envy. The way I'm built, I just never get to have the sport you two are always plotting."

"Next time, Trig," Kinnison said, "we'll really try to cook up something for you."

"I heard those remarks," came Nadreck's thought from far away. "Two of you I expect to be crude, but I'm disturbed to find out that Tregonsee is developing the humanoid appetite for violence. I find it inexplicable that Second Stage Lensmen should resort to brute force instead of sly cleverness. I am happy to state flatly that I want no part of any such escapade you three are contemplating. In fact, I feel I must lecture you, Kinnison, as Tregonsee seems to be failing. You are our Galactic Coordinator, and cowardice is a quality which you are sorely lacking. I most humbly apologize for accusing you of such a deficiency. But what is true is true, and it is not too late to correct your flaw." And without any sort of punctuation, he continued, "I have arranged to suspend my very important work, as it cannot continue without my extraordinary and indispensable talents, and will attend the conference as representative from Palain."

"Hello, Nadreck." Good, old, predictable Nadreck! "I am happy to hear you are coming in person. We meet in person so seldom. When are you arriving?"

"I should have been there as quickly as Worsel," the strange Lensman said. "I acted immediately to suspend my valuable work, but I was delayed by two Boskonian ships just after my departure. They attempted to ambush my speedster. I have reason to believe it was an amateurish trap set for me by some of the Dregs of Onlo. Perhaps we are lax in narrow-beaming our Lenses. Of course, I could have simply run away from them, as I would ordinarily do. But the thought of the Dregs moved me to take time out to destroy them. I conjured up the impression that they were not allies to each other, but foes to each other. So, they ignored me and destroyed each other. I would have preferred some survivors to question, but there were none. As it was, it took me ninety-seven minutes longer than I had estimated, which will make my arrival even more delayed. I am hurrying now as fast as I can. I implore your forgiveness. Will you grant me it, please?"

"Of course, Nadreck. Of course. And so do Worsel and Tregonsee, as you can feel. There is no deception at all in our thoughts of praise for your remarkable accomplishment while en route. But then, you are a remarkable Lensman."

Worsel's thought was strong and clear. "True, Nadreck. Very true, about your coming. We await your arrival with great anticipation. We never seem to see enough of you."

When Nadreck then had signed off, Kinnison thought, carefully by narrowed Lens, "Worsel, you snaky devil. Telling Nadreck that we never seem to see enough of him—some day he'll catch one of these sly digs of yours."

"And he'll simply type me as being silly with worthless, stupid, human-style humor. —You're not supposed to agree with me on *this* point, Treg! —You know, fellows, the more I marvel at his bizarre personal philosophy, the more I love the fractionated lug."

P'Keen and Garner felt the aftermath of pleasure of the four-way link of the Second Stage Lensmen, but, not having participated, they couldn't appreciate the exclusive intimacy of the exchange.

"That's it, Trig. With Worsel covered and Nadreck heard from, my official requests have been made to eighty-odd planets from both galaxies. It's been done with a minimum of argument. But I'm not doing any handsprings or cartwheels of joy. Ultra Prime certainly won't be overjoyed to face the invasion of such an impossibly demanding group. If you hadn't settled for the Upper Council, instead of the full Council, I probably would've yelped with pain. But it'll still be hell for a couple of days."

"Yes, of course. I understand. They are like spoiled children who are all slightly mad. Why such eminent scientists should be like this I cannot understand, for they all come from different worlds and they all have different personalities. I can only suggest that they are introverts with such superior minds that they are absolutely overwhelmed by a sense of smug superiority. But, we must admit, together they are brilliant. They will find the answers for us."

"That's just it, Trig. What answers? To what problems? It seems to me that until the tube attacks are understood, we will have no scientific questions to ask."

Then, to the growing wonder and admiration of P'Keen

and Garner, there ensued a rapid mental exchange of information and background between Kinnison and Tregonsee which was dazzling in its speed and coherency.

The flow of thoughts, lightning fast in questions and answers, became, to the two junior Lensmen, an entire review of the past and present situation of the Second Galaxy, once known simply as Lundmark's Nebula. They began with the first penetration of the Milky Way twin, the discovery of and friendship with Klovia, the first footholds of the Patrol in its battle within the strongholds of Boskonia. They touched upon the overthrow of the Thrale-Onlonian Empire by Kinnison and Nadreck with the freeing of millions of worlds from Boskonian control and the extent of destruction of the evil and barbaric conspiracy which remained. Kinnison's and Tregonsee's roles were defined and evaluated. Their separate though parallel goals were delineated: Kinnison worked openly for military stabilization and democratic peace, while Tregonsee, surrendering his independent role of Gray Lensman, "put away his Grays" to work covertly to root out the piratical remnants of the dying Boskonian cabal and to bring about its final destruction.

"Boskonia is not really dead," Tregonsee said again, as he had been saying for almost a year. "It is as the ancient Gyptian bird, a phoenix, for it is rising from its own ashes. It spawns a new trouble and evil, and we can fight this spawn only to control it, not to eliminate it. Within the limited goals of our secret services, we are more and more successful, for though their power does not diminish, yet their territory does. And it is our Special Missions Forces which have been our best weapon."

P'Keen, as one of the most gifted of the newest recruits to the S.M.F., had learned, in incredibly short order, all about the S.M.F., completely and thoroughly. The Special Missions Forces was the brainchild of Tregonsee. When Kinnison had taken over the Civilizing of the Second Galaxy, it was Tregonsee who became his right hand. The great esteem earned by the Rigellian Lensman in the Galactic Patrol as head of the M.I.S., the Military Intelligence Service, was understood by the entire Patrol. But of even greater accomplishment and value, although not nearly as well appreciated because it was not generally known, was his service as head of the Secret Intelligence Services, which he founded about the time he reached the rank of Second Stage Lensman. His advanced Arisian training had resulted in the improvement and superb performance of the S.I.S., which so greatly contributed to the final victories against the Boskonian forces near Tellus and then Klovia. However, his crowning achievement was his creation of S.M.F., which, ironically, was known by so very few. He developed his idea after the destruction of Jarnevon and presented it to Port Admiral Haynes, who, as the newly chosen President of the Galactic Council, had become the most powerful person in Civilization. Haynes had bought the plan and agreed to its utmost secrecy, subject only to the approval of the new Galactic Coordinator, Kimball Kinnison.

The Special Missions Forces, as finally approved by Kinnison under the code name of "Project Quicksilver," was the most secret of secret operations. The basic purpose of the recognized intelligence branches—M.I.S. and S.I.S.—was to collect and evaluate and dispense information, in the one case for the Patrol and its military operations, and in the other case for the Galactic Council and its general operations. For M.I.S. the principal enemy had been the galactic-wide conspiracy of Boskone and its allies, and now its concern was over the ruins of that confederacy and its offspring, the Spawn. For the S.I.S., there was intelligence concerning political and civil matters, as well as about the activities of the usual independent pirates, zwilniks, and common criminals. But for the S.M.F., there was no public or private recognition, nor could there be any, because of the nature of its clandestine work. The S.M.F. was known only to the four Second Stage Lensmen and Haynes himself, beyond the intimate circle of the Secret Missions Forces itself. Even Kinnison, technically the direct supervisor of S.M.F., felt it incumbent upon himself to know as little about the operation as possible. Even mention of its name, a simple acknowledgment of its existence, was taboo, and Kinnison consciously expunged it from his mind. He knew it to be the ultra cloak-and-dagger division of Civilization's bureaucracy, the proverbial department of dirty tricks. It was a dangerous weapon for everyone, for if it misfired it could wreak havoc on Civilization as well as on Civilization's foes.

Kinnison, however, had no uneasiness about whether or not he was following his conscience or better judgment in the operation of the S.M.F. Tregonsee was its absolute boss, and Tregonsee was completely trustworthy, possessing one of the mightiest minds of the known universe. If Kinnison had no qualms about it, Tregonsee, with his well-balanced, un-human scruples, certainly didn't.

The Special Missions Forces was a small outfit, comparatively, with enormous power, and its efficiency was astonishingly good. Next to Port Admiral, now President, Haynes, Tregonsee was perhaps the most powerful person as an instrument for progress toward the Arisian goal of peace, harmony and perfection, even considering Kimball Kinnison.

"I said at the beginning of your ultra-secret project, Trig," Kinnison said, squinting as though to recall and focus the actual memory, "that I wanted to know nothing about your operations. I will interest myself only in the results. And, through you, only the S.I.S. will get the credit. That still goes."

"However," Tregonsee reminded him, as if Kinnison needed any reminding, "I pledged to you and to Haynes that should I die or otherwise become incapacitated, the S.M.F. would immediately cease to exist and all of its apparatus would automatically become part of M.I.S., to be further parceled out to S.I.S."

"Yes, I know, Trig."

"This meeting is for my guidance. The attempt on my life has demonstrated the strengths and weaknesses of our intelligence services, especially S.M.F. Only you and I, and my three executive officers and two aides-de-camp, know that S.M.F. ends at my death. My death would trigger full disclosure to the Patrol's leaders of the existence and ending of S.M.F. Because S.M.F. has been so successful, I propose a change to insure its continuation. I propose that all records of S.M.F., in the event of my death, be turned over to Nadreck, whose mastery of psychology, and indifference to humanoid emotions, and disinterest in power for power's sake, will make him a perfect custodian. Further, I propose that you and President Haynes then decide if S.M.F. should continue under another leader. Thus, my death will bring no irreparable harm."

"You mentioned this once before, Trig, but not formally. I thought it was a good idea then, I think so now. I will so inform the admiral, that is, President Haynes, as soon as possible. I hope this doesn't mean you're anticipating your imminent death?"

"No, for I am, in fact, safer than ever. And don't be misled into thinking my possible excursion into the field on this Mando business is suicidal. I might suffer a temporary mental breakdown, but real dying, not fake dying, is not in my plans."

"What are our standing orders now?" P'Keen said to Tregonsee, referring to himself and Garner, but he was looking at Kinnison.

Kinnison chose to answer that question. "Follow this procedure just outlined. Notify Nadreck, then me, and I will notify Haynes. Put copies of your actions into the Patrol files. Only Nadreck will have access to the files. And only the president of the Galactic Council will now have the power to disband S.M.F."

"I'm satisfied," Tregonsee said, and his mental relief was felt by all. "Now to answer your original questions—the Council of Scientists must meet for five reasons. First, they must consider a defense against the Sunbeam. A faction of the Spawn has organized a strike force into the configuration of a Sunbeam weapon."

The hair on the back of Garner's neck visibly rose, and P'Keen's complexion became even paler. Kinnison, taken aback, dropped his square jaw a not-quite-imperceptible fraction of an inch. The Sunbeam! Used by the Patrol to win the Battle of Tellus, collecting and concentrating the entire energy output of a star and focusing it into a single ray of cataclysmic destructiveness!

"In fact," Tregonsee said, in his imperturbable way about catastrophic events, "a whole number of Sunbeam projects are reported by S.I.S. operators.

"Second," he continued laconically, "there is the evidence that small black holes have unexpectedly and inexplicably begun to fuse into larger, dangerous ones.

"Third, hyperspatial tube research by planetary consortiums unfriendly to us seems on the verge of controlling space-warping to produce a practical matter transmitter.

"Fourth, a plague of drones or probes of various sizes is sweeping through one end of our galaxy, collecting information for an unknown adversary considered to be hostile.

"Finally, the fifth reason, which has created this emergency, is that Boskonians and their Spawn seem to have embarked on sabotage or talent raids of our scientific establishment in the Second Galaxy. Thus, the two councils from the two galaxies are needed to meet, as represented by the Joint Senior Councils, to alert each and every scientist to the danger to themselves and to Civilization's security."

When Tregonsee stopped his thought projection, so heavy with vague and misty images of destruction and chaos, the other two younger Lensmen, stunned by the stupendous visions, were left numb. But quickly their ominous pessimism was dispelled from their shaken spirits and, composure regained, they each began to calculate what help and contributions they might make when the Joint Councils met.

At first P'Keen, wrapped in thoughts on the forthcoming conference, didn't notice the narrow-beamed Lens-to-Lens exchange between Kinnison and Tregonsee. He did so just at the moment that he received a narrow-Lensed thought himself, directly from Kinnison. "P'Keen, if you will excuse us, will you and Garner go to where the coffins have been re-arranged? One of my men outside will show you where. You'll get further instructions when you get there." There was something about the formality of Kinnison's touch that alerted P'Keen to expect the unexpected.

They both had been in the large reception room of the *Dauntless*, where the diplomatic balls were so frequently held, when Kinnison called to them. Garner, from habit, had taken his position on the high stool. P'Keen was at Meppy's coffin, kneeling, head bowed, but thinking about Kinnison, the *Dauntless*, and all the things that had been happening in—how long? One day? Two days? Three days? Or really just one, long, long day?

"P'Keen. Garner. Now hear this. There was a delicate matter I had to discuss with Trig. It seems that one of Mepauhurrat's—ah—relatives was flown in to the *Dauntless* on its last stop, as had been ordered. He has been waiting to see Trig, his fellow Rigellian. They have met. They have come to an understanding. Now, there will be some formalities there in front of the coffin. The entity, who is to be referred to as 'Two,' will be there shortly and you will handle it."

"Handle it?" P'Keen said, his placidity rather shaken by the idea and the appalling lack of preparation.

"I've no precedent to follow, sir," Garner added, even more apprehensively.

"QX, my fellows," came Tregonsee's thought. "Your good sense will see you through. Just be natural. I've complete confidence in you."

Both Kinnison and Tregonsee disconnected.

"Well," said Garner. "Here we go, ready or not."

Only moments later, a Rigellian shuffled into the room, dressed in Patrol harness, and moved heavily but nonetheless gracefully to a position in front of Garner on the stool. The two humanoid Lensmen held their military bearings, unmoving, wondering—this couldn't be the entity called "Two"?

"I am Cyclo," the big Rigellian telepathed, "Communications Officer on the *Dauntless*," and brought up one of his right tentacles in semblance of a salute. "I have the sorrow of presenting Two into the Presence. Do I have permission?"

"Certainly, sir," said Garner and returned the salute.

Cyclo didn't move, but they felt his mind reach out beyond the door.

Within seconds, a Rigellian, escorted by two pairs of honor guardsmen, shuffled into the room. He was wrapped in yards and yards of soft black fabric, trailing much of it on the floor. It wasn't Tregonsee, of course, but the sense of *déjà vu* was nevertheless startling.

The Rigellian immediately began his ritualistic greeting: "Oh, keepers of the watch. I humbly come before you to lay my just and righteous claim."

"Oh, Rigellian," replied Garner. "Although I am the senior, it is he from Ordo who will commune with you. It is he who will lock minds with you on this Sacred Occasion."

Thanks a lot, Garner! P'Keen thought to himself, but careful not to let the sarcastic rebuke slip out.

"Oh, Entity of Ordo-Ordov," the Rigellian "Two" said formally. "I have come to question the religious attention given to the departed one of my cluster. My sense of perception observes only military ceremony. Where is the religious observance?"

"For one so high in the councils of the Patrol," P'Keen answered, "the military formality prepares the way for holy services." P'Keen would have been much happier if Garner could have been linked with their communications—even happier if it could be Tregonsee. He could only guess that his performance would be satisfactory. "The Chaplain General of the Galactic Patrol is himself coming personally to take charge."

"Not that high, surely," thought the Rigellian, sincere in his wonderment.

"Tregonsee was the very highest," P'Keen said, without much exaggeration. Ouch! Now that was a mistake—even he, P'Keen, was living the deception now, mixing up Treg with Null-Treg.

"Yes, Tregonsee is a mighty one from Rigel," said the Rigellian. "But I refer to the departed Mepauhurrat."

P'Keen felt relieved that his mistake was either overlooked or forgiven and said, "Mepauhurrat was truly another self of Tregonsee, and is being treated as such." In the light of the culture of the cluster, P'Keen thought, it sounded almost as though he knew what he was talking about. So, this was one of Meppy's manufactured relatives asking for—what?

The alien was waving his tentacles about sinuously, and bouncing his barrel body up and down rhythmically, making the gauzy fabric billow. P'Keen had never seen a Rigellian act like this before, so, ah, so emotionally.

"I am reassured," the Rigellian said. "Now may I see the body?"

"Certainly," P'Keen replied, thinking secretly to himself so rapidly and clearly that he felt great confidence in himself now. "But as you gaze upon him, you must think of him as Tregonsee himself. Mepauhurrat was Tregonsee to the Civilized worlds. They must believe that way in death."

"Of course," said the Mepauhurrat relative, "the secret of my unit's profession shall stay secret with me and with the Other One in death as in life. I shall honor him as he should be honored, as Tregonsee himself."

P'Keen was elated. Mepauhurrat was placated without

destruction of the plan. The deception would be foolproof now!

"Oh, Entity of Ordo-Ordov," said Two. "I will come again with my brister Three. May Mepauhurrat dust you with peace as the watch is kept."

He did say "brister," didn't he? P'Keen asked himself. It must have been. It did make a kind of sense.

Two had stepped behind Cyclo, and, a pair of troopers in front and a pair behind, both Rigellians shuffled back out of the room, Cyclo leading the way, two big bodies bobbing in single file.

"Very well done, P'Keen," came Tregonsee's thought. "You and Garner can rejoin us now. Kim does not profess to be an expert in this case, but he feels I was right to have him lower the screens for this."

Lower the screens! P'Keen was aghast. Many could have observed that encounter! Many probably did! He could have made a mess of it! If he had known that there had been no privacy, that he had been so vulnerable,—well—!

P'Keen's nerves were settled down by the time he flopped back in the soft chair near Tregonsee. He didn't pay much attention to the discussion, still re-living the Rigellian ceremony. Then his eyes were attracted by an unexpected movement.

The center of Kinnison's desk was slowly and silently raising itself, a central core two feet in diameter, crowded with switches and meters and dials and tiny viewing plates. An orange light was noiselessly but insistently blinking. As Tregonsee paused, Kinnison depressed a button and received an oral message. "Sir. The Chaplain General is here, awaiting your attention. He's arrived with the fleet task force. There is also an unexpected arrival who came in on a privateer, LaVerne Thorndyke. He says he could not give you advanced warning because of the risk to his security, but he must see you immediately."

Kinnison, who had been leaning across the desk, one elbow on the felt top with his finger on a button, jerked in surprise and virtually shouted, "Send him in! Send them both in! Toot sweet!" He then flung himself to his feet, as though catapulted by his trick desk, and took huge strides to the door to greet them.

With much gladhanding and pats and mumblings of welcome, the two arrivals were ushered into the room.

Chaplain General Chon was a muscular, red-faced human with a military cut of gray hair and a neatly trimmed Van Dyke beard of the same iron-gray color. He was dressed in the equivalent rank of Admiral of the Fleet. After his quick and ready smiles, his face grew serious. His eyes kept flicking nervously toward Thorndyke, and his body was stiffly braced as though his companion was on the verge of exploding.

Thorndyke, Master Technician of the Galactic Patrol, indeed looked as if he were about to burst. His trim figure and military bearing had an attitude of attack. He plunked himself on the edge of Kinnison's desk, folded his arms, and said, "I don't know what kind of bad news you've been having, but I'm going to make it worse. I wasn't part of the hyperspatial tube attacks. But I do know that some of my scientist friends have been scared silly by them. They weren't as scared as they're gonna be! Kim, you've got to call a Conference of Scientists. Now get this. Somebody on the other side has sent a black hole through a hyperspatial tube! *A black hole sent through a hyperspatial tube!* I got a confidential report on that. It took place near an outpost where it might have been overlooked, except for good luck. One of our special researchers recorded it, but has been keeping it under his hat. There's a full security clamp on this information, and even I'm not supposed to know. Now you know, Kim. And you, Treg. Oh, hello, Garner. Who's your friend? . . . Good to know you, P'Keen. . . . Well, I'm here on your laboratory-warship, Kim. Tregonsee and I will immediately start an analysis. Meanwhile, call that Conference of Scientists. Every second may count. This could be a greater threat than the introduction of the tube at the Battle of Tellus!" Thorndyke took a bare fraction of a second for an introspective look at his monologue. "Excuse my tornado tactics, as you might well say, Kim. But after all, a black hole through a tube could mean the end to the Galactic Patrol and Civilization!"

8

Hero or Villain

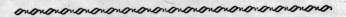

For a Patrolman who wasn't a Lensman, who was, in the opinions of the greatest scientific brains of two galaxies, a mere technician, D. D. Cloudd made a spectacular arrival at Klovia. That planet, home for Galactic Coordinator Kimball Kinnison, Ultra Prime base of the Galactic Patrol in the Second Galaxy, headquarters for the secret organizations of Second Stage Lensman Tregonsee, now the site of the meeting of the Joint Senior Councils of Scientists, was accustomed to most anything. But D. D. Cloudd's arrival, interrupting the first day's session of the conference, made a very big impression.

The tremendous thunderclap of a sonic boom over the entire capital city and the sprawling base announced the appearance of Cloudd above the roof of Supreme Galactic Headquarters.

Millions of people had rushed from buildings onto rooftops and into streets, tingling from the physical blow of the vibrating airwave.

Patrolmen and civil employees had streamed from the various cells of the hive of Ultra Prime, startled out of its occasionally impressive but generally dull routine.

Four Lensmen, the quartet of the only Second Stage Lensmen ever created by Mentor of Arisia, had been brought to their feet and out onto the balcony overlooking the private space port where lightly, like a shining, slowly spinning royal barge of some eminent visitor, Cloudd's cruiser was settling down.

Cloudd's arrival had literally and figuratively shaken up the place.

He hadn't meant to be all that eventful. He had meant to arrive with a bit of dramatic flair, proclaiming himself as being of some importance, perhaps a bit ostentatious but with dignity, distinction, and élan. As a man who was not one to shun his opportunities for excitement, he had suggested the landing maneuver. His suggestion was a command. No one questioned his distinguished status nor enlightened him that what he asked, perfectly executed, would have the result it had. His guardian fleet had come barreling into Klovian space at high speed inert. With the indisputable authority of priority orders and in full recognition of the calibre of the fleet that approached, his cruiser and its escorting vessels had been smoothly received, credentials verified, and sent on through with dispatch. They had arrowed through the opening ranks of the Home Fleet. His fleet had passed through shell after shell of defensive satellites without pause. It had circled the planet twice, in a silvery streaking line of ships in the night skies. Then it had plunged earthward. Straight at Ultra Prime it had fallen, bringing lumps to the throats of the many who had been growing aware of the developing spectacle. Every rule and regulation of landing clearance had been followed—under the waiving of the special priority—but at an irrational, breakneck speed. The ships dumbfounded the watchers as they plummeted closer and closer to the ground. Apprehension had grown as the collison course was followed—until, at the very last moment, at the edge of suicide, the pull-up had come. And the finale: the performance, under perfect execution, had ended with a spectacular U-shaped reversal under maximum G-stress, bursting open as a blossom of metal petals in the sky.

Then, the massive sonic boom had thundered down upon the people.

The four Second Stage Lensmen, inside the headquarters building in the sanctum sanctorum of the Galactic Coordinator himself, had heard or sensed the whine of the falling ships. They were moving toward the outside open door when the bang came, and they appeared, one at a time, moving at different speeds, upon the balcony which, in a huge six-foot-wide band, encircled the quarter-mile diameter of the restricted landing area.

Worsel, the big dragon Lensman, flying out like a winged snake, was on the balcony first, most of his eyes popping out on their stalks at the commotion. Since the establishment of peace, he had secretly thought of it as "ultra prim" base because it was such a showcase; this was like nothing he could have expected. He draped a goodly portion of his thirty-foot length over the railing, hanging out, gawking. He'd been so quick that he could observe the Patrolmen and office workers just now boiling out onto the tarmac and various balconies.

Kimball Kinnison was only seconds behind. His mouth was open in amazement, for only he had ever approached the base like this before. And he longed to do it still, but his worried staff had convinced him that it was complaints from townspeople and not his personal risk-taking which made them urge him to restrain himself.

The third Lensman was Tregonsee. He was no longer pretending death. The discussion with the Chaplain General aboard the *Dauntless* had decided that the maximum effect had been accomplished. There would still be deliberate mystification about the death of an important Rigellian, and the enemy would be even more unsettled by the conflicting evidence, but the masquerade shell game was over. So Tregonsee waddled out on the balcony, in full view for the first time. He did it merely to be polite and to keep his friends company, not because he was as curious as they or because he wanted to display himself as part of an official resurrection. He had early perceived the situation developing overhead and he had anticipated its finale. But, as noise meant absolutely nothing to him, he had not anticipated the effect it would have on people. The commotion was of hardly any interest to him—but the man who caused it most certainly was.

Finally there came on the scene the fourth and sole remaining Second Stage Lensman, Nadreck of Palain. That frigid-blooded, poison-breathing, Z-type being was understandably slow. Instead of his thin-skinned force-field atmosuit, he was encumbered by a bulky one, almost like a portable room. He liked the big refrigerated suit for longer visits, such as this, because he could continue his research and experiments inside it. For that convenience he gladly suffered the inconvenience of hampered mobility. He could slip more easily in and out of the fourth dimension within this supercooled suit, and he had so much more room utilizing the space-elasticity of the fourth dimension. Big suits made him feel comfortable among scientists; he could prove or disprove some of their theories within his miniature laboratory even as they were boasting about them. No, he really didn't care about being on the balcony; the coming and the going of three-dimensional people was particularly tedious to him; but after all, he was a psychologist, to his own mind probably the best psychologist in the universe, so he deigned to be out on the balcony to learn more about mass hysteria. Humanoids suffered from mass hysteria, a fascinating puzzle, and he always wished to learn more about it.

Down the ramp from the cruiser marched one medium-sized Patrolman. A technician! No high-ranking something-or-other! The Lensmen could feel the incredulity and disappointment in the air. The personnel had been turned out for days to welcome arriving VIPs, and they had been bored; this had been something different, something promising, without any command to be flag-waving greeters, so they were disappointed. Between two hastily-formed ranks of impeccably dressed Patrolmen, the technician, saluting, waving, and smiling at all, met a protocol officer. They spoke and nodded to each other and the officer led the way toward the doorway beneath the balcony where the four great Lensmen stood.

Kinnison threw his mind down on Cloudd.

"Well, I'll be damned," Kinnison said aloud and into the minds of his friends. "It's that man Cloudd you invited, Tregonsee. Curse me to the eleven hells of Telemanchia if I've ever encountered a lowly Patrolman with such impudence, such brazen assurance! We are going to meet that man now, right away! I've got a feeling—this fellow Cloudd—I'm going to like him! Something tells me we're all going to like him!"

Within minutes, D. D. Cloudd was in the presence of the mighty four. His euphoria drained away from him like the burst bottom of a waterbag. He knew he had been unspeakably reckless, rude, and presumptuous. He absolutely knew that he was about to be cashiered out of the service in disgrace. If he had known how to grovel, he would have done so with remorse and repentance.

But all he could do was stand rigidly at attention and say, "I'm sorry, sirs. Really. I apologize," and to keep thinking: I've disgraced myself and my superiors and to atone for it I'm going to blow up a Boskonian planet personally and go up along with it.

Three Lensmen were sympathetic in varying degrees, but Nadreck wasn't. He agreed with Cloudd's self-evaluation and frankly expressed himself. "Technician Benson Cloudd, I speak because there is awkward emotion in my friends. I feel your apology is an acknowledgment of errors which you intend as a kind of reparation. I also note, because of the poor quality of your mind screen, that you would act like a peevish human child and get yourself killed so we can feel sorry for you. Such is not logical, and it is irreversibly self-defeating. On the other hand, I recognize that you are potentially a very superior entity, worthy of discussing things with me. I therefore will overlook your immaturity this time and request that you tell us what you know about the illogical, aborted space battle from which you have just come. We all have a basic understanding, from the report to Tregonsee, of the appearance and disappearance of the enemy, but I humbly believe that I speak for all when I say you must organize your thoughts better and go over the facts again."

To Cloudd, Nadreck's frankness was effective. It was more effective than all the chewings-out Captain Barnard had regularly given him. Even more effective, and certainly less disconcerting, it was than the recent clinical discussion aboard his cruiser; on direct orders from HQ-T-Prime, part of a meticulous examination of him before his clearance to enter Ultra Prime, he had been psychologically poked at by the fleet's psychiatrist who had accompanied him. Of course, it had helped him, but looking so closely at himself hadn't been particularly pleasant.

Before attempting any reports to the Lensmen, there were still more preparations concerning his presence there. Cloudd was sent from them with instructions to report to the base psychiatrist, who would evaluate the psychological report from the interview on the cruiser, and then to Patrol

Credentials to have his papers and golden meteor identification pocket-case checked for his final clearance.

"Before I give you a background report on this Patrolman Cloudd," Tregonsee said, "I've got to take up the serious matters of Voddon the Manarkan and John Tsien. As you know, they are here in Ultra Prime as two of the five scientists who were victims of the tube attacks. Every one of the scientists have had their minds muddled. Both Nadreck and Worsel agree that it was a deliberate probing, not just a side-effect of the attacks. So, I have been extra cautious in my clearance of the five to be here, with complete physical and mental examinations by mind and machine. In the cases of Voddon and Tsien, however, there is an exceptional strangeness which disturbs me. I propose that we collectively examine them before they are allowed to participate in the sub-committee of the Conference of Scientists. They are here now, waiting outside for our attention."

There was full agreement to Tregonsee's plan, and John Tsien was brought in first. True to his name, he had that Tellurian oriental hereditary strain which gave him distinctive eyes and a yellow tinge to his skin. He was a middle-aged man with an exceedingly sharp and agile brain—except that there was a large black cloud of turmoil within it which no Lensman could dispel. As agreed, each Lensman concentrated on his pre-assigned responsibility: Kinnison was to fasten upon Tsien's consciousness, Tregonsee was to concentrate on the unconsciousness, and Worsel was to occupy the id's attention. Nadreck was given the crucial task of sifting through what remained.

Tsien was diagnosed as a thoroughly reliable and loyal believer in Civilization and the Galactic Council and Patrol. There was, however, Nadreck pointed out, without the slightest flicker of excitement in his mind, a very serious flaw to negate Tsien's fitness and compatability.

John Tsien had within his head, put there by fourth-dimensional surgery, an Ordovik crystal!

While the four Lensmen held the man unaware and helpless with one part of their minds, they discussed his fate with the other.

They were agreed that the crystal was there without his knowledge, that it had probably been placed there at the time of the raid against him to plunder his mind, and that whatever other function it might have, the most serious result from it being activated there, in its indisputable potential, was that it would function as a bomb. The possibility of a tube attack through it was virtually non-existent, considering that it would be through the mind of a man who could give the warning before his death, plus the enclosed condition of the crystal which would inevitably make for a disruptive explosion.

"It is, in my humble opinion," Nadreck said, "an attempt at planting a bomb in their enemy's heart—in a meeting just like this. It would be an ingenious idea, if it weren't so stupid."

"Stupid?" said Worsel. "Why so, you denizen of a deep-freezer? Is it because you consider martyrdom the height of stupidity?"

"Worsel, my friend," Nadreck replied, "you give a good example of humanoid imbecility. But no, I mean that the bomb couldn't have worked. It was so heavily shielded to prevent its discovery that it was inoperable. No wonder it took such effort by us to find it. I suggest we put Tsien in a safe place, remove the shielding, and see what does happen."

"By all that's holy, Nadreck!" Kinnison exclaimed, flabbergasted once more by Nadreck's queer ethical reasoning, "Tsien's a good man and valuable to us!"

"Perhaps he will be more valuable to us to demonstrate what could be, if designed properly, a very effective terror weapon. I'm sure Tsien would be glad to give up his life to protect mine—or any of our lives, for that matter."

"What we should do," Kinnison said, coming to the firm conclusion even as he thought of the idea, "is to make certain that the crystal really is neutralized, as you say—and allow Tsien to go about as though we didn't know about this. We may learn something. When the Conference is over we'll remove the crystal and try some other experiments."

The Lensmen, following some brief comments about such experiments later, agreed to Kinnison's idea. Then, with Tsien's departure, still unaware of his condition, they called in Voddon.

Again they went through the same procedure, although in a different manner against the humanoid without eyes or ears. Again Nadreck, without a quiver of distress, informed them that, if anything, Voddon's secret hidden within his head was even worse than Tsien's!

Voddon the Manarkan had buried within his brain, inserted by fourth-dimensional surgery, an operating transmitter! Voddon was a walking electronic spy device!

It took only a few seconds for Tregonsee to reassure Kinnison that security hadn't been breached.

"No frequencies get through our screens here in Ultra Prime," Tregonsee said. "This clears up my worry about the hidden transmitter which has been sporadically operating, and which I've had everyone searching for." They heard his mind give the equivalent of a sigh. "My big worry was that what was being blocked by us was nevertheless being recorded, to be snuggled out later, in a major security leak."

"I suppose," Kinnison said, "that's another result of the raids. Perhaps we should re-examine all the others."

"No," said Tregonsee, "these two are the only ones under any suspicion. What I am unsure of is whether Voddon is actually a traitor or not. I find his mind in unusually perfect order, but something bothers me."

"Yes," Nadreck agreed. "There is something. There is a touch of insanity to him—his brain is partially destroyed."

"What it is," Kinnison said, "is indicated by a tiny change I see. It is not a mental surgical scar, those marks left behind on a brain even when the operation is done by the most expert of brain surgeons. But it is like such a scar. It is a shadowy image of another neurological network in the mind. I'd guess that this is not the real Voddon, but a substitute, an impostor, who has had Voddon's personality stamped over his, with the other mind completely eradicated." Kinnison looked thoughtfully at the rigid body of the Manarkan, his own mind continuing to obliterate Voddon's consciousness.

"You're right, Kim," Worsel said, and Tregonsee added, "I've run over Voddon's security clearance in my head just now, and I can figure out the story. Voddon, the real Voddon, had an accident from which he recovered just a few months ago. Obviously, the real Voddon did not recover. His identity died or was murdered. The impostor took his place. The blanket in his mind, hiding the change in his brain and the transmitter, was excused away as being a result of the accident. The static from the disrupted mind, plus a reinforcing artificial static and cloaking device, would deceive all but the most thorough investigation such as we just had."

"However," Worsel said, "that makes the status of Voddon's brain unclear. Is it a reconstituted Voddon or a latent impostor or what?"

"I'd call him," Tregonsee said, "just a shell, ripe for a take-over at any time by an outsider, not dangerous in himself alone."

"Note this," Kinnison said, "he was—he still is—a Manarkan. Why the transmitter? Why doesn't he use his natural telepathic powers?"

"That's what's so diabolically clever. The re-animated corpse is not evil, thus he is above suspicion. Add to this the fact that no one would dream that a Manarkan would use a machine in his brain to do what he should be able to do naturally, to transmit messages mentally."

"What tipped you off, Trig?" Kinnison asked. "Tsien complained of his headaches. Tsien acted peculiarly. What led you to re-examine Voddon?"

"Thorndyke just the other day reported on the tiny black hole which had come through a tube. Everyone discussed it and it was finally decided that this was not as bad as first believed. The fact is that such holes can be very small, as small as the size of their constituent particles. They can be as light as ten millionths of a gram, moving as fast as average galaxies do, around five hundred miles per second. Such ones would fly right through Klovia or Tellus, although the system's sun would stop them. Thus, the danger is considered unexceptional. If it were a bigger black hole, well, that would be another story."

"Why do you tell us this, Trig?" Kinnison said, very puzzled. "We all know these facts."

"Precisely. These are the facts I mentioned to Voddon, telepathing my question about a certain small black hole. To my amazement, this investigator of the black hole phenomenon expressed his disinterest. Then I asked about a report I had received of a tiny black hole passing through hyperspace produced in his laboratory. He said it hadn't happened. But I persisted. I said someone had identified a track on a photographic plate as being a miniature black hole. Oh, that was really an energetic-proton, he explained. Yes, but might it not have been a trace of a hyperspatial tube, I asked? Of course not, he said, actually it was a vortex. I had my doubts, so this morning I personally checked with Philip Strong, who is the conference's specialist on vortices. He said he had heard rumors, had asked Voddon about them, and that Voddon had denied everything. The inconsistencies led me to the unmasking of Voddon."

Tregonsee felt the appreciation of his detective abilities from the Lensmen, who recognized and understood the unmentioned details, and blocked their undeserved praise by an admission. "The irony of this situation is that I have subsequently just confirmed that there was in fact no attack nor a hyperspatial tube in his lab and that, inexplicably, Voddon himself started the rumor, evidently just to receive attention by us. I suggest Voddon be treated the same way as Tsien. Let him think things are normal, but watch him, and confront him openly later. We'll scramble his transmissions, as we've been doing, and keep looking for the receivers."

When they had all agreed, Voddon was restored to consciousness, unaware of what had happened or of the instrument in his own brain. He was dismissed. Then Tregonsee moved to another subject.

"Technician Cloudd is now back outside. Let me go ahead with my summary of information on him which has been prepared by my office."

By his ideographic memory and his pictographic perception, Tregonsee recited Cloudd's background:

"Cloudd, number 1-1-1-12057818-569003," he began, using the Tellurian civilian identification based upon the old Solarian Patrol system. The first three numbers were easily recognizable as the third planet of the system of Sol in the sector of the Milky Way galaxy where the Galactic Patrol was created. "He is known as 'D.D.' and 'Double-D.' Real name is 'Benson.' Friends started calling him D. D. because, when the spelling of his name came up or when he introduced himself, he would say, 'That's Cloudd, with a double D.' He started to get away from the 'Double-D' nickname, but when he began to be identified with datadrone research, the 'D. D.' description for datadrones revived the 'D. D.' description for Cloudd. As a youth, his life was unstructured. He flitted around among the more obscure planets of the First Galaxy.

His natural sense of adventure was tied to a growing feeling of identification with the humanoid races and Civilization. Because of the combination of his daring and experience, he was recruited by S.M.F. With the conquering of the Second Galaxy, he quit S.M.F. His report of service was excellent, but he was recognized as restless and difficult to discipline, so he was not made part of our Patrol reserve, as is most often the case. Freed from any obligation to my secret organizations or to the Patrol itself, he joined in a partnership to form a sector space line carrying passengers and cargo. He and his company, struggling for survival, were approached by the zwilniks of the drug trade, as well as other criminal elements, with offers to bend and sometimes to break the laws of the space lanes. He could have done so profitably, but he resented any idea of anyone controlling his life, so he refused. Pirates, financed by the zwilniks, began to hit his space line very hard. The racketeers applied pressures to make him capitulate. He resisted angrily, increased the armament on his ships and, with Patrol help, began a small war. On one of his business trips, his best space liner was attacked by a force of Boskonian warships. These Boskonians, powerful remnants of the elite of Boskone, had been organizing the zwilniks and pirates into the Spawn of Boskone. Cloudd was on board with his betrothed, a young female from a Tellurian colony. The liner was cut to pieces, but several lifeboats did at first escape. They were, however, hunted down and destroyed. His bride-to-be was killed. Cloudd should have died, too, but his tremendous willpower, fueled by a fierce passion for revenge, kept him alive. He was rescued, the only one who survived from a casualty list of nearly three thousand entities.

"Thereafter, Cloudd became like a madman. With the loss of the liner, his partners forced him out of the company as a much too aggressive troublemaker. He attempted to re-join S.M.F, but his psycho-profile identified him as unreliable and a potential security risk. He was not in control of himself. He considered joining the Patrol, but, once again, the discipline, he felt, would be unbearable. He took his few assets, mortgaging his future, and purchased a miner's ship. He spent the next year poking around the fringes of explored space acting as a freelance agent for S.I.S. and the Patrol. His ship was loaded down with weapons, and his object seemed less to find his fortune than to kill Boskonians and pirates. This was how he was one of the first to observe and report datadrones.

"Cloudd felt that the datadrones were a new development of the Spawn of Boskone. Therefore, in his burning hatred, and believing that this was the strongest blow he could deliver to them, he became dedicated to learning everything he could about the datadrone probes. He faithfully reported everything he learned to S.I.S. and thus to the Patrol. He made himself our most valuable researcher on a worrisome situation which was constantly increasing in scope. I personally made mind-to-mind contact with him and convinced him that he could best serve the interests of himself and Civilization by joining the Patrol. He accepted the position of a technician, giving his assistance and advice, if not having actual command, for a squadron of observation and research ships, semi-officially under the direction of S.I.S. and secretly a project of S.M.F.

"That is what brings Benson Cloudd to this meeting of scientists."

"I can appreciate what this fellow Cloudd has gone through," Kinnison said, his mind rapidly turning over the dramatic events in his own career. "Sounds to me as though he now deserves to be trusted with further responsibility. What are your plans for him, Trig?"

"He is about ready to be a part of the inner circle of the Secret Missions Forces, as an officer. I know he now is anxious to do so, but he will have to pass the various psychological screening tests first. I must stress that he has not yet passed my scrutiny."

"What's his family background, Trig? I gather he's one hundred percent Tellurian. I know the name. There is a Cloud who is a neucleonicist back in the Milky Way. I recall that for a time he was more famous than I was. As the Vortex Blaster he practically single-handedly saved Tellus from destruction, but you must know all about that. Is this Cloudd here any relation to that Doctor Cloud?"

"Not really," Tregonsee said. "You would describe him as a tenth cousin. They have never met, according to security checks in depth. There's the difference in the spelling, too, single dee as opposed to double dee."

"Hmm." Kinnison was pensive. "Why do I have such a strong hunch that they're somehow very close?"

"It's the similarity in their personal lives, I believe," Tregonsee said. "Both men had that aura of personal tragedy which strikes a sensitive at once. The doctor's wife and children were killed, in a vortex explosion. Afterwards, he became despondent, inordinately fearless, dedicated to finding out the cause and seeking revenge. He worked with the Patrol and proved to be a genius."

"Yet never became a Lensman."

"Correct, Kim. As often happens under the strict requirements of Arisia, Neal Cloud failed Lensman's Exam on the very first round."

"Yeah, I know friends of mine," Kinnison said with some sadness, "smarter than me, better than me, I swear, who failed."

"Superficial comparisons make them seem similar, but they're not. This Technician Benson 'D. D.' Cloudd is no genius, but he is very smart and clever, and grows more mature each year. My reports so far show he'd make a good Patrol officer and has the potential of being a Lensman if he channels his talents and aspirations properly."

"You have plans for him, Trig?"

"Yes, provided he disciplines himself by his own choice." The texture of Tregonsee's mind abruptly changed. "And provided something else that is very important."

The Lensmen felt the ominous vibration in Tregonsee's thought.

"I've been having several intensive investigations into his life. He's got the makings of a real hero—or a real villain—plenty of potential, but so far with just superficial Patrol training." Tregonsee seemed to be reluctant to make his charge. "He may be another like Tsien or Voddon. Or worse. He may be a traitor."

In view of what had just happened, there was no shocked response by Kinnison or the other two. They simply waited to hear more.

"Cloudd is carrying an Ordovik crystal around with him in his pocket. My aide P'Keen sensed it and Lensed it: the thing is tuned. Tuned like a homing beacon. P'Keen has kept

Cloudd under constant surveillance for the past few hours. P'Keen tells me the crystal is, as he phrases it, heating up. Right now Cloudd is outside, waiting. I'll call him in now. This is my warning, friends. Be ready for anything."

9

Cloudd Faces Four Lensmen

∿∿∿∿∿∿∿∿∿∿∿∿∿∿∿∿∿∿∿∿∿

Benson Cloudd did not know that he was under suspicion when he was called back in to face the Lensmen. His contrition had, by virtue of his lonely waiting, been changed into a resolution to raise his standards to honor the Lensmen who sought out his help. Never again would he give any reason to be called "a peevish human child." Never would he risk being labeled with a belittling sobriquet. But the atmosphere had changed since he had been away.

"Benson Cloudd," Kinnison said. "We understand you've brought an Ordovik crystal with you to this meeting. In fact, you seem to carry it with you everywhere. Can you tell us why?"

"Well, sir. It's very valuable. It's part of the mystery of the datadrones, at least insofar as I'm concerned. The safest place for it to be is right here in my pocket. That's where it's been since I left my ship." Under the stress of the moment some of the richness in his baritone voice was lost to a slightly higher pitch.

"That makes sense," Kinnison said. "Ordovik crystals are common enough. Millions of Ordoviks carry them. The larger, purer, better-crafted ones are worth much money to men and women of many races. Nadreck, as a gem collector, values them highly. All that being so, what is it that makes you obviously value it so excessively, so singularly?"

"Well, of course, you indicate it's beautiful, especially

104

after it's been shaped. And we know it gives a sensual pleasure when held or worn. But it's the stimulation of people's mental powers which makes it so often valued, particularly for those people who are native to Ordov. It's been proved that the crystal has a memory matrix. It records all sorts of things in patterns which can be nearly felt and sometimes read. Now take this crystal..." Cloudd put his right hand in his pants pocket and, as each Lensman watched and perceived with eye and mind and Lens for a questionable move, brought out a stone the size and shape of an egg on the palm of his hand. It was many-faceted, reflecting brilliant sprays of shifting lights. There were not, however, polygonal planes or faces covering it; the faces were polygonal convex surfaces, like hundreds of smooth bumps. As they looked in silence, the stone perceptibly flattened, fitting into the hollow of the hand. An Ordovik crystal, harder than a diamond, always was reshaping itself, round, oval, teardrop, its reflected light patterns constantly shifting.

If ever there had been felt a passionate emotion from that most placid of all creatures, a Palainian, it was felt then and everyone present recognized that remarkable fact. Nadreck had given the equivalent of a long, low, emotionally charged moan.

"It is one of the most beautiful I have ever seen," Nadreck said. "I will personally examine it, for within it I can read that it is my destiny to do so." And with that enigmatic remark he allowed not another thought or comment to escape from him for the many minutes which followed.

"No wonder you want to carry it," Kinnison said. "It's striking. What about its memory matrix...?"

"As I was saying," Cloudd continued, "this crystal is special. It's been cooked, cut, and polished by an expert. I'm positive that its intrinsic quality of retaining imprints of all radiations, spanning the range from visible light to mental waves, has been enhanced during its perfection. I'm not an authority on these crystals. I feel you Lensmen must see and examine it."

"Why?" said Tregonsee.

"Because even if none of you can actually read its memories, you may be able to suggest how it might be done."

"Why?" Tregonsee persisted. "What do you hope for someone to find?"

"The crystal was found next to the drone that a technician had tampered with. If the crystal came from the collection box of that drone, we might be able to read the location of the place it came from. We might be able to see or understand how it was actually collected. There was an explosion, caused by the drone, which killed the technician. We hypothesize, that is, I hypothesize that it was caused by a matter-anti-matter convergence. The crystal may have a record of the event on all wavelengths. On the other hand, if the technician was actually the carrier, it will tell us that. In any case, we will have some clues about anti-matter, which drones are proved to carry sometimes, but may be carrying at all times. Right now we have few clues as to the function, character, and utterly alien qualities and properties of drone anti-matter."

"Benson Cloudd," Tregonsee said. "You've been on trial now, without knowing it, for the possession of this Ordovik crystal. You are right about it being special. A property of it has been discovered about which we did not know. It is what is known as 'tuned,' that is, a guiding beacon for focusing certain energy forces. It may be identical with those used for the hyperspacial tube raids, and thus an instrument of our enemies. My responsibility for security makes me careful and I certainly had to be careful with you, a relatively unknown human being coming right into the centers of power. You've been having your mind thoroughly examined by us while you've stood there. We know nothing about the details of your life beyond what is public knowledge, or any of the facts which you should consider private and inviolate—but now we do know your personality, your motivation, your intrinsic worth, and your moral and ethical code of conduct. Because we are experienced and practiced, and you are unsophisticated in the use of telepathy, perception, and other such parascientific powers, we have been able to do this without your knowing it. You are now taken by us at face value. We now recognize you as a true and loyal Patrolman, to be treated by us, within your limitations, as an equal. Please take this crystal you hold in your hand to the doorway you entered, and give it to my aide, P'Keen, who is waiting for it.

In a little while, Nadreck will give it the examination you have requested."

When he had done so, Cloudd said, "Gentlemen, you expect much of me. I will do my best. To symbolize my resolution, I will strive to be known as Benson Cloudd. 'D.D.' and 'Double-Dee' are nicknames of the past."

"Very well, Benson Cloudd," Kinnison said. "We will remember that. Now about that battle with the phantom fleet. . . ."

Cloudd told them once more what he had experienced.

Then began an analysis of the event, which Cloudd could just barely follow and not completely understand. The experience of having such legendary Lensmen open up his mind telepathically so he could follow their discussion was indescribable. The thoughts which washed so freely through his brain were not an oppressive load to bear. They were somehow soothing and stimulating, and gave him a sense of greater awareness and intelligence than he believed himself capable of. It gave him an insight into his own mind, and stimulated within him a craving for personal mental improvement for which he now knew he would always hunger.

The Lensmen went through the possible explanations rapidly but carefully. Was the original encounter with the enemy fleet by chance or by design? By chance for the Patrol, unknown for the enemy. Did the enemy increase its forces to do battle or to scare away the Patrol? They had acted as if to do battle. They should have succeeded. They may not have been fully armed, or they may only have been in training—then they would not have gone into attack formation unless it was to frighten the Patrol into retreat. In this case, when the Patrol went into a frontal assault, they would naturally have failed to stop the Patrol and they would have retreated, themselves, as they did. Such was the first logical explanation.

So, it would seem, the enemy ships were scouts which the Patrol had stumbled upon. To attack the Patrol or to defend the scouts, the enemy had arrived in strength. Nearly frightened into retreat, the Patrol, instead, had broken through a lightly armed enemy. Or an inexperienced enemy. Or were allowed to escape.

Nothing sinister about this analysis, except possibly the idea that escape had been permitted.

However, there were other disturbing facts. The enemy had increased in number in a phenomenally short time. Did they have a new propulsion system? Did they have a new cloaking device? Did they have a new, ultra-dimensional commitment to battle? Or was the enemy simply well-organized and capable of instantaneous responses to instantaneous commands? That last possibility, bad though it was, but more reassuring than the others, was probably the truth.

Why did the Patrol missiles miss their targets? Why did the super ray beams fail? Poor equipment or training of the Patrol? No. New defensive equipment or tactics of the enemy? Probably. Local space-time conditions, naturally or artificially present? Possibly. An illusion, showing no destruction when there was, or enemy ships where there weren't any? Possibly.

At this point, Kinnison said, "I want Thorndyke here with us with data on space-time conditions!" and gave the order. And Worsel said, "I want Lalla Kallatra here with us with her latest research on Delgonian Overlord illusions and the Eichwoor." Whereupon Kinnison flashed a quick question about the current physical status of "that robot-girl Lensman" and received back from Worsel the immediate assurance that she was "progressing excellently, both personally and professionally."

Kinnison revised his order by an immediately Lensed command. "Send for Lensman Lalla Kallatra, too," and repeated Worsel's specific request for her data.

The brainstorming continued.

Why did the enemy's supposedly weak apex of its formation show the greatest power? Why did the Patrol's beams strike defending screens there, but no other place? How could the enemy retreat so quickly off the Patrol's screens? Answers to these questions depended on the answers to the questions asked earlier as to how and why the enemy appeared in the first place.

They had gone through the problem now, but had formed no final conclusion except for a tentative one from Worsel.

"I have an uneasy sense, an intuition," Worsel said, to break the reflective silence, "about an illusion. This may have been a phantom fleet, a spell of the mind. Or it may have been ghosts from another plane of existence. I have that feeling. I know that the instruments registered material things. And some very real exchanges of energy on a massive scale by offensive and defensive armaments were reported. But I still have that feeling. Thorndyke and Kallatra may have some contribution, and they should be here shortly. Meanwhile, before we take up Cloudd's primary mission here, about the datadrones, I suggest we check the progress of the conference of scientists, considering that so far none of us have been able to attend."

Kinnison summoned an aide, who silently placed a memo clipboard with a one-sheet summary on the oversized right arm of his chair, his miniature communications console desk.

Kinnison said, "Great!" and slammed his two hands together with a simultaneous *crack*! His voice and thought were enthusiastic. "Great news! Listen to this!" A flip of a switch brought a large video screen to life at one end of the room. Sir Austin Cardynge of Tellus, chairman of the conference, appeared, his aged and fragile body magnified far larger than life.

"Mr. Coordinator, Council members, members of the Patrol. We have taken up the second most urgent matter, the Sunbeam weapon. I am happy to report that there is no problem. Since the original concept by Kimball Kinnison and its construction by LaVerne Thorndyke, individual council members continued their research on it. They recognized the probability that Boskone would build and use this terrible weapon.

"As will be recalled, there was a 'winking phenomenon' when the sun's power waxed and waned as the Battle of Tellus began. The wavering was caused by Boskonian defenses, which almost succeeded. They made, however, a fundamental mistake.

"First, for your understanding, let me recapitulate:

"The quantity of energy used in the operation of the Sunbeam is unthinkably enormous, concentrating as it does the entire fantastic power of a sun or star by using other solar bodies to form a mammoth vacuum tube in space. And in direct ratio to it is the unthinkably enormous inefficiency of the weapon created. Consider that the process is to draw off from the prime source and focus on a target its total energy. As in the actual case of old Sol, itself—a moderately sized star—the total energy amounts to four and a half million tons of mass converted every second into neutrinos and gamma rays. The wattage of such released energy every second equals the number of kilograms of the mass destroyed multiplied by 90 million billion, the meters-per-second velocity of light multiplied by itself! Although this incredible power is collected into a beam and directed at its target, only a fraction of it drives straight ahead, due to the inconceivable turbulence and back-pressure. Even so, there is nothing to compare to it in effective raw power. Some radiates away, proportionately to the length and thickness of its beam. The power beam which penetrates its own turbulence and strikes a defensive screen is absorbed rapidly up to that screen's capability. The screen dissipates the incoming energy over the screen's total area. For these reasons, the Sunbeam, if defended against properly, is no more dangerous than the concentrated fire power of a large fleet.

"I emphasize that most power is wasted, and that which strikes a screen is absorbed rather than punching through as a coherent beam. Therefore, if defensive screens are expanded into large, if weakly thin, curtains, the sunbeams will themselves be spread out, absorbed, and thus stopped, or at least drastically reduced in efficiency. The titanic magnitude of the Sunbeam's intrinsic energy thus should never be realized.

"So, as can be seen, the Patrol's defensive screens, even of that period, if linked together as in a very large fleet, could probably have handled a Sunbeam weapon if it had been turned on us. The Boskonians did not allow for the dissipation of power. They contracted their screens for greater shielding, a natural reaction. They should have, instead, expanded their shields to dissipate the energy. They simply burned out their screens by the wrong defense.

"The Patrol can defend against the Sunbeam, if Boskonians themselves succeed in inventing it. The secret is in defensive tactics, not in any new technology.

"The council points out that the Sunbeam could be used to make an opponent spread his screens thinly and then to be attacked with needle-rays, but believes the logistics make it not viable. The conclusion of the council, therefore, is that Civilization need not fear deployment of the Sunbeam.

"This report ends.

"We are now assembling facts on the other items on the
110

agenda. Our preliminary findings are that, first: small black holes may be serious inconveniences if manipulated, but, as yet, large ones cannot be, and pose no major threat. Two: datadrones, like small black holes, are at present only an annoyance. And, finally: the use of hyperspatial tubes is now considered potentially catastrophic, particularly as it relates to the health of every scientist. The council feels that even a small loss of any of its members by injury, kidnapping or death is completely unacceptable to the members. They believe that they are the most valuable assets that Civilization has.

"We are drawing this conviction especially to the attention of Kimball Kinnison. So pay attention to what I'm saying, young man! The Galactic Patrol must defend all scientists as its first priority. Is that clear? Frankly, I'm surprised that Tregonsee, who is usually so reliable, should have had such slip-shod security for some of our most important brains. If this is negligence, it is inexcusable and will not be tolerated by me. Or any of us. You've given me cause to criticize you in the past, but you're older now, and shouldn't allow yourself or others any mistakes. You must realize, young man, what great responsibilities you and Tregonsee have.

"The conference will not adjourn until it feels it has understood and solved this problem.

"Cardynge out."

The screen flickered in many colors and Kinnison turned off the power.

"Well," Kinnison chuckled, "I guess Sir Austin has told me off good and proper! And it's really very reassuring—that peppery old man is still full of beans."

"Full of beans?" There came to Cloudd's mind a more vulgar expression. Cloudd, unfamiliar with the idiosyncrasies of both Cardynge and Kinnison, was both perplexed and disturbed by what seemed to him such intolerant language. Kinnison's picturesque phrasing, picked up from the faddish regional culture of his boyhood, frequently bewildered the uninitiated.

Kinnison noted the troubled thought. "Still firing on all jets," he clarified. "I suggest we all jointly Lens our sincere congratulations to him for conveyance to the scientists assembled." The four Second Stage Lensmen promptly did so, expressing also their thorough agreement that the Galactic Patrol would defend them as its first priority. The scientists sounded scared stiff; no wonder their bickering had so far been kept at a surprisingly low level.

"It's only right for me to point out to you, Cloudd," Kinnison said, "that Cardynge isn't really worried about himself. That wispy little scientific wizard has the courage of a bantam cock—it's the others he's speaking for, with genuine concern, too. As to be expected, the conference is doing a fine job—although, as is also to be expected, they're exhibiting a mixture of complacency and imperious exaggeration. Now let's get back to the question of the datadrones which they so lightly dismiss."

Once more Cloudd was interrogated, both inside and outside his mind, and the discussion began.

Where were the datadrone probes coming from? From a source inside one of the galaxies? From beyond the galaxies? But there were no life forms beyond the twin galaxies, mostly because there were practically no planets elsewhere. Nothing conclusive. Arguments could be made for either source. But they were definitely coming from some unexplored region of space, and were most active on the edges of the two galaxies. Most likely the source could be a globular cluster, outside the galaxies proper, but part of either one of the galactic systems.

What were they? Most obviously, they were parts of an information collection system. Did they have any other function? Unknown.

Who could be collecting information? Boskonia? Highly improbable. The Spawn or other pirates? The most likely possibility, but recently partially discounted. An undiscovered alien race? Quite possible. A secret activity of one of the Civilized planets? Highly unlikely, but just possible. There were some strong clues present, based on Cloudd's examinations. The technology was not alien, could be definitely identified with Civilization. It had markings suggestive of humanoid culture: reversed-S symbols, wedged-shaped symbols, painted for the visible light optic spectrum of Tellurians and Tellurian types.

When did this probing start? Was it increasing? It was discovered not much more than a year before, in the First

Galaxy. It had spread to the Second Galaxy. It certainly was on the increase.

Were the Civilized planets suffering any ill effects? Not really. The datadrones avoided dangerous situations: caused no transportation system foul-ups; interfered with no communications or other frequencies. But they did cause apprehension and unrest by their presence alone.

What did they actually do? They just seemed to drift around in vacuum, rarely in atmosphere, observing. Sometimes they actually took small objects. A dozen or so complex mechanical parts had been found in drones, all broken or worn out. They had, the inevitable deduction seemed to indicate, come from discarded parts, trash dumps, or junk discarded from spaceships. Why? Obviously so as not to disturb the normal functioning of the culture probed? Why weren't they obvious on the surface of planets? Why so considerate? Why so cautious? Perhaps there was a fear of alerting too many ordinary people? Perhaps they were building a tolerance? Perhaps they weren't even collecting anything, but were serving merely as monitoring or warning devices? Why? Why? Why?

What happened to the objects collected? Cloudd concluded that they were scanned, analyzed, tested, and jettisoned, sometimes unchanged and sometimes as atomic particles. They were used only as articles for examination, that seemed definite.

Were they a threat to Civilization? Unknown, but for that very reason they had to be considered as a potential threat of great magnitude.

How did they operate? Small probes passed information on to larger probes, which transmitted such information, encoded, by an undiscoverable method. Significantly, all datadrones contained sizable amounts of anti-matter with unexaminable shielding. Why? The only purpose the anti-matter seemed to serve was to inhibit the Patrol from examining the drones thoroughly. One mistake and there was a violent explosion. It had happened. Propulsion was a form of universal energy picked up by each probe in a so far undecipherable way. The use of sub-ether or Nth space was being investigated.

"We have examined all aspects of this situation, Trig,"

Kinnison said, concluding the exploration of the subject. "It certainly is mysterious, but it doesn't seem to be any immediate or dangerous threat. Why are you so concerned?"

"My investigators indicated that there is definitely an organization known as the Spawn of the Boskone, and that this Spawn is attempting to solve the riddle of the datadrones. Cloudd, without being influenced by me, has independently come to the conclusion that the drones are considered inimical by our foes in the field. They may think these drones are ours. They may be as worried about them as we are. And they may succeed in finding out about them before we do. The possibility exists that they may discover something to use against us to our great, perhaps fatal, misfortune. I emphatically feel that this may be, eventually, one of the greatest threats we have ever faced, insidious because it is so mysterious."

"I take your point, Trig," Kinnison said. "But Thorndyke is outside now, and Kallatra is ready to join us by Lens while she's en route from her lab at Research Park outside of town. We will get back to the datadrones later."

Thorndyke came in, not nearly as agitated as when Kinnison had first seen him so many hours before.

"You know the problem, Thorny," Kinnison said. "Was the enemy fleet involved in a space-time warp of some sort?"

"No," Thorndyke said. He told them his reasons for his conclusion, and went into a lot of technical detail, using readings from the Sector Patrol Task Force's battle recordings, to indicate that the encounter was far more mysterious than the Lensmen had been considering it. Cloudd couldn't get a clear picture of Thorndyke's reasoning because Thorndyke was not a Lensman and the telepathy to Cloudd's telepathically undeveloped mind, which was dependent on re-transmission by the Lensmen, rendered the conversation fuzzy. Cloudd felt a great kinship toward the dynamic non-Lensman who was the greatest technician in the entire Patrol. Here was a man Cloudd could identify himself with without losing a bit of his own self-assertiveness.

"I've been listening, sirs," came another mind. To Cloudd it was firm and clear, and he knew from the warm greetings of Kinnison and Worsel that this was Lalla Kallatra, a woman Lensman. Cloudd had never met a woman Lensman, and he was intrigued by the prospect. The mind was certainly impressive, moving and touching like a cool, sweet running brook.

"I've been listening and I have something very serious to offer. I believe Worsel is on the right track. There is more than just a touch of the psychic involved in this. Deuce O'Sx, the Voice-from-Beyond-the-Grave, has told me to beware. I suggest that the Chaplain General, who has grown to know my extramundane work so well, be summoned to this meeting, too. The phantom fleet of the enemy was really phantom. I believe the ships did not exist!"

10

Conspiracy on Kresh-kree

In the center of the domed room there blazed a sphere of great beauty. Its surface swirled with all the hues of the spectrum, brilliant and dull and intense and faded. Shimmering bands streamed in one direction, then in another. Sometimes the ball sparkled and revolved vertically, sometimes it flamed and turned horizontally. Fast, slow, pulsating, one moment as small as a human skull, another moment ten times as large, it sprayed dancing light from curved floor to ceiling. The sculptured crystal pendants, which hung like numberless clusters of stalactites, glistened, sometimes with streaks of color, sometimes with specks of light.

This was a force-ball, created out of pure thought by a mighty race of entities. Its simplest function, to which use it was now being put, was as an intra-galactic communicator.

Emanating from this sphere, which ironically was as overwhelmingly gorgeous and pristine as the creature which created it was overwhelmingly ugly and evil, came a thought:

"Imperial Kalonians! Acknowledge your Master!"

On the floor, sitting in pairs to form a large circle, were six male and six female Kalonians, dressed in purple silken lounge suits. Only their styles of hair and their individual jeweled necklaces or strings of beads set them apart. The flecks of color passing across their bare arms and shoulders and faces accentuated the blue skin tones of their flesh. They were all beautiful, the features of the men strong and sharp, the bodies of the women soft and full. Physically, in fact, they were too perfect, smoothly, artificially prettified products of the wealth of aristocrats of the defunct Thrale-Onlonian Empire.

The voice from the sphere had an immediate effect. Each male grasped the coiffured hair of his mate and pulled her head back, exposing her bare, arched throat. Each male pulled from a scabbard at his belt a long knife and placed it against his mate's throat. The razor sharpness of the blades in two instances, slight though the pressure was, sliced the perfect skin, so that purplish drops of blood began to trickle down.

One Kalonian male, marked by wearing two golden chained, bejeweled ornaments, said, "Say the word, Master, and we will each kill our favorite childbearer for you. Thus do you know we follow you without question."

"I hear you, Imperial Kalonians, I acknowledge your fealty. Shall I ask a token killing now? Six? Five? Four? I free you all. Three? Two? Shall I ask it of you, Two? Or should it be One? I free you, Two. Now as for One. You would enjoy killing! I free you, One."

The knives came down and the women lowered their bodies in front of their men, sprawled face upward. On the bare abdomens of their women, exposed by the cut-out panel of their clothes, the men laid their naked knives.

"Death to Lanion the Traitor!" the men spoke in unison. "Long life to the Master! Long life to the New Empire!"

"Bah!" said the mental thought. "I despise you all! Do you think the blood of your women will satisfy me? I want power! I want death to my enemies! I want wealth! Do you think a cheap trick like this will blind me? This is no substitute for what you have promised me. Pander to me—I will enjoy it! But do not pay me worthless coin. I know you Kalonians—you believe that only your men are Kalonians. Your women are expendable at your whim. They have been subjugated into mere playthings and baby-making machines. Sacrifice your women to me? You offer me no more than spit! I want wealth, power, deaths!"

The Kalonians were frozen in their postures as they heard these thoughts. The men were still sitting, their women supine before them, but the leader slowly rose. He held one forefinger to his lips while his other forefinger made a brief circular motion at his right temple to indicate insanity. With another sign from him, the men put away their knives while the women crawled to the edge of the room and crouched in fear.

"We are fulfilling our promises, Master. Are we not?"

"What have you done with the tubes? Using them, you swore, would bring wealth, power, deaths. You have used the tubes, so fulfill your promises!"

"We have explained, Master. Patience is needed."

"Aargh!" came a fierce, choking sound. "Don't lecture me! You act imperious! You are not yet Imperial Kalonians! Do you think me mad? I am totally sane. I am much too considerate. I am much too gentle with you. Perhaps this is my madness. I am crazed with anger at you. You say your matter-eating weapon will gain you an empire, and you promise me an empire of many empires. Where is this matter-eating weapon?"

"It is not yet ready, Master. Patience is needed. We are perfecting it. Yes, slow progress can be maddening."

"Patience, is it, Kalonians? Soon I will have no more patience. Then I will show you what madness is. This is your final chance. The next time you deny me I will take, not your cheap females, but each of you, one by one. I am magnanimous now only while I wait to see if your hyperspatial tube attacks are all the success you claim."

"Thank you, Master," said the leader, a sneer creeping from his voice and into his features. "You are so reasonable, so obviously sane, Master. Thus you will see how the tube attacks will bring us victory. Our Kalonian promises are not idle boasts. Our lives will be nothing but pain and unhappiness while Lanion the Traitor lives. And yet we did not use the tube to murder him. Does that not prove that we have greater plans for the tubes for winning our greatest victories?"

"That does seem true. You are not fools. Nor are you fools to ignore the fact that Lanion the Traitor is probably too well protected by the Galactic Patrol. Lanion and the Patrol still fear that there may be counter-revolutionaries just like you. Yes, you are right by saying we must weaken the Patrol first. I admit, they are already reacting to your raids. They are already showing their panic by calling their greatest scientists into an intergalactic conference. Tregonsee's death has been a stunning blow to them. They are pathetically parading an impersonator at their headquarters at Ultra Prime, but we and our allies will not be deceived. Soon you will be able to call for an uprising on Thrale, and Lanion the Traitor and his Council of Advisers will all die.

"But why is not your weapon ready? I know of your tube raids on the scientists. I know you kidnapped the expert, John Tsien, from whom you said you would wring the vital knowledge to make the black hole weapon work. You are able to manipulate small black holes. This I know. Why haven't you done as you promised?"

The sparkling sphere was angry in its color now, spitting off long, hot sparks.

"It is only a matter of time, Master." The leader of the Kalonians had his hands planted on his hips, annoyance on his face. "We do not wish our enemies or your enemies to live one second longer than necessary. Their doom comes nearer, faster and faster. John Tsien has given us what was in his mind, that is true. The secret of black hole guidance is ours. The ability to concentrate gravitational collapse is within our grasp. We have already sent a black hole down a hyperspatial tube, much too tiny to cause any trouble, we admit, yet a promise of greater things to come. However, we must have caution. What we may start, we may not stop. What we do, we may not undo."

The sparkling sphere was deep red. It no longer spun. From it radiated an oppressive wave of mental hate.

"Weakling! You disgust me, One! You falter—and you will collapse and fail if your hatred is so puny and your passion for revenge so vacillating! I want a small black hole dropped on Klovia. I want it to sink rapidly to that planet's center where it will devour that cursed world with great violence. I want another black hole dropped on Tellus, the earth home of the contemptible Homo sapiens. I do not just want this—I *demand* this! But we do not stop there. Such is not enough. One world, two worlds, a hundred worlds of Civilization—they are not enough, not a fraction of a fraction enough to sate my need for deaths, deaths, deaths of our enemies! A million planets must be snuffed out, and then another million. And it will be our black hole weapon which will do it. We will eliminate them like insects swept up by a tornado. Our black hole will feed and feed and grow and grow until this energy eater, this cosmic suction cleaner, will suck up into its maw all of Civilization, its Council, its despicable Patrol!"

"Madness is not profitable, Master." The Kalonian's face had slowly hardened into a ruthless mask. "One does not sink the boat which carries you because it carries your enemy, too. Nor does one wring the neck of all the fowl which lay the golden eggs because one of them has pecked you."

"We shall see," said the sphere and its color gradually lightened and it spun once more, but not sparkling again. "One way or another, vengeance will be done. You can see that I am disappointed by your unfulfilled promises. I have good reason. I revealed to you the power of the hyperspatial tube and the secret of focusing it with a tuned Orodovik crystal. I gave to you seven crystals. I supervised the preparation of seven tubes. But you have used them with no wealth or riches to show for it, few deaths, no conquered planets. Your reports are much too meagre. Oh, I've heard how you caused the assassination of the Rigellian Lensman Tregonsee. I've heard that you kidnapped five of the Galactic Council's best scientists. And right from under the sniveling noses of Tregonsee's secret agents. Buy why did I hear about it first by rumors? Why? Why do you hide things from me?"

"Master, have we not told you of the death of Tregonsee? Have we not told you of the unfortunate passing of Mando the Vegian, killed by the dying Tregonsee? Have we not told you of the confusion brought on by the death of the Rigellian?"

"Yes, but not quickly enough. And that is not all."

"Have we not told you of our penetration into the brains of the scientists? How we have soaked up the concealed knowledge they possess? Have we not forwarded to you transcripts of certain secrets they had?"

"If you did not take their bodies, too, why did you not kill them when their knowledge was taken?"

"For many reasons. And alive we might have further use for them. I ask again, did not you receive from us their secrets?"

"Yes, some secrets. But not sent quickly enough. You did not say how many scientists. How many tube attacks were made on scientists?"

"Four attacks. Four scientists. Four crystals. Plus the fifth used against Tregonsee. Five used crystals were returned, degraded, to you. Crystal six was not used in the fake attack on Voddon, but is lodged in Tsien's head. The seventh crystal has not been used."

"Liar! The seventh crystal has been used!"

"We do not lie to you, Master. The six are Tsien, Cardynge, Strong and Ehht, plus Tregonsee, plus the bomb in Tsien's head. The seventh still awaits usage."

"Then I will tell you how the seventh has been used. My spies tell me that the Patrol is responsible for the thousand mechanical spies that are flying now throughout space—and you have used the seventh crystal to discover their secret. I think you were successful there, too, but you will not share the information with me. I demand to know what you have found!"

"We found nothing, Master. That attack was never made. It was our one failure. We did not report it because there was nothing to report."

"Because it was a failure, you mean! That is why you did not report it! Well, I want to know your failures, too. I will know you by your failures as well as your successes."

"Perhaps the attack will still take place. The seventh Ordovik crystal was taken aboard a Patrol ship by a zwilnik who was well paid. He assumed the identity of a Patrolman he had murdered. The ship was for research on the project known as datadrones, and he was to place the crystal in the work area or datadrone material of the technician in charge. The zwilnik was killed, but the crystal is now in possession of a man named Cloudd. Our raiding party assigned to this crystal has kept track of it. This Cloudd has taken the crystal right into Ultra Prime base. At any moment the raiding party could attack out of the tube, but there are too many Ordovik Patrolmen around. If the crystal is activated by the beginning of a tube materialization, an Ordovik will sense it and defensive measures will be taken against it. So, we have our alternative plan for the other terror attack, more murders. If not through a raiding party, then through an assassin. We of The Council of Six have been attentive and are patient. An appropriate time will come. We will reward whoever succeeds in a spectacular manner. We have promised special payment—

much money, official power in our movement, a monopoly on the thionite trade. That is what will be done with the seventh Ordovik crystal and the seventh tube."

"Who is paying these special payments? Not me. I did not agree to pay extra."

"The Council of Six will pay."

"Then this plan is a good one. But why did you not tell me of it? I suspect that you may still be trying to take some kind of advantage of me. I will give you three days to use the tube and crystal, otherwise I demand that it be returned to me."

"We will use it, Master, or we will return it."

"I feel better, now that you have explained with a reasonable story. But you have not told me all."

"We told you about all the scientists. Have we not told you about the crystal bomb planted in the head of John Tsien, which will explode when he is in the presence of the hated Kinnison? Do you not know how we will monitor the confidential notes of the Council of Scientists by the sub-etheric transmitter planted in the brain of Voddon the Manarkan?"

"Yes, but that is not all."

"Have we not disclosed our plans to attack by tube the pregnant wife of Kinnison and to destroy mother and unborn child? We can be delayed only because we are not yet able to place the tuned Ordovik crystal within her heavily guarded residence. But we shall succeed, for we have an Ordovik traitor who will carry the crystal into her presence within days, perhaps hours, disguised as a gift of a precious gem—authorized under the very seal of Tregonsee's office!"

"Yes. Good. But that still is not all."

"There is nothing more, Master. Is there?"

"There is. I refer to the tricks you are scheming there on your planet of Kresh-kree."

"Tricks, Master?"

"Don't pretend you don't know of what I speak. You are liars and murderers. I have praised you as the blackest of villains and the vilest of evildoers. So, I trust you no more than you trust me, for all your protestations of servility to me, your so-called Master. You will kill your closest companions if it will serve your purpose. But I am the mastermind of our new force against the Galactic Patrol, and I must know of your plans concerning the Tansers of Tanse and the Qu'orr of The Moon of Lost Souls."

Five male Kalonians, though provoked, were afraid, but the leader was full of arrogant courage. "We honor you, Master, because you are more powerful than we. We do not worship you, but we respect your power. But we are powerful, too, and we know that you respect us for that. We are working together for our own selfish ends. We want our Empire back. You wish to build your own, larger than ours, covering the galaxies now, perhaps later controlling the universe. You now are the speaker for the mysterious organizers of the Spawn of the Boskone. They are really the masterminds, not just you. Yet we call you Master anyhow. The epithets you hurl at us are compliments to us. Let us be honest with you—you are a master of great skill. You deserve to be called Master, although you are just one of your small group. But from now on you will not treat us as servants. No one will treat us so. No, we shall, instead, be allies of equal rank. For now we know as much as you once did and more, with a world of two hundred million Kalonians and one hundred million slaves. Kresh-kree is a world with high technology, with a thriving drug trade, and a criminal network in an entire sector of the galaxy. Yes, Master, we are strong now, perhaps stronger than you. And we have secrets which you yourself have begun to fear. Report that to your fellow plotters. The Spawn does not yet rule like Boskone."

The force-ball had been spinning faster and faster, a blur of ugly hot colors, throwing off embers of pure energy. Now it was nearly twelve feet tall, nearly touching the jagged crystals of the ceiling and the polished black marble of the floor. Instead of the solid globe it had been, it was now like vapor, a dull orange mist, slowly changing into a bilious green. Inside it was forming a vision. At first it was humanoid. But the face was melting. From the face were growing many eyes and slavering gray teeth without a head, just stuck upon a skinless mass of shapeless flesh. Not shapeless, no, a hundred-armed octopus, with the eyes melting like red wax balls in fire, dripping into many mouths in which the teeth had become tiny, wriggling worms. The skinless flesh was heaving, uncovering hideously shaped organs, as though a repulsive monster had been turned inside out, twisting now into an amorphous shape in puddles of fourth-dimensional haziness.

All the Kalonians were hiding their eyes, mind shields up as tightly as they could manage, except the standing blue-tinged man in the purple costume, whose hands, with pointed fingers, were thrust forward toward the misty sphere in the manner of one trying to exorcise it.

"I know who you are, Master. You are the dark and cold Onlon who deserted Kandron, your superior. You fled into the poisonous depths of the now infamous Green Parricide Nebula, known before the Boskonian infestation as the placid Green Parrot Nebula. Kandron himself has told us your secrets. Yes, I did lie—for his information I gave him the right to pick the seventh target for the seventh crystal and it is being placed into position for a trap he is setting. He knows you by the real name under which you were disgraced. Your fellow deserters call you Ish-Ingvors, which means 'He-is-to-be-called-a-Hero-not-a-Coward.'"

The sphere shrank and grew opaque again, in ugly orange-red pulses of energy, and for the first time, actually an impression within the minds of the Kalonians, it gave off a nauseating, rotten smell.

"Know that we have a better weapon," the Kalonian said. "Better than the black hole one with which you would disintegrate and send into another continuum the disassembled matter of your enemies, some allies, and most of the stars and planets of our own two island universes. We, on the other hand, have a weapon of control. Of control, Master. We would not destroy, we would *control. Enslave the galaxies!*

"Our time has come. The Tansers of Tanse now bow under the power of we Kalonian-Kresh-kree of Kresh-kree. And from the Tansers we have wrested the secret of the Qu'orr. The Tansers are no longer necessary to our plans. The Qu'orr will be harvested only by The Chosen Six. The Qu'orr power is not like mere thionite, bringing worthless drug-induced dreams. With the Qu'orr there comes a new reality to existence.

"You will no longer be given the pleasure-dreams of the Qu'orr by us, Master. There is no price you can pay us to continue. Nor will the Tansers help you, for we have become their gods and you have become their devils.

"You cannot stop us, Master. Kandron cannot stop us.

"You cannot even interfere, Master. No one can.

"The galaxies will soon begin to fall under our *control.* *Our* control, not yours.

"Which one of us has the better goal? Which one of us will succeed?

"You are Ish-Ingvors. Now will you know my name and it will make you tremble. I am Helmuth-the-Younger, Number One of the Chosen Six, Overseer of Kresh-kree. As Helmuth's son, I myself *now* speak for *you*, Ish-Ingvors, and *for all the Bosko-Spawn!"*

Three telepaths were in deep concentration. Each one was on a different world. Two were agents of the Secret Intelligence Service of the Galactic Patrol, and between them was developing the answer to a terrible secret. Theirs was a discourse, passing through the ether from the planet of Kresh-kree to the planet of Tanse, that would affect the peace of the Second Galaxy and the future of Civilization. The third telepath was an agent of evil who took care to make no ripple in the stream of silent sound. He crouched, scarcely breathing, on The Moon of the Gods, and listened, over-hearing—on the verge, just on the verge, of understanding.

"Ulie! The Council of Six has decided—they will harvest the Qu'orr!"

"No! Oh, no! You must stop them, Seena! When is it to be?"

"The time of the harvest has been set for the sacrificial period following the next one."

"Then we must act now, Seena! I can do nothing here on Tanse without help. Can you stop it there?"

"No, Ulie. The raiding party is already in position on The Moon of the Gods. It is there, or on Tanse itself, where they must be stopped."

"I can't do it alone, Seena. I must have help. I must have Lensman help. Do you agree?"

"Yes, Ulie, I agree. How soon must help come? Do we have until the period after next?"

"No, no. We must act before they do; perhaps we can be prepared to stop them, then. We must act within three days."

"Impossible, Ulie! There's not one unattached or Gray

Lensman here on Kresh-kree! I will have to contact my S.I.S. link, who is already waiting word from us, and have him Lens my recommendations directly through to Tregonsee. That will take at least two days!"

"To Tregonsee, Seena? Then he's not dead? Thank Klono! You told me of the rumors last week..."

—*On The Moon of the Gods, the enemy agent caught the name,* Tregonsee! *Everything else had been a distant blur, like whispers covered by the hiss of a flowing stream. Yet the name of* Tregonsee *was a powerful word with powerful connotations and it sprang out of what was unintelligible and was recognized in his brain. More and more he concentrated to strain out the essence of this faraway dialogue—thoughts coming, he now knew, from enemies deadly to him—*

"No, Ulie, Tregonsee is not dead. Word came through to me that it has been a deception. Strangely, it was my report of the rumor of his death which was the first of all the rumors in the galaxy that HQ-T had received."

"Ah, that sounds as if Kresh-kree must have been in on the plot!"

"Yes, it seems most likely. That's the very reason I was asked to trace further the source of that rumor and I did. A hired band of assassins under Eramista the Manarkan—"

—*Eramista! His name! He could hear his name in that indistinct mumbling of thought waves. He listened harder, and the sweat came out upon his brow—*

"—under Eramista the Manarkan struck by hyperspatial tube while T was on a visit to Preeko. T managed to kill Mando the Vegian, who came out of the tube, but Eramista then killed T. At least, that's the story. I also learned that this was one of a series of attacks aimed at other Lensmen."

"Other Lensmen, Seena? Did others die?"

"I don't know. But certain scientists were kidnapped, or nearly kidnapped, the sense is not clear. According to the underworld here on Kresh-kree, the different raiding parties were hired by the Overseer and The Council of Six. The hyperspatial tubes were obtained from an unknown enemy of the Galactic Coordinator, believed to be an Onlonian named Ish-Ingvors. Have you learned anything new there on Tanse, Ulie?"

"Nothing new, but I've confirmed my own theories. The

Qu'orr are probably things growing on Tanse Moon One—the moon called The Moon of Lost Souls because none who go there can return. I certainly don't care to, even though I've found a way to go. That's why a Lensman, a special Lensman, is essential. Only one with the most developed sense of perception might be able to scan that moon. If anything, Seena, the whirlpools of mental turmoil which surround it like an aura are getting worse. T must send his best. As for Tanse Moon Two—The Moon of the Gods—I have caught the faintest thought waves from there. A raiding party, you say? Those few, faint mental waves tell me they are arrogant, over-confident and careless." There was a long, dead pause. "That is why you have been so cautious in the narrow mental beam that you are projecting, Seena. And that is why I have been so careful to do the same. We are a matched pair, aren't we, Seena?"

"Yes, Ulie, we are. No other two in the twelve digits of A's could be better matched than we are."

"Can you sense anyone reaching out for us from Moon Two? Do you think the tightness of our mental beam could be pierced?"

"Never. Not for two like us, Ulie. This is so, even though it is Eramista, who is perhaps the most accomplished of all Manarkans. It would be just like him to be arrogant, over-confident, and careless."

—*Eramista heard his name again and didn't like the feeling of the name. The hair rose across the bridge of his nose, and he opened his mouth to make an outlandish, mute snarl from a throat that never had a larynx. Annoyance grew into frustration and frustration was growing into hatred*—

"If anyone can succeed in harvesting the Qu'orr, Seena, it will be a wretch like that Manarkan outlaw. He has the ruthless mind to do it."

"How will he get there? By the way you have found?"

"I don't know. My way is by a spaceboat here on Tanse."

"A spaceboat? On Tanse? I don't understand!"

"The spaceboat, hard to believe, I know, is the sacred coffin used in the sacrifices. It's used to carry the victims to and from the moons by remote control. I'll explain that all later to you, Seena. Anyhow, I have used that spaceboat often in the past few weeks. I steal it at night and return it before dawn. I've surveyed much of this part of the planet. The jungle is impossible to penetrate very far on foot. I tried twice to fly to Tanse Moon One, but the strange effect which the Tansers call the Turmoil of Lost Souls was a real mental force which threatened my sanity. That's why I stress that the highest caliber of Lensman is needed. Perhaps—I know it's too much to hope for, but—perhaps, a Second Stage Lensman might come.".

"I will try for the best. There may not be enough time to get any kind of Lensman. How will the Lensman—even a Patrolman or two of Lensman caliber—get to Tanse to meet you? The Kalonians' on Moon Two will be on the watch for outsiders. We do not have the Lens. How will you guide them in under the inward eye of Eramista and his band?"

"I will use the spaceboat. I'll fly in it to a planetoid I've marked on the far side of Moon Two's orbit, putting Tanse between us. There I will rendezvous with the Lensmen, who will have to come in under a cloak of invisibility. I'll do that tomorrow night. If they do not meet me there tomorrow night, I will fly to the same place the following night. That second night will be the eve of the sacrifice, so our margin for successful action will be very small indeed. From there I'll steer them back to Tanse. I want them present at the sacrifice because it is then that I think they can penetrate the Turmoil of Lost Souls. They can follow with their sense of perception the sacred coffin carrying the victim to the moon of the Qu'orr."

"Sounds workable. I will try to get someone there by tomorrow night or the next. What are the coordinates?"

"Eye eks hyphen one point forty-two sigma. Repeat. Eye eks hyphen one point forty-two sigma. Use Tanse star chart GP-Tanse twelve. Repeat. Tanse star chart GP-Tanse twelve."

"I've got that, Ulie. Do you need any muscle? A Valerian star warrior or two?"

"Good idea. But no Valerian. Somebody Tellurian in size, at least as powerful as me. A human barbarian, preferably, to work with me in the tribe."

"Maybe Kimball Kinnison?"

—*Eramista jumped as though he had been shot. Kimball Kinnison! The name came through clearly, like a bolt of electrons riding a laser beam, and stunned him. And then he*

128

thought he felt laughter. Laughter! Women's laughter! And his fear was gone, and his burning hatred increased in him like a thermonuclear flame—

"That's the right idea, Seena! A good, husky Tellurian Lensman who's looking for a real brawl!"

"I'll get on this immediately, Ulie. You'll hear from me tomorrow evening when Tanse Moon One is low in the sky, shielded from you. One way or another, you'll get your help. And will you be ready to come in to shelter afterwards?"

"Perhaps. My work seems done now. It's up to a high-tension mind. I'll be glad. I've missed you, Seena. Remember, whatever happens, you have my love."

"And all my love goes out to you, Ulie. I will pray for you. Until tomorrow evening, then. I touch my forehead."

"I touch my forehead, loved one."

—The thought transmission ended between the tawny-white-skinned Ulie and the purple-tinted-skinned Seena, while the raiding party on Tanse Moon Two, three Manarkan renegades led by Eramista, listened. Eramista, greatest of natural telepaths, had listened well, but the stream of thoughts had been perfectly controlled. The meaning had been incomprehensible. His mental sensitivity lines had criss-crossed that stream, like a net, but he had not been able to catch a single coherent idea. "There is a telepath on the planet Tanse," he projected to his deaf-mute companions. "In two days, when we go down there, to jump off to The Moon of Lost Souls, I will find that telepath. And if he—or she—is anyone except a personal friend of mine, I will butcher that one up into little pieces".

11

Two Only for Tanse

෴෴෴෴෴෴෴෴෴෴෴෴෴෴෴෴෴෴

Near the center of Ultra Prime base rose a low complex
of black stone structures, like huge building blocks tumbled
in an untidy pile. This was Headquarters, Patrol Intelligence
Services—known more familiarly as HQ-T-Prime.

Deep within the pile was a conference room honeycombed
with many cells. Each of these separate cubicles was capable
of turning itself into an authentic environmental replication
mimicking any one of a hundred or so different planets, from
A to Z in the first digit of planetary classification. Any
atmosphere, any gravity, any temperature of any of the major
Civilized planets, along with a lot of minor ones, could be
quickly reproduced. A conferee in that conference hall could
relax and feel at home.

Like the most austere of harsh prisons, each cell was like
a windowless, sealed box. No windows were needed, so no
windows were provided in the stacked cells; it was expected
that senses of perception would be commonly used and the
walls would simply fade away; for the primitives, full wall
screens for viewing could be used.

To those who used the conference rooms, it seemed that
all races were mixed together freely, each somehow comfortable in his own environment.

In each cubicle, arranged in and around one another for
closest three-dimensional intimacy, were the conferees especially invited to this meeting. In the exact center, in his own

box the same size as the others, there firmly stood on four thick feet the host himself, Tregonsee.

On one side, Nadreck writhed luxuriously in his frigid, poisonous simulation of Palain VII, his four-dimensional form seeming to flow out of his fully opened suit.

On another side, Worsel was draped on a Velantian resting-pole, serpentine body touching from wall to wall, flexing his wings and sniffing odors of home.

Kinnison, above, with his two scientist-mathematician friends, Sir Austin Cardynge and LaVerne Thorndyke, sat in one of the leather easy chairs in a room more like Klovia than Tellus.

In another cell, Ehht the Nevian was partially immersed in emerald green water, sometimes allowing himself to slip entirely down into the liquid which filled half his room.

John Tsien and Voddon the Manarkan, the impostor, shared the light gravity and oxygen-helium atmosphere such as each of their satellite laboratories contained.

In the final compartment, under Tellurian conditions, were Philip Strong, the Tellurian scientist-Lensman, Benson Cloudd, and Lalla Kallatra. The older Strong sat relaxed on one end of a couch and the younger Cloudd sat stiffly at the other end. Kallatra, who was the youngest of all, stood unmoving in the center of the room, frozen rigidly into a mannequin-like stance, the lights shining off the polished metal skin of her face in bright, starry points.

"So," Tregonsee was thinking, "we have heard from Kallatra that the phantom fleet is not an astral projection from beyond the grave. Worsel's concern that it could be another attack by the Eichwoor can be laid aside. Nadreck argues that it is some kind of hallucinatory effect, but cannot explain how dials and meters can be affected except by some kind of ectoplasmic manipulation which neither Kallatra nor Worsel can explain. Nadreck does not believe it is Nth or hyper dimensional. Our conclusion is that some new kind of weapon is being developed and that M.I.S. and S.I.S. now have a high priority task to find out more."

Tregonsee was strongly telepathing his thoughts, for of the dozen persons present, only six of them had Lenses. The exceptional talents of the Second Stage Lensmen made the mental exchanges easy, even for a neophyte like Cloudd. He could not project, so he had to have his thoughts pulled out of him by Tregonsee.

Cloudd found the setting weird, unable as he was to see anything with his own eyes, except in that single room with Strong and the android, Kallatra. He found the communication easy, but a bit unpleasant, having his mind picked over. As for the situation itself, he could only describe it to himself as bizarre, a feeling he manfully tried to hide. Through the minds of the others, he could intellectually perceive the entire group in a hazy way—all except for Nadreck, that is, whose compartment was an opaque frozen cloud of noxious-looking, varicolored gas-like particles through which occasionally some monstrous horror might be seen. Strong asked to sit with him because that tall, quiet man had thought him a relative of a former co-worker. Kallatra had chosen to be near him, she freely admitted, because the base psychologist had told her that Cloudd could use "some help." "My field is psychic research," the monotonic voice intoned from somewhere within her blouse, "but I also am an expert on prostheses. For obvious reasons." There was a noise which he interpreted, after a puzzled moment, as a chuckle.

Through Strong's perception, Cloudd saw a handful of Patrolmen coming into the conference room and along the connecting passageways. They didn't look ominous, but he could feel that, for some reason, they were. They were mulling around the doorway to John Tsien's compartment. Then the vision shut off as Kallatra's audible voice jarred him.

"I can fix those fingers of yours," she said. Perhaps because the voice wasn't human, he felt insulted and irritated by her presumptuousness. She grasped his left hand in her surprisingly flexible, human-appearing metal fingers, and peered at the two stumps critically. "The prostheses will look, feel, work like real ones. They'll be flesh-colored, of course, not like mine." There had been and still was no expression on her death-mask face, and there was no compassion in her mechanical voice. Cloudd, tactfully trying to keep the thought out of his mind, forced himself to believe that this thing should be treated like a woman and not like a machine. After all, her mental waves were seductive and beguiling when he could feel her thoughts. But when she spoke, her inflectionless mechanical sounds grated on his nerves. Perhaps if he were a Lensman he wouldn't find her appearance repugnant and her touch repulsive. "It's so very simple," she continued. "Each finger, done in my shop, will be an efficient digit, hardly noticeable as other than the real thing." When he failed to answer, his mind black with annoyance, his thoughts desperately screened, she mistook his reaction. "Of course, if you feel funny about wearing them, there's the expensive Phillips regenerative treatment." He told her thanks, but no thanks.

For one very brief moment Strong's mind swirled through his and then withdrew. Cloudd had a sense of some utterly revolting action or procedure taking place before his unseeing eyes and uncomprehending brain.

The moment, perhaps several moments, passed, and Kallatra was speaking to him again in a robot's voice. "Worsel told me that you have found a very unusual Ordovik crystal. I would like to examine it. It may be significant in my work. Will you show it to me later?" He had replied, "Of course," but he hoped it could be avoided. She made him too uncomfortable.

He had a sudden impression that John Tsien had collapsed and that a group of Patrolmen were carrying his stiff body out of his tiny room. The vision should have been alarming to Cloudd, but his instincts did not respond that way.

"You know, I'll do your fingers for free."

Outwardly keeping control, he fought to keep his irritation from escaping. Damnation! If she was what women were like from being Lensmen, aggressively asserting themselves, then he would be happy to be a male chauvinist. Why was her hard mind preserved while Lucille's tender mind was lost? His unreasoning resentment against her, stimulated by such slight things, he introspectively recognized. This was his loneliness for Lucille working its way out of his system because of that oh-so-clever-base psychiatrist. The doctor had read within his private heart about the white scarf, Lucille's, which he wrapped around his neck, like a knight of old, when on his missions. Damnation! The old do-gooder was right! Childishness! He had pledged to Kinnison that "D.D." Cloudd was another person put away in the past. He had to work on that. So, as for Lalla Kallatra—well, he was sure she must be a good person and a fine Lensman, but he'd rather try to relate to Nadreck than to her.

The vision came again. Tsien was at the entrance to Nadreck's room, stretched out on the floor, and some writhing amorphous limbs were coming out of the door—*through* the door—wrapping around Tsien's head—going *into* his head! Cloudd, with great effort, vigorously shaking his own head, managed to dispel the vision.

Cloudd was now suddenly conscious of having missed part of the discussion, having missed also some outré melodrama. Something had happened, was happening, in or about hyper space. Voddon the Manarkan was having his brains picked—*actually* having his brains picked! The five scientists who had been involved in the hyperspatial tube attacks were present: Cardynge, the experienced expert specializing in hyperspatial mathematics; Tsien, top man on gravitational fields and black holes; Ehht the amphibious Nevian, whose lifetime ambition was to invent matter transmission; Voddon the Manarkan, who was not well-known but had been considered valuable enough to be a potential victim; and Philip Strong, who actually knew Dr. Neal Cloud, both specialists on the atomic vortex phenomena.

Cloudd was now aware that Tregonsee had just reviewed the situation concerning the hyperspatial tube attacks.

"You're right," Tregonsee was saying, evidently agreeing with Cardynge. "That's the reason you were all attacked."

What reason? was the startled thought Cloudd had. The answer came from Strong's lightly attentive mind: "It's agreed that the five scientists were attacked to be neither killed nor kidnapped. There was a temporary abduction during which they had their minds scanned quickly but thoroughly, all their knowledge secured, and then the raiders left with some kind of recording out of their brains."

You mean, Cloudd thought, we were supposed to be deceived? To believe in bungled plans for assassination or kidnapping? But actually a successful plan to steal minds? Clever!

"Yes," said Strong. "A clever success. The L2s just finished close-scanning us all, the victims. We have the scars on our synapses which only they could notice. John Tsien was found with an Ordovik crystal in his head and—"

"What?"

"Where has your mind been wandering? That's why Tsien and Voddon have both been put into a hypnotized state within the cubicle they are sharing—so they can recover from Nadreck's surgery."

"Surgery? Voddon? Something was in his brain, too?"

"My, my, Cloudd. You have been daydreaming!"

"Forgive me," Kallatra said. "I'm really to blame. I noticed you, Cloudd, slipping into some introspection and self-analysis, and my intuition told me to let it happen uninterrupted. So I sealed you off from what's been going on here. Now don't fret, my friend," she said, when Cloudd's blood boiled up at the invasion of his privacy and free-will. "I did not look into what you were thinking. No Lensman would ever violate your right of privacy without permission. I just caught your mood and gave you the peace to pursue it. The base psychiatrist told me—"

"Damn the base psychologist!" Cloudd exploded. "He has no right to bring you into my private life!"

"Psychiatrist, not psychologist," Kallatra corrected. "And on the contrary, sir. Considering your importance to us, he has every right. And, because of my own past psychic troubles, he asked me to help."

"Sorry," Cloudd said, quickly recovering. This new life of "Benson" instead of "D.D." was not coming easily to him. "I do understand."

"And please accept my apologies, too," Kallatra said. "I had no desire to upset you. I can tell that you found your insights, just now, profitable. I am happy for you. So now, let Strong bring you up to date."

"Voddon," Strong continued, taking this all in his stride, as though nothing unusually emotional had happened, "had a transmitter in his head."

"A transmitter!?"

"Yes. Seems as though he's been transmitting everything that's been going on here at Ultra Prime in which he participated."

"That's disastrous!" exclaimed Cloudd.

"Not at all. No transmissions got through. We're too well safeguarded."

"How could this be? I thought Lensmen couldn't be fooled as easily as this."

"We can't be fooled easily. Sometimes, though, with difficulty, we can be temporarily fooled. No harm done, and the crystal and the transmitter are safely boxed up in shielded containers."

"Boxed up? But...? When...?"

"Kallatra did a good job on you, didn't she? Tsien and Voddon each had a fourth-dimensional extraction performed by Nadreck. Right here. Zip, zip! And they never knew a thing about it. Excuse me, Cloudd. I'll get out of your mind. Did I give you the whole picture?" Cloudd knew Strong had tried to print upon his brain all the details, but really hadn't succeeded. Cloudd wasn't yet that receptive, but he said yes anyhow; he did have the bare facts. "QX, Tregonsee, Cloudd's, yours."

Cloudd was now conscious of Tregonsee calling him, asking for his report on datadrones. With his mind still whirling from the disclosures of enemies within their midst, of a brain implanted with a bomb, of Kallatra's presumptuous prying—distracted by all this—Benson Cloudd gave his report almost automatically. He tried to limit himself only to the technical facts that they didn't already know:

"How are datadrones powered? They are not jet propelled. Not by liquid, solid, nuclear, nor any discoverable fuel. They do, though, have atomic particle emitters as control jets for precision steering. A datadrone's power plant seems electrical, in a general sense, a mix of gravitational and electromagnetic emission. These drones, therefore, sometimes sail by cosmic pressures—sometimes are propelled by electromagnetic induction—sometimes ride anti-matter or Nth space waves. Whatever, the force is almost infinite in strength and availability. No drone need carry any fuel. Even the retro-fuel is from matter collectible in the most empty places of space."

"Is the drive inertialess?" Cardynge asked. "Like the Bergenholm drive? The Patrol has found these drones traveling at the speed of light, even encountering them in free flight."

"They have to be inertialess, but a new energy source, or a new principle or combination, is involved. Mass enters significantly into this. The datadrone mass is extremely small, so we couldn't drive our warships with its power plant. Like a helium dirigible, the lighter the weight, the smaller and more efficient the vehicle can be. Large engines of the drone type would no doubt be clumsy, and maybe not even work. At best, such a system would reduce the size of personal speedsters to something much smaller, maybe suit-fitting, if it's worthwhile to do so. There is probably a limiting factor of acceleration, this system growing more efficient at light speed and beyond. Unlike Bergenholms, it would take time to build to maximum speed. That's, no doubt, why we've been able to capture so many, catching them just as they are beginning to accelerate."

Cloudd was finding this mix of communication modes less strange now. He accepted the fact that he talked aloud, but had his words heard by only half the group—while the others knew his thoughts even before he was through expressing them.

"What I find most fascinating is the capacity of their memory banks. With the right key, they are capable of absorbing the knowledge of an entire planet with a small drone. If they can scan a book, they can copy it. If they can understand the language, they can transcribe records instead of stealing files. They understand Tellurian English perfectly. And all the other languages which I'm competent to test. They can scan in three dimensions and through barriers that aren't too thick, such as filing cases and unarmored space-ships. They recognize and record all wave frequencies, including, I suspect, thought waves. The datadrone Type-2X1 is an incredibly sophisticated investigator and memory bank—but nothing else. The datadrone Type-50 re-records the information gathered by the Type 2X through the Type-8, evidently functioning to evaluate and eliminate duplication and transmitting it into Nth space to an unknown destination. Nth space transmission could put the user on the other side of the universe, or any place in our own neighborhood which isn't blocked by the activities of the Patrol."

"Who is collecting this information?" Kinnison interjected. "Why are they? Is it dangerous for us? What can we do about it?"

"Well, let's consider the communications links. Some kind of exchange takes place. Probably it's only in one direction, back to its base. Perhaps simple commands might be sent to each separate drone—simple instructions to return to its mother ship or to destroy itself."

Cloudd felt that the pictures of charts and graphs which he was recalling as he spoke were being seen by the Lensmen as though they were pictures he was presenting. He noticed that both Tsien and Voddon were conscious, with the group, unaware of their experience.

"Of course, much of this is guesswork. But a single 2X1 contains billions of chips. That's a lifetime of work to examine all their combinations. That's an infinity of permutations. The chip circuitries would have to be taken to a laboratory such as on Medon for examination."

"Can you answer my questions?" Kinnison said. "Who? Why? What?"

"No, I'm afraid not, sir. I don't know who is doing this nor do I know why. As for danger, that's relative."

"Let me answer the question of what we can do about it," Tregonsee said. "We can increase our security—that is already being done. And very successfully in highly populated and advanced technological areas. But very poorly in lowly populated and low-level technological cultures. Datadrones are becoming more of a nuisance than of a threat to our secrets. So, from a defensive point of view, we certainly have the upper hand, if not complete control. Not, however, offensively—due mostly to our desire to capture them unharmed, and avoid deliberate destruction. The drones seem to be increasing in number, so we've decided now to let no drone escape. It's either capture or destroy. That's the current situation we have to live with."

"I don't seem to have been much help, sir," Cloudd said to Tregonsee.

"Don't underestimate yourself, Cloudd. You've helped us understand the situation. It's up to us all to get more data to work with. After P'Keen does his tests, Nadreck will scan the crystal as you've suggested. Now, gentlemen, let's consider the latest conference reports. From persistent evidence, one problem remaining, of some magnitude, is about some kind of super-black-hole experiment. This could be a super-weapon development undertaken by outlaws with Boskonian financing or direction, or maybe both." Tregonsee began to reel off statements, papers, and statistics so fast that they became a blur in Cloudd's mind.

Cloudd spent the next hour, while the Lensmen conferred, writing out a plan for himself on future action to be taken on the datadrone problem. When the meeting ended and he was leaving the room, Kallatra whirred over to him, using the wheeled platforms on the soles of her knee-high boots instead of stalking.

"I beg your pardon, Cloudd," Kallatra said, "but I've heard rumors of a so-called 'mech-planet,' anything from several hundred to several thousands of miles in diameter. Of course, this myth has been around a long time, but lately such tales have been heard more often. It strikes me that this suggests a gigantic datadrone or a drone collection station. Have you heard anything like this?"

"No, I'm sorry to say, I haven't. Not lately, that is." Cloudd felt self-conscious about looking directly at her metal face, a Lens imbedded in the middle of her forehead. "Thanks for the thought. It sounds provocative." Only her eyes moved. Were they organic? They seemed natural, a bluish gray, sparkling with life. She had no hair, a cloth skull cap, cut to go around her human-shaped metal ears, covering her head down to the nape of her neck. Her chin-high collar probably covered the swivel joint at her neck. The rest of her body, except for those metal hands, was covered with a standard tunic-and-pantaloons uniform of the Patrol.

He wondered if the silvery face really was in fact a death mask of the person she once had been. Rather boldly, he took his longest look yet. No, it wasn't—the representation was insipid. However, hadn't that been what had been implied when he had been introduced to her by her "godparent," Worsel?

Worsel himself suddenly came into his mind. "I caught my name, Cloudd. You're asking me about Lalla?"

"Not really, sir." Cloudd felt his face growing red. "But—while you're here—with me, that is—well, how do I treat her? As an android or as a real human?"

As suddenly as Worsel had come into his mind, Cloudd suddenly possessed the essential facts about Lalla Kallatra.

She and Worsel had had a remarkable past battling Eichwoor ghosts. Her body had been destroyed, but Worsel had saved her brain. She'd been a normal, very young woman, only the second woman Lensman known by Worsel to exist. And now, although her body was gone, she was still alive as a much matured, undamaged brain. Treat her as a human being, Worsel said. Someday, if Worsel had anything to do with it, she'd have a natural face like the face she should have had, and Cloudd wouldn't be so uneasy.

Had Kallatra been staring at him? He caught those bluish eyes flicking away from him. Had she heard what just had been exchanged? He was conscious of his ears being red and his cheeks being flushed. Cloudd was finding his association with Lensmen at this close and intimate range a trying experience. He was growing into a new awareness, that was what was happening. He was mentally growing, and he felt he had no limits.

"A datadrone collection station. That's a fascinating idea, Kallatra," he picked up where he had left off, finding it easier now to say "Kallatra" without feeling he was anthropomorphically talking to one of his own servo-mechanisms back on the old ship. His face was cooling down. This mind might be more stimulating than Lucille's had been, but Lucille had been physically attractive. The contrast made him much more aware of his loss. And it again made him aware of his obsession. He would have to start exorcising the ghost of Lucille, by having girlfriends again. He would start now, as Benson and not as Double-Dee, to rejoin reality. Maybe he could start with that attractive assistant that Thorndyke seemed to have....

He daydreamed along, feeling uncommonly good about it, all the way out to the roof to catch an aircab to his quarters. He was there on the roof waiting when Tregonsee called him by telepathy and changed his plans. No doubt about it, he was getting quite accustomed to this method now, and it was really not unpleasant at all!

"I want you to go to see P'Keen immediately," Tregonsee said. "It's about the crystal."

Cloudd finally got to see P'Keen after an hour's wait.

"Sorry to keep you waiting, Cloudd," P'Keen said, "I've been in contact with Mrs. Kimball Kinnison's home about delivering a present for her expected baby and got a real scare. Tregonsee said he's received a report warning of an impending attack on the Kinnison household. We checked out all security and found nothing. We've made things tighter than ever, and we're convinced there's no danger. Anyhow, what you're needed for is to let me probe your mind to see if there are any details you've overlooked or half-forgotten about the finding of that Ordovik crystal of yours."

For the next fifteen minutes Cloudd and P'Keen worked together, but nothing new seemed to emerge.

Then came another call from Tregonsee for Cloudd to meet him immediately in Kinnison's office.

When Cloudd came in there were only three men present, Kinnison, Tregonsee, and Chaplain General Chon. Kinnison and Chon nodded, and Tregonsee jumped into his mind immediately.

"We have a dangerous mission for you, Cloudd," he said, "if you want to take it."

"I'll take it, of course!" Cloudd said. "Great! Danger is my middle name." He used to tell people that all the time, when they asked him what "D.D." stood for.

"First, I'll tell you what it's all about. Then you can volunteer." Tregonsee explained that his mock death had succeeded in pinpointing the source of the personal tube attacks. He credited "two of my best agents, Seena-KK-45 at Kresh-kree near the inward side of the Green Parrot Nebula, and Ulie-KK-46 on Tanse, its distant neighbor" as having established the irrefutable evidence and briefly described the grim situation: a group of Kalonians, unrepentant aristocrats who had fled the overthrow of the Thrale-Onlonian Empire, were identified as one of the most serious focal points of continued Boskonian resistance. They were probably responsible for the recent tube attacks. They were interested in a new and terrible weapon. Perhaps it concerned the black hole rumors, but it also concerned some kind of new power discovered on a moon of Tanse among its neighboring star systems. This immeasurable power could affect organic minds and had so far blocked all mental attempts to investigate it. There was also some kind of force barrier preventing any life form from approaching it, except along a narrow channel directly from its mother planet. There was a deadline to meet to keep this power from somehow unleashing the ultimate of destructive forces against the Patrol and Civilization. A Patrol force with Lens capability had to go to Tanse immediately before the deadline and find out what was happening. Personal danger to the strike force was warned as being extreme. It would first require exposure to a savage culture in which physical death and torture were commonplace. Then, the next phase would be exposure to an unknown mental force, in which torture of the mind leading to quick destruction seemed to be inescapable if pursued.

"So," Tregonsee said, "a Second Stage Lensman is needed there immediately—in person, as the force barrier between it and the moon is too strong for mental projection. Worsel has his own task, assembling a Patrol fleet to go out to the edge of the galaxy in the vicinity of Green Parrot. Nadreck has agreed to join the fleet in his flitter and be on hand to evaluate possible Nth-spatial or multi-dimensional causations. That leaves available just me and Kinnison as L2s. Two hours ago we agreed to go together, along with another Lensman—planning for me to be in space, Kinnison to be on Tanse, and the other Lensman to go to the deadly moon. This plan now seems impractical, yet the deadline for departure has come. I must make an immediate decision." Tregonsee's attitude and his speech seemed so stiff that to Cloudd the Rigellian was like another robotoid, like Kallatra, a strange, inhuman hulk, unmoving, expressionless, but behind its brain case a very intelligent mind ticking over. As for Kinnison, he was inattentive, seemingly occupied with other things. Cloudd couldn't see what Tregonsee was leading up to. He, Cloudd, wasn't a Lensman, so where was his dangerous mission?

Then Cloudd found out why Tregonsee was so solemn.

"The other Lensman was to have been Frank Garner," Tregonsee said. "Garner can't go. I'm suggesting you, instead."

Cloudd was flabbergasted.

"Me?" Cloudd said. "Me? With you and Kinnison? What do you mean? Are there others with me in this, ah, Patrol force?"

"Does it matter? Would you go if we two were the only ones?"

"I'll go!" Cloudd said. "I'll go alone if that's best! You bet I'll go! I wouldn't miss this for anything!" Was he dreaming?

"But why me?" He looked at Kinnison, who caught his eye and smiled. He looked at Chaplain General Chon who looked sombre, much as though he was professionally at a deathwatch.

"A sturdy, muscular Tellurian type is called for, Cloudd," Kinnison said. "And you fit the bill."

"But I'm not a Lensman," Cloudd protested. "Don't get me wrong, I'll *love* to go! But will I be good enough?"

"Frankly, Cloudd," Tregonsee said, "I don't have much choice. I need a Tellurian body, as Kim says, a man of youth, strength and agility; he has to fit into this barbarian culture we'll be stepping into. Being a Lensman could be a disadvantage when we face this 'Turmoil of Lost Souls' thing; I suspect that the stronger the mind, the stronger the reaction by this unknown force. Religion, human sacrifices, gods, and lost souls are some of the ingredients in this unique picture, so Chon, here, was considered to replace Garner. But he's really not young enough, and there's a chance that his automatic responses from his religious consciousness might be a detriment instead of a help. I'm happy to have someone like you, unsophisticated, metally untrained, not privy to a lot of Patrol secrets. I think you can more easily pass yourself off as a barbarian."

Cloudd, for one fraction of a moment, was a bit chagrined to realize that he was being chosen as much for what he wasn't as for what he was. But that moment was fleeting; he wasn't all that egotistical to think that he could really stack up with Kimball Kinnison and Tregonsee of Rigel IV.

"Good," Tregonsee said. "Now I believe you deserve to know why you are substituting for Garner. My information from my agents indicates that the Kinnison family is being threatened by an Ordovik who is a member of or masquerading as a member of the Patrol. My staff member P'Keen is an Ordovik, of course, and that has complicated the matter. Garner must stay behind to monitor P'Keen. P'Keen could be a dupe or an impostor. I don't think so, but we must consider this as a possibility. P'Keen reports that his investigation of you and the crystal proves that you were supposed to be one of those scientists attacked by hyperspacial tube. The technician was carrying the crystal and attempted to initiate the attack so that you would be attacked while examining the datadrone, and thus the raiders would also retrieve a datadrone along with the information in your head. All four L2s confirm this as substantiated by the crystal's recorded impressions." Cloudd by now wasn't surprised at this revelation. "P'Keen is delivering to the Red Lensman a packaged gift which we know to be some kind of crystal. Garner is monitoring this situation. As you can see, Garner could not make the trip."

"Yes, I see," Cloudd said, but not quite seeing.

"Now I tell you all this, to emphasize that you are important in replacing Garner for your human shape and splendid muscles." Tregonsee's thoughts were now quiet, considerate and a bit troubled. "What you next must know is that Kimball Kinnison has decided not to go."

Not going! Cloudd now really was confused.

"Damn it," Kinnison said, aloud, more to himself than to the other three. "Everybody is right—and if I wasn't so pig-headed I wouldn't have questioned my friends' advice—in fact, I would have probably made the suggestion first myself. I can't go, and I'd smell like a hunk of Limburger if I didn't honestly feel that my Red Lensman must come ahead of a good time. Damn it, Tregonsee! You know I'd go if I was convinced you absolutely need me! But I must look after my family—I'd have Mentor burning my tail if I didn't!"

Tregonsee waved some tentacles. "I know that, Kim. Everyone knows that. Your disappointment hurts me, too, as a friend, but you're not essential."

"Now, if I really believed—" Kinnison started to weaken. "—that I was needed . . ."

"Don't worry about it, Kim. Your decision is correct. I don't really need you."

For a long moment Kinnison had no reply. Into the look of disappointment on his face there came an uncomfortable and singular touch of mortification. Then he said, quietly, simply, humbly, "You are right, of course, Trig, old friend. My place is here. But to think of you going alone—I have serious doubts—you're not a fighter, physically, I mean. It's just not, well, the—ah—the Rigellian way."

"Do you forget, Kim, my most dangerous assignment? On that hellish planet Trenco, where we first met? Did I stay inside? Or did I venture out into the wild storms in which other Lensmen died? Do you remember that when the President of Medon gave you the name 'Keen,' he gave me the name 'Strong'? Don't worry for me, friend Kinnison, for my Rigellian cautiousness will not allow me to jeopardize my life recklessly. There's great danger, yes, but I'm not foolhardy. I'll retreat if I have to. But a Second Stage Lensman is needed on the scene—this cannot be handled at long distance."

Kinnison was reluctantly nodding in agreement.

"Also, there's a selfish reason I'm going, Kim, one you'll easily understand—it's for my own joy and pleasure. Mental puzzles and unknown challenges are there for me to face, the intriguing things I look for in my secret service work. Other Rigellians can't understand my curiosity, but you do, and you know it makes me a true successor to the first Rigellian Lensman, Dronvire. Going to Tanse is right for me to do."

Kinnison smiled understandingly, in his mind as well as on his unseen lips.

"Remember, too, that I won't be alone, for you'll be Lensing me as much as possible and Cloudd will be with me. I may suffer humiliation, but it is Cloudd who may suffer death."

Even before Tregonsee spoke these words, Cloudd had been seeing the whole situation in terms of himself and the fate of Civilization.

"Only the two of us?" he said, awe in his voice, his eyes shifting back and forth between Kinnison and Tregonsee. "Can you really believe me to be good enough to be your only partner?"

"But I do think that, Cloudd, precisely that. Worsel's too big. Nadreck's psychology is wrong for a bunch of barbarians. One Class XIX High-Tension Thinker, like me, and a top Tellurian intellect with muscle, like you, will do the job. In fact, Cloudd, it really is for the best. You and I will be the perfect team!"

Within two hours, the head of the Galactic Patrol's secret services and his tyro were in Tregonsee's tiny speedster en route to the planet of Tanse toward the edge of the galaxy.

What no one knew, except himself and the other two Rigellians of his three-unit-cluster, was that Tregonsee was in mental fusion. He had locked mind-souls with his bristers, "Two" and "Three." Across the immensity of distance from galaxy to galaxy, Tregonsee had the unshakable mental anchor of his two other empathetic psyches. Never before had he used them in his work nor would he ever use them that way again. He was prepared for the vast and mighty forces of the alien minds, fully as deadly, calamitous, and fateful as anything expected from the ghostly Eichwoor.

12

Into the Black Hole

The planetoid was tiny, scarcely more than a mammoth boulder tumbling slowly in space.

As Tregonsee's decelerating flitter approached it, he could see that it was a perfect place for a clandestine meeting, irregular in shape and pitted with holes, depressions, and caves. The position of IX-1.42-Sigma given to him was only nine minutes off the mark. They would easily reach Tanse itself, many hours before sunrise, the time when any chance of arriving unobserved would be gone.

Beyond the planetoid was the huge globe which was the mother planet itself, dark orange against the star-filled void, a thin, radiant crescent of sunshine along one side. Neither of its sunside moons was to be seen.

As the flitter swung around the rotating rock, passing from the sunlit side to the shadow, Cloudd could see a moving humanoid figure on the rugged surface. The image sharpened before his eyes, turning brown to silver—an adjustable Patrol suit, Cloudd thought, its reflective properties switched on for higher visibility.

He saw an arm waving.

"That's Ulie-KK-46," Tregonsee said, and Cloudd realized that the Rigellian was mentally in touch with her.

The flitter was now fixed above the figure, turning end over end in synchronized movement with the planetoid, staying in the shadow. The figure below disappeared in a hollow. Then another object appeared. It was a rectangular box, covered with blue and green and red symbols—he had never seen one before, but he knew it to be the coffin that was a spaceship!

The gaudy box spun around once and began to move away toward Tanse. Tregonsee moved his ship in pursuit.

"We're masked from the two moons by the planet," Tregonsee said, "but we're not taking any chances on being sensed." Cloudd was slung in a hammock, swinging just above Tregonsee in the crowded cockpit. "We're using no telepathy and have our minds blocked off. You must try to keep your own mind blank, although I don't believe you will ordinarily radiate enough mental energy to be noticed at this distance." The rest of the trip down to Tanse was in silence.

The night was still its darkest when the two ships landed in a small glade in the middle of the jungle. The suited Ulie climbed out of the coffin and squared it up more exactly on the altar pedestal upon which she had landed. Then she half draped herself over the flitter, holding tightly to some hand holds while Tregonsee maneuvered above the trees and then along the carpet of leaves for some distance before lowering once more to the ground through the forest. The flitter rested on the spongy ground, half buried by the thick undergrowth.

Ulie silently began stripping off her suit, gesturing for Cloudd to do the same with his uniform. The air was hot and humid, water dripping down from overhead. Her face was uncovered first, tanned and human, a bit beefy, with a wide and generous mouth and sharp, brown eyes. It was a pleasant face, filled with strength, and Cloudd liked it. What followed next was unexpected and a shock to Cloudd. When she shrugged out of the top of her suit, two large, bare breasts came out; when she slipped off the lower part, she was all naked, browned skin, with flat stomach and pale round behind. While she was folding up her suit, she again gestured to him, this time impatiently, to take off his uniform.

Cloudd didn't know what to do until he heard a gentle nudge from Tregonsee, "Take off your uniform, Cloudd, and put it in my ship." Tregonsee, who always looked undressed anyhow, was unbuckling his harnesses and stowing them aboard. His Lens he took from the depression in his forehead and shoved it up out of sight under one tentacle. With no clothing and no Lens, his symmetrical body lost all front-to-back relationship, thoroughly muddling Cloudd, who now had no reference point upon which his human orientation could be keyed.

Cloudd stepped out of his own clothes, removed his watch, Meteor case, I.D. bracelet, and necklace with Lucille's locket, and placed them together next to Tregonsee's things. He felt embarrassed and could not bring himself to look at the very shapely and surprisingly muscular Ulie, keeping himself half turned away. He was also self-conscious about his own appearance. He was unwashed, unshaven, his fingernails ragged and dirty, his greased hair hacked into a mop, his skin stained brown, his hands rough with manufactured calluses. Within a few hours the S.I.S. specialists had succeeded in making him a filthy mess.

Tregonsee's soft thought, so narrowed that he could hardly catch it, came to him. "You've been in Tellurian culture all your life, Cloudd. On their own ground, most other races wear few or no clothes. You'll get used to it. Pay attention to Ulie; you won't embarrass her."

Cloudd looked around then and was alarmed to see a big hairy animal approaching him. The animal was holding out a fur coat for him. Then he realized that it was Ulie in a kind of thick, hairy wrap who was handing him a similar black garment, signing him to put it on. He did so, with much relief. To his surprise, he discovered that the covering was actually made of some kind of light metal strands, much like hair, extremely flexible and comfortable, and not heavy at all.

Tregonsee had two more garments under two of his tentacles. There was equipment under the other two.

Ulie beckoned with her arms for them to follow her.

In a few moments they had gone down a trail lit by the slender beam of a flashlight she had in one hand. After about twenty minutes of hard going through overhanging brush and across vines and logs, they came to a clearing. Tregonsee set down his things and, opening one of the boxes, pulled out a light energy screen, erecting it with the snap of a few buttons releasing the pre-formed frame. Within thirty seconds, they were inside. Ulie slipped the covering off her head and Cloudd did the same. Their faces were covered with perspiration.

"Now we can think and talk," Ulie said. "Hello, Mister Tregonsee." She lightly punched him on his leathery chest in a casual greeting. "Hello, Mister Cloudd." She stuck out her hand, grasped his in a very firm squeeze, and said, "I've got a lot to tell you. I'm telepathic, but not good enough to compensate for your untrained mind. It's better that we talk, anyway, to foil any mental eavesdroppers. First, you tell me what you've picked up from Tregonsee on your flight here."

Cloudd went through it slowly, trying to make it perfectly clear to himself: The Tansers of the planet Tanse are barbarians with a non-technological culture. Human in shape, they are all a mixture of diverse ethnic backgrounds similar to those found on earth. They are much like Stone Age tribesmen, but they have and use many products of higher cultures which have been given to them as gifts from the gods as payment for their sacrifices. Like miracles, the gifts come in the coffin transporter. The big difference from human Tellurians is their great variety of sizes. The smallest is two and a half feet tall, the largest is eight feet tall, with intelligence in inverse ratio. The smallest is about as smart as a primitive savage, the largest not much smarter than a dog or bear.

"Smarter than that," Ulie corrected. "They all can talk and comprehend. The difference is more in the individual speed of their thinking processes. The dumbest are awfully dumb, but they seem worse because they're so slow at thinking."

The Tansers—Cloudd continued—are gathered in small bands of one or two hundred. Each band is jealously independent and fights each and every other band regularly within their areas of contact. Their only interests and abilities are to hunt, to fight, to destroy, to raise families—and to worship.

Their religion is simple. When the two moons, Tanse Moon One and Tanse Moon Two, seem to approach each other at their closest in the Tanse sky, a human sacrifice is made on the altar of the gods of Tanse. This human sacrifice is placed in the traditional ceremonial coffin one evening, as the moons approach each other when both are full. The lid is screwed in place, and the coffin rises in the air and disappears. Sometime during the night or following day the coffin reappears and the lid is taken off. The victim is still alive, but now is in a mystical state or trance. The lid is replaced and the coffin again ascends in the air and disappears. This coincides with the optimum position of the moons. The following evening, as the moons begin to move away from each other, the coffin reappears and the lid is again taken off. This time the coffin is empty. It stays empty, sometimes disappearing and reappearing, often with the miraculous gifts, until the next mating of the two moons.

"You're doing fine," Ulie said. "Tell me about the moons."

On the first evening—Cloudd again continuing—the victim is supposed to go to The Moon of the Gods, which is Two, for the surrender of his life to the gods and preparation of his soul for heaven. On the second evening, the victim, purged and prepared, returns to tell the worshippers, by his presence, that the gods are pleased, and then makes his trip to The Moon of Lost Souls, which is One. Sometimes the gods reject a sacrifice by returning him or her not in a trance, but lifeless. Sometimes heaven, or paradise, rejects the sacrifice by returning the dead body.

"That's enough of that," Ulie said. "Now what do you know about this unique tribe?"

The smartest small Tanser of the tribe acts as the high priest or priestess and is the one who chooses which of the tribe goes. He always picks the largest smart one, the one who would seek to replace him. Sometimes, when the chief is overthrown because his rival's strongest champion is defeated in combat by the rival's strongest champion, the deposed chief becomes the sacrifice.

"Very good," Ulie said, when Cloudd had finished. "You know the basic information. When the dawn comes I will point you the way to my tribe's camp. Tregonsee knows what is expected of you, and he will give you mental instructions from time to time. You must do everything that Tregonsee or I tell you to do. Come here." Ulie took Cloudd's hand, fondling it as though she had a romantic right to do so, and led him out of the metal-foil tent to a pile of leaves. She kicked them aside. Underneath them was a body of a man about six or seven feet tall. "Bury this corpse," she said. "I killed him last night to provide an extra armor-skin for Tregonsee." She stepped a few paces to her right and kicked away some more leaves on the ground. "Put him here next to the others." Cloudd could now see that there were three rather fresh graves, crudely disguised.

Cloudd looked at her a bit incredulously. She saw the look and squeezed his hand. "Life is cheap on this planet, Cloudd, my chum. It's kill or be killed—and I've been at it for months now." She pulled him back inside the tent. "There is no love on this planet. You don't know what that means, to be without love for so long. I mean love and affection, not sex. There's plenty of that around. You're the first humanoid with Civilized human feelings I've touched in what seems like years to me. I have to go now. Remember, this is a planet of bloody death. If you get into a fight, you'd better kill first before you're killed yourself." She handed him a bag made out of gigantic fresh leaves. "Take this. There are four scalps in here. These will get you into my tribe for the few days we need. Tregonsee will tell you the details. Good bye—see you later." And Ulie was gone.

Tregonsee told him the plan. He and Cloudd were to go to Ulie's camp after sunup. Cloudd would claim to be from another tribe, seeking a new home, and would present the scalps to show that he was a warrior worth having—

"But I can't talk the local language, can I?" Cloudd said. "English, French, German, Spanish, Spaceal, Chickladorian, that's my limit."

"No problem," Tregonsee assured him. "Their language is simple, rudimentary verbalism—there's so little to talk about. All the tribes have different languages and can't understand each other. Just make up something. Use noises you humanoids are so fond of using, grunts, groans, whatever. Then use gestures. Use your imagination. Don't worry about it. If I sense a problem, I'll plant a solution in your mind."

"And you? What about you? You can't pass yourself off as a barbarian."

"No. I'll be your, ah, your horse."

"What?" Cloudd didn't think the thought had translated itself right. "Horse? My horse? Did I hear you right? Are you going to use some kind of spell to make them think that?"

"No, my friend," Tregonsee said. "You are marching into

the camp, covered with your armor-fur, bag of scalps in hand, pretending you are a great warrior, and I'll be following, covered also with armor-fur, pretending to be your riding animal. It will work. Trust me."

"Sure, if you say so, Tregonseee," Cloudd said, shaking his head, making the perspiration fly off his eyebrows. "These guys will have to be awfully stupid . . ."

"You are right. They are awfully stupid," Tregonsee said, "but a little bit of hypnotism now and then will help." He rose on his four feet. "We'd better bury that body now. And pick out the best axe and knife for yourself. Let's go. No Tanser goes out at night, but come sunrise they'll be out on war parties looking to scalp each other."

When they had done the job, Tregonsee began to lead them down a trail toward their destination. Cloudd found that dawn didn't penetrate the vegetation, but it did bring an increase in the heat and humidity, if that were possible. The cloak he wore was surprisingly light for its density. He asked, "What's this material made of?" and was intrigued to be told it was an alloy of high technology. "One of the gifts from the gods," Tregonsee said. "It's very valuable to the Tansers. It's a form of chain mail and has a special property by which when struck above a certain force or speed it acts like a solid surface. No spear or arrow or axe or projectile gun can penetrate it."

"So how do people get killed, then?"

"As you say, they're stupid, so they make combat mistakes."

"And about guns. There are guns, with bullets, on this planet?"

"Yes, and other weapons you'll never expect to see. Ulie tells me that the gods give away all kinds of things when the mood strikes them. And if they are overgenerous and give something which might upset things too much, they don't have to worry. Let a few weeks or a few months pass, and those items will be lost or broken and discarded as useless."

"These gods, just who are they, anyway?"

"The evidence points to Kalonians from Kresh-kree. We don't know the full story, but a group of Kalonians have established a base on Tanse Moon Two, or The Moon of the Gods. They've interfered with the culture of Tanse so that they are the gods who are worshipped and who grant the little comforts, ornaments, or manufactured items. They've supplied the sacrificial coffin which takes the victim to them. There they seem to enslave the mind of that Tanser, send him back to Tanse and from there on to Tanse Moon One, or The Moon of Lost Souls, where the slave obtains from the native Qu'orr something of some great power. It was several sacrifices ago that a victim returning from The Moon of the Gods babbled the name of Mando, Mando, Mando! It is for us to find out what is going on."

Cloudd was by now plodding wearily down the broadened trail toward a crude bamboo stockade several hundred yards ahead of him. On some of the pointed sticks were human heads, hairless, in various stages of decomposition. Tregonsee himself had been making effortless progress in a unique and fascinating way.

Tregonsee had turned himself into Cloudd's "horse." He was in a horizontal position, suspended above the ground. His tentacles hung down and were moving rhythmically, like legs, but actually he was supported by a miniature force field, the pressors working like invisible legs. The hairy armor was thrown over him, hanging within inches of the pathway, and even to Cloudd, who knew better, he looked like some shaggy beast.

"Tregonsee," Cloudd said, overcome by the absurdity of the situation. "Do you think I ought to come into camp riding on your back?" The image in Cloudd's mind was so clear and ludicrous that he burst out with a couple of barklike laughs.

"I don't believe that will be necessary," Tregonsee replied. There was a very short mental pause. "Oh," the Rigellian said. "Tellurian humor. Just like Kinnison. That's a good sign. You were a good choice for me."

In the pathetic camp, which was a patch of trampled mud, a few scraggly lean-tos, and a dying fire of logs and moss, there were different sized barbarians shuffling around when the two of them appeared. There were about a hundred, seemingly in a hundred different shapes, colors, and states of hairiness. Some of them wore the armored cloak, looking like big furry animals and small furry animals, and some of them even without any cloak at all looked that way, too. Others, in contrast, were nearly bare skin naked, but painted with thick, greasy smears of red and blue and green.

Most of their faces were all of a sameness, simian, but a sizable minority were almost decently human looking and unmistakably female. Ulie was one of them.

On one edge of the camp was a placid group of shaggy beasts milling around. Several looked like Tregonsee. In fact, Cloudd noted with a slight shock, one of them was, indeed, Tregonsee!

Cloudd began to do the obvious things. Following either his intuition or some subtle guidance by Tregonsee, he dumped his sack of scalps in front of the smallest barbarian and jumped up and down beating his chest and shouting nonsense. The chief, his bare head sticking out of his cloak, smiled, picked up the scalps, smiled some more, pointed at the biggest and most naked man, and smiled again.

"Now you must fight him, Cloudd," said a voice within his head. It was Tregonsee re-transmitting Ulie.

Fight him! Cloudd thought to himself. The man was a giant, rippling all over with muscles! He didn't have a chance! Ulie must have known this would happen, how could she not have warned him?

"Don't worry," said the voice. "You'll do all right. Just remember you're smarter than he is."

The fight began. The big man lunged at Cloudd. Cloudd, instead of retreating, charged ahead, under the flailing arms, delivered two kidney punches, dropped on his shoulders and drove his feet upward into the giant's groin. The giant went over sideways, off balance, and Cloudd was on him in a flash, axe raised. For the tiny fraction of a second while he hesitated, the giant twisted away and upset Cloudd. Again they tumbled about. Cloudd felt more confident with every passing moment. This big man was strong and fast, but he didn't have a chance against the practiced moves of a Patrol-trained man.

"You could have killed him half a dozen times," the voice said. "Next time knock him out with the flat side of your axe, then throw the axe away and drag the man to the feet of the chief."

Cloudd tried to do as instructed, worrying not that he would not be able to flat-axe the man, but that he wouldn't be able to drag the hulk in front of the chief. Somehow he managed it.

The chief was delighted; he motioned for two other lesser giants to drag off the unconscious body and offered food and drink. Cloudd was dripping with perspiration and, although the liquid was unpleasantly sulphuric-tasting, with mental reassurance, he drank much but did not eat.

All the tribesmen came up to lay hands on him, including Ulie, and then they ignored him, doing different tasks. Ulie, through Tregonsee, reassured him that everything was fine and that they needed only to rest until the time for the sacrifice.

Two gorgeous moons rose in the night sky that evening. One was blue, The Moon of Lost Souls, the other pink, The Moon of the Gods. They threw their light down on the tribe assembled around the coffin, two grotesque shadows dancing in time with each dancing Tanser. As the time drew near for the coffin to rise into the air for its trip to the pink moon, Cloudd had a voice in his head again, saying, "We'll take no chances on your mind giving us away, Cloudd. You'll be one of those who fall into a religious trance for the next full period." As some Tansers dropped down in a self-induced fit, Cloudd felt himself slip and fall and his mind blanked out.

When he came to consciousness again, he thought only seconds had passed. The scene seemed identical.

"A day has passed, Cloudd." This time it was pure Tregonsee in his mind. "The victim is about to leave for the moon. I am about to mesmerize the whole tribe for a few minutes. I will give you time to open up the coffin, pull out the senseless victim, and crawl in there yourself. Ulie will clamp down the lid, while I put part of myself into your mind to guard you against what is certain to be a difficult mental ordeal for us both. This past day, during your sleep, I tried to penetrate the barrier around Moon One; it's no exaggeration to say that the blanket of mental turmoil guarding it is incredibly powerful and undoubtedly mind-destroying. As the coffin carries you to The Moon of Lost Souls, Ulie will dispose of the victim and I will be following you in my speedster, monitoring you every minute. Don't worry, Ulie and I have figured this out today. You'll be able to get through to the moon this way with my help, even though Ulie won't be able to follow with me as a body. She'll be covering me, just as I'm covering you. Now, move!"

Cloudd sprang toward the coffin even as bodies began to collapse around him. In less than a minute, he was inside with the lid clamped shut. He noticed that panel lights had come on to the left and right of his face, showing many small dials, with switches and buttons running down both sides from his shoulders to his waist. Then, once more, he lost consciousness.

About 3,000 parsecs or 9,600 light years beyond Kreshkree, partially obscured by a bilious feather of the Green Parrot Nebula, toward the edge of the Second Galaxy, a frozen star hung in space. It did not move, it did not blaze. Over its dully shining surface, fixed like a thin, spherical shell of ice, there was a strange sense of energy annihilated.

A solitary Patrol ship tangentially approached the terrible, fearful thing.

"God of Gods!" said the ship's captain. "It's a collapsing star. Our fleet is gone!"

On his ship's screens, magnified at full power, the captain saw the horrifying sight. Suspended in the star's shell, like flies stuck in some monstrous spider's web, were one, two, six, a dozen tiny spaceships. It was that ship's mother fleet, or rather the image of the fleet, caught there for eternity, the actual ships gone into the heart of the star, drawn down, stretched like putty and crushed, atoms compressed a million million times in black hole space.

"How? How?" agonized the captain. "How can it be? He knew that no Patrol ship would ever knowingly approach the event horizon so close as to risk falling within the Schwarschild radius. To do so would be a one-way voyage to oblivion—at least in this universe. The thought of the consequences and the recognition that his friends had been somehow deceived to plunge to their deaths made the captain react violently. He personally punched the buttons to fling his tiny scout craft away from the terror that lay ahead.

The second-in-command, along with the celestial navigator, brought the captain the sector charts. Much of the area was unknown and uncharted, but all the significant and potentially dangerous objects and situations were there, clearly identified. Or they should have been. Where the black hole was forming, according to the chart, there was plotted a neutron star.

"Look," said the captain, pointing at the chart and glancing at his other two officers. "It must be that the neutron star has suddenly collapsed. We must get this information back to Ultra Prime immediately. It's a puzzle, but the greater puzzle is—how did the sector fleet, granting normal navigational readings, stumble into such a disaster?"

The captain was interrupted by a double-voiced warning from his Posenian perceiver, who was on full alert duty in the sensory room. "Captain! The collapse is complete! The star is gone! It's now a black hole! There's another star moving in its direction. The readings are—unbelievable—they're changing rapidly, even as I watch!"

The captain glanced at the rear screen, looking back to whence he had come, and saw the incredible sight of a star attenuating, stretching an arm of matter toward where the invisible black hole should be. The flaming matter of the star was forming a tiny teardrop, pointing toward the black hole, stretching out under the cataclysmic forces. With some alarm, he deduced that he could see this only because his own ship was traveling so slowly.

"God!" said the captain. "That star's being sucked in! That black hole is growing beyond any laws of nature that I know of!" He glanced at his indicators. His regular space drive was operating at full power, but the ship was not accelerating! "I'm going to throw in the Bergenholm if we slow too fast or approach zero readings. I don't know how much time we have before we leave the area, but I want every man aboard to make every possible observation and to take every possible reading!" He called to his Posenian, "Let Number Two take over from you! See if you can project back to Ultra Prime and make contact! Call on any of us who can help intensify your mind beam."

Under the stresses of the moment, time seemed to be unmeasurable—whether it was quickly or slowly, whether it was easily done or with difficulty, a mind link was forged by the Posenian and read by the captain, who was now in the Posenian's brain. The link was with Kimball Kinnison himself!

"Sir! This is Captain McBane of Scout SC-1212G. We've run into something fantastic!" McBane reported what had been observed while Kinnison's mind link grew stronger with the awesome excitement. "I'm slowly losing power! I'm ready to slip into Bergenholm drive, but I'm hanging in to give you my latest readings." The ship gave a definite lurch. It was an experience the crew had had before only with a fishing tractor beam.

"Sir! It's incredible. One star is disappearing into the black hole. And I can see another one moving in its direction. My God! There's another! And another!"

"Captain!" This was Kinnison. "Give me readings as long as you safely can. I want everything. Your Posenian is a great projector; boost him as best you can, and send through the readings, but also send through everything any of you can think of; we'll sort out the clues later!"

"Yes, sir!"

"Captain, make a judgment! Does it look to you like these stars are being manipulated? Is the black hole stationary or moving? Do you sense unnatural forces or intelligent forces at work?"

"Yes, sir! The stars are being moved around now like fireflies toward a magnetic center! There's a whole sector of space out there in motion! It's a dazzling display! It's stupefyingly beautiful! By the Klono of Klono, there're thousands of planets and stars going into that black hell! There must be billions of life forms, billions of people out there going to their deaths!"

"Captain! Keep the readings coming. Try to keep your mind under control!"

"Sir! The black hole—*I think it's chasing us!*"

The ship lurched again, as if it had hit a stone wall.

"Captain! You've discovered our worst fear! You've entered space the Patrol wasn't expected to be in and you've come across the Boskonian black hole weapon in operation! Keep the readings coming as long as you safely can!"

There was a void now in Kinnison's mind.

"Captain! Captain!"

There was nothing. Scout SC-1212G was gone.

13

The-Moon-of-Lost-Souls

Two tiny spaceships, streaking in line almost end to end and acting as though they were one, plummeted down into the thin atmosphere of Tanse Moon One, The Moon of Lost Souls. The first was the blue-green-red-marked flying coffin containing the unconscious Benson Cloudd; the second was Tregonsee's flitter, with the very much awake Second Stage Lensman from Rigel IV cradled within, steering both ships. And the tandem was in serious trouble.

Almost from the start of their journey, Tregonsee had been confronted with firm resistance. Steadily it had grown in his mind until he had now been pressed to the limits of his powers. His difficulty was really because of Cloudd. The Rigellian had thrown a protective covering over the Tellurian, which had stretched to the edge of collapse his Second Stage capabilities, as enormous as they were. Without Cloudd, he would no doubt have been able to keep himself from drowning in the turbulent seas of mental energy surrounding them. The firm rocks upon which he was fixed to keep himself from being washed away to madness or oblivion were "Two" and "Three." Fastened to them, he was secure. But even so, his companion Cloudd was in danger of being incinerated within his skull.

"Cloudd!" Tregonsee called out. "I'm slipping, but if I slip too far, I will send you back. Don't worry!"

Tregonsee meant his words, although the unconscious

160

Cloudd might not hear them. He wasn't certain, however, that he could save Cloudd, even now. He was, therefore, worried. Seriously worried. The unit-cluster, though life insurance for him, would not be able to save Cloudd.

"Rigellian!" came a soundless thunder vibrating through the dome of his head. "Rigellian! Hold on! Safety lies ahead. Ahead there, you can perceive it now. Build yourself another pyramid with the last whit of your strength, and there you can recover and face your task ahead."

This was the voice of Mentor the Arisian fusion.

The omnipresent and omnipotent Mentor knew the past and knew the future and knew Tregonsee would succeed. But serious setbacks were possible. On occasion, during a crisis, a touch of help was appropriate for those who wore the Lens of Arisia.

Mentor observed that his encouragement brought a burst of speed by the ships as Tregonsee, in fusion with his bristers, fought his suffocation. Mentor felt the determined, though faltering, entity from Rigel IV find his final reserves of strength. No more help was needed, if, indeed, any had actually been given. The Qu'orr had met their match in Tregonsee and his unit cluster.

Mentor knew the story of the Qu'orr and regretted that Arisia had come too late to help them:

Eons before humanity rose out of the primordial slime, when the eternal conflict between Arisians and Eddorians was first developing, there was a race of beings which prospered in a star system called Quilquid. Among the new worlds formed on the edge of the Second Galaxy emerging from the Coalescence was the fourth planet of that system of Quilquid called Quilquidor. All the happy circumstances of nature combined to make Quilquidor a triumph of successful evolution. Its glory came quickly. Before any other beings had developed brains capable of climbing the time-stretched ladder of intelligence, the Quilquidorrians had built a culture of harmony, peace and wisdom. Then, into their simple society of simple desires, fashioned as it was around their nearly attained goal of complete blissfulness, came the evil Eddorian presence.

The Eddorian lust for power was insatiable. After they had obliterated all competition within one universe, they had searched countless others for life forms to dominate. Finally, steering their planet into the Second Galaxy, they had found millions of developing worlds offering prospects for a new Eddorian empire. In the forefront of the developing, fresh life forms were the Quilquidorrians. To them came the insidious Eddorians, turning paradise into hell, introducing them to sin. Their ambitions became wicked, lusting for conquest and pillage, and the technological gifts pressed upon them by the Eddorians gave them the tools. With nuclear fission and atomic power, they planned aggression against the stars. Then fate, not the Arisians, intervened.

The subverted Quilquidorrian intellects became demented. Crazed, they fragmented, fought among themselves, and ultimately came to a planetary war of nuclear devastation. Burrowed within the mountains, thinkers, pacifists, and cowards survived, but decimated by epidemic sicknesses which swept the planet. Abandoned callously by the Eddorians, having no present and no future, they left their stricken planet in their untested spaceships. In a pathetic exodus, they hoped to find some other world and a new beginning.

Drifting through space for thousands of years, successive generations of Quilquidorrians became resigned to an aimless existence. When the three remaining space arks passed into an unknown system, two of them crashed into a moon, killing most, while the third plunged to a fiery death in the molten seas of Tanse.

The ancestors of the Qu'orr, the Quilquidorrians of the large heads and puny bodies, had come to spend the rest of eternity on Tanse Moon One, the blue world, all technology forgotten.

Tregonsee and the other Lensmen would eventually find out most of these facts, but of the Eddorians none would know. The truth could never be revealed to any entity below the third level of intelligence. Soon, though—Mentor knew the future to the last detail—those special babies would come . . .

As Tregonsee, his building of mental force completed, released his bristers from fusion and fell down unconscious, he sent out a message. "Thank you, Mentor!" But he had built well and that message traveled no farther than a few feet, stopped by the pyramidal wall he had just finished.

Hours passed before Cloudd, at Tregonsee's side, was able to shake himself awake and stagger to his feet.

As his eyes focused, he spread his feet and put his hands on his hips. His naked body took the stance of a defiant Tanser barbarian. Dirty and unkempt, with a loincloth of woven leaves and a necklace of strung thorns, he straddled the round head of Tregonsee, whose tentacle tips wound themselves around the human's ankles as Tregonsee's mind reactivated.

The two of them were enclosed in a transparent, ten-foot-high, five-sided pyramid. In front of Cloudd, not many feet away, stood a pyramidal twin containing a tall, immaculate Kalonian in royal robes, his bare blue arms wrapped around his upper chest and neck, hands grasping his shoulders. His eyes and mouth were open, giving his handsome face a vapid expression.

The expression on Cloudd's own face was now also becoming weird. His eyes bulged, his eyebrows lifted, his lips and teeth twisted into a painful, unfunny grin. Tregonsee had entered his mind unbidden. He had become Tregonsee. He himself was the interloper in his own head.

Cloudd knew automatically that the pyramid in which they were had been constructed by Tregonsee and was held together, in place, by the power of that prodigious mind. Somehow, Tregonsee had, almost in a twinkling, duplicated the original which sparkled before them. Without their pyramid they both would be dead or demented, joining the rest of the "lost souls."

From the mind of the Kalonian, on a thin mental thread thrust by Tregonsee between the two shelters, there flowed a story of the Qu'orr.

The ancestors of the Qu'orr corrupted, then ruined, by a malignant alien race, had come from another part of the galaxy on three spaceships, two of which had survived a crash on the moon. Despite the harsh conditions of the inhospitable environment, the Quilqu'orrians, Quilqu'orr, or Qu'orr, as they came to call themselves, managed to survive. Small groups built rock igloos and lived as hermits, growing food on the floors of their dwellings and rarely going outside, keeping in touch with the others of their race through telepathy.

As the milleniums passed, the Qu'orr literally became

rooted to their little patches of ground. The hands and feet that sifted the soil and harvested the fungus foods began to digest and absorb the nutrients directly from the plants and the soil itself. The Qu'orr sat immobile year after year, passing the 'time in mental exchanges and in dreams. The centuries rolled on; their dwellings disintegrated down around them and blew away as dust. The Qu'orr were plant people now, half vegetable, half animal, all sensory nerve endings gone except for touch, but with their receptors for seeing, hearing, smelling, tasting, still within their brains. And within their brains they did see and hear and smell and taste their dreams.

The Qu'orr had become The Dreamers.

Quickly the rest of the story came to Tregonsee. Now the Rigellian Lensman knew all. The mystery of the phantom fleet was solved. He withdrew his mind from the Kalonian's and allowed Cloudd's mind to return partially.

"I can understand up to the point where these plantmen became The Dreamers, Tregonsee. But the rest of the story—you left me behind. You understood it too quickly. I can guess that the Qu'orr found life only in their dreams, their total existence. They probably dreamed and redreamed their racial memories, dreams of their long-gone culture so beautiful before the incursion by the maleficent beings."

"Yes, they did. In their minds, joined together as a unified mental beehive, they found fulfillment. Imagine a half million minds ebbing and flowing, sometimes separately, sometimes massed as one. Life was gentle again—nothing disturbed them—until the Tansers came."

"What about the Tansers? How do they fit in? And, please, Tregonsee, will you relax my face? It aches."

"Sorry, my friend," Tregonsee said, blinking Cloudd's eyes, closing his mouth, and flexing some of the man's muscles. "The Tansers are related to the Qu'orr. Quite closely, as a matter of fact. The Tansers—much like the way the races of Civilization are related to the life spores of Arisia—sprang as a new evolutionary breed from the original seed of the Quilquidorrians. It seems that the other spaceship deposited the essence of the Quilquidorrians on Tanse even as it had been swallowed by the all-pervasive corrosive liquids there. So, as the moon survivors evolved into the Qu'orr, the life forces from the other survivors grew into the Tansers. The two races were distinctly different—yet between them was, still is, a strange linkage of minds."

Tregonsee let Cloudd look out over the barren landscape with Rigellian perception. In the distance, like dried-up stalks of corn, grouped in a bunch here and there, were—? "Yes," said Tregonsee, "those are Qu'orr."

"Different? I'll say they're different!" Cloudd said. "The Tansers are meat-and-blood musclemen with almost no mind, and the Qu'orr, well—"

"But there's an affinity between them. And it's not a good thing."

"But the Tansers, how did they ever get to meet the Qu'orr? Each race is isolated."

"The Tansers came to the moon of the Qu'orr by accident. Blame it on the old Kalonians who had explored this section of space seeking recruits for the criminal army of Boskonia. They found Tanse inhabited with brutes who'd make fine slaves. But the Kalonians had to leave Tanse Moon One unexplored. Too much brain-searing energy emanated from it. What the radiation was they couldn't figure out, so they contented themselves with establishing a slave port on Tanse Moon Two from which they operated their lucrative slave trade.

"Inevitably, a time came when a slaver crashed on Tanse Moon One. Rescue was impossible. The Kalonian masters soon died here, but the score of Tansers, all huge, stupid beasts, survived. They broke off pieces of the local shrubbery, the only possible food on the entire planet, and found it nourishing. Nourishment, however, brought with it a mental bombardment of painful, frightening dreams while awake. Despite the terror and the pain, hunger forced them to continue—Tansers eating Qu'orr."

"How awful!"

"No worse than the distant relatives you humans eat. Anyhow, the Qu'orr were intelligent beings, so they soon manipulated the Tansers into eating only the renewable leafy parts of their bodies, a parasitic situation which each could tolerate. When the Tansers ate the permissible parts they had pleasant dreams; when they ate the forbidden parts they had wideawake nightmares. One day, to the Qu'orr's misfortune, a Kalonian spaceship had a forced landing. Most of the crew went insane and died horribly, but the ship did get away under emergency repairs—with a few Tansers found on board. From them the Kalonians soon knew enough about the Qu'orr and the antipathetic symbiosis to try a new kind of slavery, a slavery of the mind instead of the body. The Kalonians wanted to have those sensual experiences for themselves. Obviously, no uncontrolled thionite dream could be as pleasurable as the directed power of the Qu'orr. Think out the basis of your dream and begin to torture the Qu'orr—the Qu'orr would buy you off with detailed pleasure."

"But the Kalonians couldn't go to the moon. . . . Or could they?"

"They tried. They tried in every way to get here themselves without the impossible mental ordeal. They simply couldn't. With static on all frequencies, no kind of telefactor or probe would work, either. So they sent the original moon Tansers back by pre-programmed ships to uproot and return with living plantmen. The results were unsatisfactory. The Tansers' minds eventually fatally deteriorated and none of the transplanted Qu'orr lived for long. But the Kalonians did discover that although they could not get dreams on command from the moon across space to another planet, they could get the Qu'orr to create visions *outside* the minds of the Kalonians. Three-dimensional images would appear, naturalistic, with movement, sound and smell. And, to the amazed and enraptured Kalonians, the images could be *handled as real objects*! They had all the properties of existence without existing!"

Cloudd looked ahead, into the other pyramid, at the blue Kalonian with the folded arms, frozen in the same position as when he had first seen that figure, hours, perhaps days?, before. A Qu'orr illusion? Surely not a real Kalonian where a real one could not exist?

"The Kalonian is real," Tregonsee said, knowing with a fraction of his mind everything that Cloudd thought. The rest of his mind was solving the problem of the Qu'orr. "He's really real. And remember, labeling the Qu'orr images as 'illusions' is wrong. They are objects that exist, manufactured by very special intellects. As for that poor, half-dead Kalonian, he's a story in himself, which I'll get to.

"Just consider. Put a clear image in the uncomprehending mind of a Tanser, send him to the Qu'orr with a nerve gun or a heat ray for applying torture, and get your desired image by coercion."

"A clear image in the uncomprehending mind...?"

"Qu'orr can create images only of things they understand. Women and sex, or spaceships and weapons. They can create only things having counterparts in reality out of their experience or racial memories. The Qu'orr would create the product for any place chosen, such as on Kresh-kree itself. All the way from Tanse Moon One. A thing that was practically real. But a pattern is absolutely necessary, either from the Qu'orr itself or from some other mental image.

"What a market for such dreams!" Cloudd could see a greater demand for it than thionite. "What fortunes can be made!"

"It doesn't work out that way," Tregonsee said. "If you can have every material thing you want, what do you need money for? Why sell this product which is so difficult to obtain? The Kalonians soon saw that. They would keep it for themselves; that is, for the small elitist group who could exploit this power. But how to harvest the fruits?"

Cloudd saw the answer then. Or had he just now recalled what Tregonsee had so swiftly learned? The Kalonians instituted a religion. They planned it so that a steady supply of mentally immune slaves could be sent to the Qu'orr. So on the moon they called The Moon of the Gods they brought the sacrificial victim and indoctrinated him with their desires. Back to Tanse went the special spaceworthy coffin with the barbarian catalyst. There it would pass along the mental track between Tanse and its other moon through the racial linkage between the two offspring of the Quilquidorrians. Torture a Qu'orr, torture many Qu'orr, and make them give up an image or many images, to save themselves from agony.

"Some Tansers die, and many more Tansers will yet die, but the Qu'orr enslavement grows stronger and stronger."

Again Cloudd saw the logical conclusion. "Spaceships and the phantom fleet!"

"The day some Kalonian," Tregonsee agreed, "caused a spaceship to be created was the beginning of big trouble for the Galactic Patrol." Tregonsee drew Cloudd's attention to the living statue of the Kalonian before them. "There's the genesis of the phantom fleet. Right there!"

"So, if we destroy him," Cloudd began to suggest, "then..."

"No. The idea has been passed on to the Qu'orr. The Kalonian has already done his dirty work. It will have to be the Qu'orr who are stopped."

"But what role does he play? How did he get here? How could he succeed in living here when others had failed?"

"He came in the same way the Tansers came, in a coffin shielded enough to get him through the barrier and on to the moon long enough to accomplish his mission. That was his success, but he, too, has had his life destroyed, although technically his body still exists. He was sent in order for the Qu'orr to make a better warship.

"The first spaceships they made were exceptionally good. They had doors that opened and rooms that could be walked into. The ships could actually carry passengers at the instantaneous speed of thought. But they were not real, so they did not really work. Passengers would die from lack of life support systems or be crushed by unneutralized acceleration forces, nor would they have viewing screens or communication equipment. The ships existed, but they were only just pretty full-scale models. The woman-hating Kalonian male might love his beautiful female creation, as manufactured by the Qu'orr, but she would never serve him by bearing him his children. That was also true of his fake warships. They were supposed to fool by an appearance of powerful numbers, so they didn't have to really work, but unfortunately they did not look as if they really could work. They were much too obsolete-looking; after all, they were reproductions of the quaint, old Quilquidorrian warships. Something more modern and convincing was needed. The Qu'orr had to be given a detailed blueprint to make a realistic warship, one that could be scanned *inside* and *outside*, showing believable engineering and registering *full crews*. Such a warship had to appear sophisticated enough to deceive the Patrol instruments and perceivers, and it had to be visualized solidly enough to make the thought substance firm enough to be mistaken for material substance."

"So," Cloudd concluded the idea, "this Kalonian was the one who transmitted the plan. He was the sacrifice for the Kalonian cause."

"Correct. And a gruesome sacrifice it is, too. He was a special person with an exceptional mind. His father, Helmuth's son, obsessed with the magnitude of his idea, chose the best Kalonian he could find. The victim was his own son, Helmuthyounger-the-Son. Obviously it worked for Helmuth-the-Younger. He got what he wanted: thousands of Qu'orr, tortured into a frenzy, by a hundred or so Tansers, produced the phantom fleet."

"By Klono!" Cloudd could see utter confusion for the Patrol when the enemy could flood space with billions of warships! Any kind of defense might become impossible!

"There is a limitation," Tregonsee said. "One Qu'orr equals one small ship. And there are only a half a million Qu'orr."

Only half a million! thought Cloudd. That could still be disastrous by mixing them with real ships. He shifted his attention from the future to the present. "What's the purpose of the pyramid?"

"It is a mental matrix constructed by the Qu'orr to contain the insane Helmuthyounger-the-Son. He arrived on this moon as a crazy man. The Qu'orr took the images of spaceships from his mind, but the Kalonian did not die. He ran about, throwing his mental waves around like darts and daggers, like slashing sweeps of a cutlass, so they quarantined him. His intellect is gone and, although the brain still lives, he will slowly die, his madness fading away until the danger is gone."

"And the Qu'orr put us in this pyramid to save themselves from us?"

"No. I did it," Tregonsee said. A few of the tendrils of his tentacles tightened on Cloudd's ankles, as if to give evidence that his body was still alive and in a trance by choice. "The assault upon us by the Qu'orr was almost overwhelming. I couldn't even call for help from other Lensmen. We're cut off from everyone beyond this moon—especially so, as we're in this isolation pyramid. This is the first time I haven't been mentally battling the Qu'orr defenses. With help from my

Lens, I discovered the matrix pyramid, recognized it as a temporary haven, and constructed one myself. I dragged your unconscious form in here, just in time, I think."

"What went wrong? I thought I wasn't supposed to be affected? Obviously I didn't pass as a Tanser."

"You certainly were rejected as an outsider. It wasn't the large bulk you have, I'm certain, and my mental disguise of a Tanser, in which I encased your mind, should have worked. Must be that the past assaults by the Kalonians have sharpened the Qu'orr's defenses. Anyhow, I have, during my recovery period since our arrival, formulated a plan which should work. I am going on a reconnaissance utilizing the body of Helmuthyounger-the-Son. I will try to stay in contact with you, but if I don't you must not worry."

There was a blankness, then, in Cloudd's mind, and in front of him he was aware of the near side of the other pyramid shimmering. A blue form seemed to drift out of a blue fog. It was Helmuthyounger-the-Son. The Kalonian, royal blue robes swaying with each stiff step, stalked slowly toward the distant clump of Qu'orr.

Cloudd followed the figure with his eyes, but there was no sound, nor a single feeling or thought wave touching his mind. Minutes passed in an agonizing crawl, with only the blurred vision of a blue figure and some tall sheaves to be seen motionless together. Cloudd's body was aching with tension by the time some movement was seen again. The Kalonian came shuffling back and, as Tregonsee once more dissolved the pyramid wall, returned to his original position. Cloudd felt Tregonsee's presence once more in his own mind.

"As I had hoped," Tregonsee said, his mental projection ended and his mental waves strong within Cloudd, "I hid under the madness in the Kalonian's brain, masking my presence from the Qu'orr. I approached them with no threats, and they treated me with indifference. I was able to study them closely, and made some very profitable observations as to the way they think, so that I might communicate with them. I told them I was a spirit come to save them and that I would return. I am now going to undertake the same trick with you as with my vehicle. My body again stays protected in this mental matrix of a pyramid, and we go out together— your body, my mind over yours. I saw some Tansers nearby when I was out there. We must be alert to the sudden appearance of any imbecilic slaves who are probably wandering around terrorizing Qu'orr with their heat guns. I hope your physical reflexes can match the quickness of my commands, but then I did believe when I chose you that you would measure up. I don't want to, but be prepared to inflict just enough torture, if necessary, to keep the Qu'orr deceived and quiet."

Tregonsee then acted. He altered a solid side of the transparent case to a fluid consistency and pushed Cloudd's body through it. Cloudd was conscious, but Tregonsee was in control. Cloudd could feel the sharp grains of sand through the thin fiber soles of his crude sandals, and the air in his lungs was acrid, pricking his nose and lungs like pins and needles. His feet went up and down, carrying his body toward a bunch of Qu'orr.

The plantmen, who at a distance looked like withered stalks of corn, up close looked entirely different. To Cloudd, each Qu'orr was a cluster of long, flat-bodied snakes joined together by a network of fibers. The end of the bundle of snakes which was spread out over the ground was almost a giant hand, with many fingers buried in the reddish dirt; the fingers were actually moving, pulsating, *clawing* into the dirt. On the top was a bulbous growth, a kind of naked cortex, with thick and thin hairs waving and wriggling like blood-red worms.

As his body approached, the score or more of Qu'orr leaned in his direction, hairs directed at him as if from a gentle breeze blowing from behind them.

Cloudd's hand involuntarily came up with a heat gun in it and his finger rested on the rheostat button, ready to scorch the sides of the snake bodies. Tregonsee's shaped thought wave squirted out into the turbulent ether like a phosphorescent slash from a colored dye marker. "I am the good spirit in the mind of the bad Kalonian, returned once more. I have demonstrated that I am able to control your foe. I am truly the savior who has come to save you. I must know the price you pay to appease the devil. Show me the dream you are making! Picture it for me there on the ground!"

For one nauseating, crucifying moment Cloudd felt the fires of hell consuming his mind and body, accompanied by a despairing, soundless wail, and the gentle, peaceful response of Tregonsee saying, "I give you no pain. I am the good spirit. Show me the dream so that I may help you!"

The agony was gone. Before Cloudd's aghast stare there slowly formed, a few feet off the ground, a score or more of toy-like warships of Boskonian design and markings!

Tregonsee moved Cloudd's body faster than Cloudd had ever thought possible. It ran to the next nearest clump of Qu'orr where Tregonsee repeated his performance.

Again there appeared, suspended in the air, part of a Boskonian battle fleet!

As they watched, glimmering bands of color radiated away from the tiny ships. They began to dart about, spreading through a wider and wider area. Flashes of colors burst silently among them. Miniature fields of force glowed, expanded, contracted. Beams were lancing out now, crossing and recrossing, splashing against invisible fields of force. Red, orange, purple, green, the flares burst everywhere.

The little fleet was in battle with an invisible enemy! Tregonsee threw part of his mind back to the first group and saw the same thing still happening. He merged the two images and they meshed perfectly. They were in a coordinated effort against some foe in some place—some *real* foe in some *real* place! The conclusion was inescapable.

"It's happening, Cloudd," Tregonsee said. "The main Patrol fleet which Kinnison ordered assembled out in that sector where you first met the phantom fleet—well, it's happening—the Patrol is being attacked! Look around at the Qu'orr, as far as your eyes will see, and as far as I can perceive. There will be a half-million Boskonian spaceships facing our comrades! I can almost hear Kinnison saying now, The devils! What are they up to? What's the ace they have up their sleeves? And Kinnison's reaction will be right. What are they up to? Can they really believe a grand fleet of the Patrol can be defeated by phantom warships? There is something much more sinister going on here!"

14

The Doomsday Machine

Kinnison closed the door to his wife's room and stepped over the body of Voddon the Manarkan which lay in a pool of blood in the hallway. His house guards were carrying the wounded P'Keen to the waiting ambulance.

Cris was safe and the threat was over.

"Well done, Tsien," Kinnison said. "Kind of hairy, wasn't it, when Voddon tried to take off the top of your skull?"

"Very!" Tsien agreed, his face flushed sallow. "I still can't believe I had an Ordovik crystal in my head. Or got fourth-dimensional surgery. Voddon sure didn't suspect it had been removed. What a bizarre plan to destroy your children—to kill Mrs. Kinnison, and perhaps you, too, before they were even born!"

"Yes," Kinnison said. "Grotesque and vicious, the idea of a mad Onlonian called Ish-Ingvors, according to what I picked out of the dying impostor's brainwashed memories."

"Who was that impostor?"

"A clever, singleminded jewel thief, I gather, who agreed to impersonate Voddon just to meet Cris. He didn't know the involved plan to get him to Klovia, or that his own identity would be destroyed. He didn't know of the double murder plan. All he knew, I'm certain, was that he had the simple job of getting himself and you together as visitors to Cris. He didn't know his real goal, so neither did we. It was a remarkably insidious plan which only P'Keen, with the special abilities of a variant Manarkan-Ordovik crossbreed, partially sensed.

"I didn't know about the crystal in my head, how did he?"

Kinnison picked up a heavy security box from a table, raised the lid, and showed Tsien the microelectronic ball inside.

"From this transceiver," Kinnison said. "This told him. This is what was implanted in his head, the thing Nadreck removed. P'Keen monitored it as a mental bridge between it and Voddon. P'Keen was literally a circuit breaker. Despite this, Voddon still received his instructions."

"How could that be? You said no alien transmission could get through here in Ultra Prime. Then P'Keen became a safeguard."

"We were fooled. The transceiver did not receive. It had a built-in program for Voddon. These instructions it transmitted, activated by some key phrase, such as Mrs. Kinnison's voice saying, 'Hello, Voddon,' or 'Manarkan star-drop.'"

"Manarkan star-drop?"

"That was what the impostor, the thief, was personally after. The fabulous Manarkan star-drop, Cris's engagement ring." Kinnison picked out of his breast pocket with thumb and forefinger a gorgeously mounted scintillating gem of overwhelming beauty. "Looks real? It's a fake. This is what Voddon was going to switch. It didn't matter to him what ransom or payments Cris was expected to pay under threats or blackmail, or perhaps kidnapping or hostage-taking. He wanted the real ring. The poor fool. He was victimized from the start, doomed to die along with you."

When Kinnison left the shaken Tsien and returned to his headquarters, he was feeling downcast. His personal concerns were over, but he was missing the momentous events out at the frontiers of his realm. His administrative burdens now seemed intolerable. It was his depressing, bureaucratic role to stand by, almost helplessly, while Tregonsee and Worsel and Nadreck bore the brunt of the problems.

Tregonsee had already left for the Kresh-kree-Tanse troubles when Kinnison ordered a full military response to the danger at the galactic rim. Immediately, Worsel and Nadreck, accompanied by Thorndyke and Kallatra, had themselves rushed off for the action. Kinnison gritted his teeth and stayed behind.

The clues had undeviatingly led to that far distant corner of the galaxy, millions of suns away. The troubles had been traced there. The best of the Patrol, ships and men, were on their way and, without a doubt, the inevitable climax was about to happen there. Even the two enemy Ordovik crystals were no longer a threat, no longer promising Kinnison some action there on Klovia. Cloudd's crystal was now far away, deemed too great a risk by its "heating up" to be kept in Ultra Prime. Nadreck was guarding it as if it were an egg about to hatch a demon. As for the other, the crystal from John Tsien's head, it had been untuned and rendered harmless even as the injured P'Keen was fighting for his life.

But though Kinnison now felt like an ordinary bureaucrat, he was no ordinary man. He was a great leader with enormous intelligence, and he was determined to be of help. He had been pondering the problem. Now he acted. He set up a colloquy between the not-yet-dispersed scientists and Ultra Prime's analytical computer, GOMEAC-Mark 34. And then he created a link between them and the front-line warriors.

Within hours he had the scientists on standby, each furnished with a Rigellian or Posenian telepath and a GOMEAC terminal with operators. He programmed GOMEAC with all the available facts and every speculation he could think up or collect. The first results from G-34, a variety of conclusions with weighted probabilities generated by the contributions of the scientists, were further analyzed by him and were sent out mentally from his remarkable mind into the depths of space at a speed which covered a light year's distance in less than a thousandth of a second. No other entity, even with Arisian assistance, had ever projected thought faster.

Worsel, aboard Admiral Raoul LaForge's hastily assembled force of Patrol warships as Kinnison's personal representative, tuned into the link almost at the moment of its creation, well ahead of Tregonsee on Tanse Moon One and considerably before Nadreck who was at his side. The Velantian dragon made the connection even as the main section of the "Grand Fleet" in which he traveled was reaching its peak acceleration in negated space. Patrol ships had been flowing in steadily from all sections of the galaxy to swell the ranks along the line of free flight, based on pre-determined mobilization plans. The properly-designated "Grand Fleet" was not as grand as such ones had been in the recent past, but it was still of enormous size and power. As usually happens after a long and hard-fought war, the victorious side, in this case Civilization and the Galactic Patrol, had allowed its forces to deteriorate too rapidly and beyond prudence. It was a tribute to Kinnison's far-sightedness and organizational ability that the Patrol was able to react as strongly and as quickly as it was doing. Within hours the Grand Fleet would be dropping down into inert condition to support the advance party and to deploy in battle positions. Already the vanguard was in contact with Spawn ships and disrupting the enemy formations, which gave every indication of spoiling for a fight.

Kinnison's sub-etheric mental waves came in firmly to Worsel while the main section of the Grand Fleet was reaching its peak inertialess acceleration. He described the GOMEAC-scientist association and its availability through him for immediate counseling. Nadreck's mind was there for the briefing. Tregonsee, however, had not even acknowledged the call.

"Your primary job, Worsel," Kinnison stressed, "is to anchor your end of this link. I've never encountered greater etheric static, interference, or resistance—from both sources of energy: nuclear and mental. You'll be under strain every second, Worsel, I regret to say."

"You'll have your link," Worsel promised. "Go ahead and worry about something else."

"Thanks, old snake! My first worry is about the safety of the fleet. Make sure Raoul sees the real danger, Worsel. He's not going into a conventional conflict of massed fleets. He must assume that some kind of trap is being laid for us, probably based on black hole force. Maybe it's a weapon, maybe an enormous energy generator. Whatever it is, scan it thoroughly and send back every scrap of information. Use as many Rigellians and Posenians on the battle staffs as possible in addition to the Special Perception Force we created. Worsel, probe the hole. And Nadreck, you probe the surrounding space, multi-dimensionally."

Nadreck broke in. "Pardon me, Kinnison, but I've been

176

prospecting mentally around here since we arrived. And so has Lalla Kallatra, a willing and intriguing pupil who understands I have much to teach her. It is even possible I might learn something about this other dimension where spirits of the dead are supposed to go. Worsel seems to understand. I suggest you get a reading from GOMEAC about this, as I confess, with humiliation and remorse, that I seem to be quite ignorant about things Kallatra and Worsel have experienced, and their talk about phantoms."

"Find anything new, Nadreck?" Kinnison asked.

"No. I would have told you immediately. I've investigated black holes for years, need I remind you, and my reports merely confuse our scientists. Fundamental laws seem to be destroyed, and we haven't been able to sort out the chaos. What more can you expect of me? Certainly if I myself expect to contribute little if anything, then Worsel's perceptions will be worthless. However, if you are expecting only the pragmatic, I may be able to make a small contribution."

"Do your best, Nadeck. I'm sure you'll be of help. We're looking for observable facts. Is there one hole or more? Are they fusing? Are quasars involved? Neutron stars? Coalescing collapsars? Are the holes electrically neutral? Are they spinning? What's the rate of gravitational radiation? What's the magnitude of its mass? What are the characteristics and extent of its charge?" Kinnison's quick list of questions were being simultaneously fed into Rigellian and Posenian minds.

"Got you, Kim," Worsel said. "But space has been scanned where SC-1212G disappeared and we've found nothing. We'll be out of free flight in another hour. Perhaps we'll find something then. Where's Tregonsee?"

"QX. As for Trig, he's reached his objective, but hasn't reported his progress yet. Clear ether."

Worsel, at ease, and curled around Nadreck's refrigerated atmosuit, was idly tickling his nose with the tip of his tail. He exchanged some quick thoughts with Nadreck. Tregonsee behind on his reports? Highly unusual, but hardly worrisome. Worsel tried to worry only about real problems, now that he had healed himself of his Delgonian traumas. And Nadreck, who said he worried about everything, actually worried about nothing; his concepts and personal psychology were hardly humanoid; at the most, Nadreck regretted the foolish exposure to danger in which Kinnison and Worsel indulged themselves, something the sensible Tregonsee would never do.

"I've given some deep thought," Worsel said, "to that crystal you're carrying. I mean the one Cloudd brought us. I've asked myself how its attraction for a hyperspatial tube can be nullified, or used defensively. A tube needs a special energy force to produce an oscillating coherent wave, which rotates normal space in an undeviatingly exact 180 degrees out of phase. In effect, it cancels space by overlapping positive space with negative space. Cardynge has called this 'out of phase rotation,' but an easier visualization is imagining that the *second* dimension has been eliminated. Normal space cannot exist without three dimensions, or four, if you want to get technical, Nadreck, my four-dimensional friend. Eliminate a dimension and *normal* space cannot exist. To do that is to eliminate all normal space from the point of generation of the tube to the point of terminus. Thus, you have hyper space, or non-space, or whatever you want to call it. Distance, therefore, simply doesn't exist from one end of the tube to the other end. That makes the paradox—the tube doesn't exist on the inside, but it exists on the outside. So, we have a tubular phenomenon with most of the properties of a tube."

"Obviously," Nadreck said, unimpressed.

"Well, let's reverse the process. Or re-reverse it, to be exact. Rotate 180 degrees of space another 180 degrees and what happens to the tube? It vanishes. Replace the second dimension and hyper space disappears. Granting this, take another crystal, duplicate the tune frequencies of the original, and reflect the second into the first. The original tuned crystal is neutralized. Or perhaps I should say, the reflected tuning *cancels out* the tuning in both crystals. There it is! Place an untuned crystal against a tuned one, not less than, say, 40 percent smaller, and it will, by harmony, replicate. And silently, invisibly, and instantaneously all danger of a homing device for tube materialization is gone."

Nadreck said nothing.

"Well," Worsel said, "admit it, you amorphous know-it-all. That should become standard operating procedure for the Patrol. That's the answer, isn't it?"

"I admit it," Nadreck said, as if to say he had known it all along.

Worsel flicked his tail and vented a long, hissing sigh.

When the bulk of the Patrol throttled back to normal space, the battle was already under way.

While Nadreck began a systematic search for any indication of the presence of a black hole, Worsel surveyed the tactical situation. No Patrol ships had been destroyed or even seriously damaged. Minor damage had been reported from conventional, though weak, energy beams, and there were no casualties. Nevertheless, the Chickladorian Admiral of Task Force who was being relieved reported that the opposing force was overwhelmingly superior in quantity and quality, and that he had been operating a collapsing defense, unsuccessfully inviting a foolhardy response at minimal risk. His stalling for time, however, had succeeded; the Grand Fleet had arrived; the two sides were now of virtually equal strength.

"Where in damnation did the Spawn get all their warships?" Admiral LaForge said to no one in particular in his war room. "There are ten times as many as there ought to be. Even if every Boskonian warship at large and every armed pirate in this half of the galaxy managed to get out here on the edge of nowhere without being reported, they would amount to only a fraction of the size of the fleet we face. What does M.I.S. have to say about that?" The M.I.S. colonel, once a Null-Treg who now was also LaForge's intelligence chief in his G-2 section, had no excuses. He simply did not know.

Under LaForge's orders the Patrol assembled itself into a double crescent formation, crossing at the centers to form a sort of four-pronged claw in space. Fanning out in front was the same Sector Patrol Task Force which had first skirmished with the phantom fleet with Cloudd aboard.

As soon as LaForge was in position, he began his attack. Operations took its orders directly from the admiral as he formulated them with the linked minds of his two tacticians, Worsel and his G-1 Lensman, Cliff Maitland. From LaForge's mind the orders went directly into that of the chief Rigellian Operations Executive. From him they were distributed mentally to the scores of Rigellian switchboard operators, who in turn flashed them out along the communicator beams to the pilot rooms on every one of the tens of thousands of Patrol ships. As the orders were received and the different units moved into attacking positions, the smaller craft of the Task Force and the screen of scouts for the Grand Fleet slipped back through the ranks, out of the way of the expected explosive spray of interlocking power beams.

There were three ways for Worsel to observe the enemy: eyes, sense of perception, and telepathic input. Using all his eyes, he studied the battle tank, looked at the electronic screen at various magnifications, and did a direct telescopic scan. He compared this to the various impressions from the other observers whose thoughts filled the battle room. Then he projected his perception out into space and swept it back and forth at incredible speed.

The results were utterly confusing to his logical, compartmented mind. None of his comparisons roughly matched. There were five hundred and thirty-eight thousand enemy ships, give or take fifty thousand. Fifty thousand! There was no understandable reason why there should be a ten percent difference between his own perceptive powers and the electronic monitors. Then, too, he could detect only one-twentieth of the life forces which should have been present to man that fleet. The "phantom" issue was definitely present. Even within the three dimensional tank, display lights would alternately flicker strongly or weakly at a five percent rate. Some even appeared and disappeared. Everyone noticed the effect and attempted various explanations, the most common one being attributed to ships slipping in and out of Nth space or the fourth dimension.

"No," said Nadreck. "It's not fourth dimensional. I don't believe its Nth dimensional, either. If anything, it reminds me of an etheric dimensional transference, which is theoretical and never before observed by me."

"Etheric!" Worsel said, a deep ripple of emotion shaking his thoughts. "That sounds nasty, sort of Delgonian, sort of, sort of—" He was reluctant to say it.

"—Sort of like Eichwoor!" Worsel's thought was completed by Lalla Kallatra. To her, a possible return of disembodied

Woor of the Eich from another existence was excruciating, and she knew Worsel, who had joined with her to drive the evil Eichwoor back into its supernatural world, felt the same.

"You have some reason to be superstitious," Nadreck said disdainfully in his peculiarly impersonal, yet smug, manner, "but do not become paranoid." Granted that the Eich had been, were still, among the most baneful of Civilization's enemies, near the top of the Boskonian hierarchy, Nadreck did not find frigid-blooded poison-breathing entities like the Eich and the Onlonians instinctively repulsive, as humanoids did. As for the Eichwoor, he had looked for those dead spirits and had found nothing. "I admit other dimensions beyond our time and space, unknown even to me. But the unknown doesn't have to be unnatural or supernatural. I have been patiently explaining to Kallatra, who listens, even if you don't, Worsel. I have no evidence of a spirit world, therefore I find your fears irrational. Eichwoor ghosts, indeed! They are ghosts from your minds." The story of Kallatra's dead father, the quasi-robot Deuce O'Sx, his ethereal soul on guard in the spirit world against the Eichwoor, was exceedingly irritating to him because so many Lensmen accepted as a fact something Nadreck couldn't prove. "There's more of a young girl's sentimentality than scientific logic muddling your mind, Worsel."

Admiral LaForge did not allow himself to be inhibited by the confusing observations. The orders continued to flow out to his captains. The double crescent spread wider, the tips twisting into an arc, growing into a clockwise circle.

LaForge projected an accelerated countdown—5-4-3-2-1—and a hundred thousand beams of prodigious energy flew from a hundred thousand Patrol ships to smite the enemy. There were three pulses. One flash followed another followed another. Raw energy flickered against the sides of the enemy. Yet there were no spitting balls of force splattering against defensive screens! There were no roiling clouds of thermonuclear fire, no incandescent clusters of miniature suns! Instead, the focal points of power seemed to be swallowed up by a corresponding shield, sponged up without a trace, with answering fire returned fully as powerful. One, two, three pulses. The hundred thousand Patrol ships flared around the edges, rocked and quivered, their screens absorbing the sledgehammer blows with brilliantly sparkling curtains of resistance.

Worsel heard LaForge's amazed and discouraged comment meant for no one else's mind. "Klono, no! How did they do that? They've invented the perfect screen!"

The damage reports were coming in. There were no serious casualties, but half of the attackers had suffered some minor damage. The enemy's ray guns were at least as powerful as the Patrol's, despite any power drain by their screens in dissipating the attack. LaForge's plan to force the enemy into a defensive posture, to minimize the equipment loss and bloodshed on his own side, was obviously impossible.

There was a quick council of war. Worsel made an emphatic request. "Try one more volley, Laf! I think I've noticed something."

Again there was a quick countdown and again there were a hundred thousand stabs of energy, nearly as powerful as the first time. One, two, three bursts. And as rapidly as they struck, there was return fire. One. Then another. Then a third. Again the Patrol ships reeled and shivered, but held to their formation of a cartwheeling circle in the blackness.

"Reflections!" Worsel said. "That's not their fire, that's our fire! They're throwing back our own beams at us!"

Admiral LaForge's response was calm but pained. "That practically disarms us. We can lob some duodec bombs at them, but..." Maitland and Worsel were busy exchanging ideas.

"We sent out about a hundred thousand triple bursts on the first volley," Maitland said. "We got back about ninety-five thousand. What happened to about five percent?"

"Five percent of our fire missed," Worsel suggested.

"Impossible," LaForge said. "Our gunners, with the type of aiming systems we have, should be practically perfect."

"Nadreck and I have the answer to that," Kallatra said, injecting herself into an exchange where she normally should have stayed out. "Those missing beams were fired at ships with fluctuating mass. They weren't really there. They were flickering in and out between reality and unreality. Our beams went into empty space. And five percent was the first time. Our second volley was twelve percent wasted."

The fleet continued to swirl in formation, but space was empty of any missiles or beams. The enemy tactics were identical to the Patrol's. Like a gigantic mirrored twin, the Spawn fleet itself rotated in space less than ten million miles away. Most of the men of the Patrol were watching the Spawn now, each one by his own convenient method.

What they then saw were like visions in a nightmare. The Patrolmen didn't want to believe their eyes, their instruments, or their senses of perception. They double-checked, they triple-checked. The nightmare visions remained.

"Giant spaceships! GIANT spaceships!"

They had suddenly appeared from behind the half-million Spawn ships. The uniform size of the mammoth superships staggered their imaginations.

The largest ships of the Galactic Patrol were basically the maulers. They were gigantic and cumbersome, but they were far more powerful than any other type in the Patrol's arsenal. They were, in fact, mobile fortresses packed with titanic accumulators, their large-throated projectors capable of clawing an enemy's defenses into shreds. When the super-maulers had been built a few short years before, it was assumed that they perhaps would never be surpassed.

These new Spawn ships were five times larger than the Galactic Patrol's finest warships. Except for the lack of GP markings, they were exact but expanded copies of the GP super maulers. Five times larger could mean twenty-five times more powerful!

The Spawn superships hung in space just behind the wheeling front line of the enemy vanguard. The rest of the Spawn ships had faded into the background, by contrast now looking insignificant.

"By Klono's carballoy claws!" LaForge said. "My instruments tell me they are real, but my instincts tell me that they're not!" For the rest of the Lensmen and fleet command there was stunned silence.

"Obviously illusionary," Nadreck said, his thought waves to the others incomprehensibly phlegmatic, "images of our own ships. But there is a substance of reality here. My calculations show that my theory of reflectivity is correct, but my statistical deductions are wrong. We did not lose five percent on the first volley. We did not lose twelve percent on the second volley. We lost double that amount each time. That means that there are some real ships, perhaps five to ten percent, firing their own weapons, mixed up with those which are merely reflecting our power. Therefore, we must be ultra-careful. These illusions of super warships may have some extra sting to them."

For the first time, Kinnison's thoughts came to the others on the flagship. "I've already monitored your speculations and extracted all the facts you've been observing. We'll be going over them here on Klovia. Meanwhile, fellows, Tregonsee has been reached by me and he's making use of his Lens. He's got some facts for you to consider.".

Tregonsee's unperturbed thoughts flooded in on them, boosted by Kinnison, who had assumed the role of informational processor. "I've heard your discussion. Your deductions are right up to a point. Ninety-five percent of the spawn fleet is quasi-real. That is, for every one hundred metric tons, there are five metric tons of conventional warship." As quickly as possible, Tregonsee told them about the Qu'orr and their ships. "So the Qu'orr, using another space-time continuum, are turning energy into matter. The medium is analogous to Nth space, where the laws of matter and energy as we know them are different, but existing as a material place, unlike the Eichwoor's plane of existence. The objects they shape by manifesting ectomatter through mental energy are pseudo-molecular structures of substance, with the appearance of reality without the properties of reality. They therefore have measurable mass, comparable to the original pattern. The enormous energy needed could be derived by their pervasive minds from standard cosmic sources, such as mini-black-holes. But they are ersatz bits and pieces glued together by an alien willpower, reflecting and repelling normal matter as if they had the properties of a solid. Most remarkable is the ability of this thought-matter to absorb and use our own thought-energy to reinforce the illusion of what we think we see."

"All well and good, Tregonsee," LaForge said, exasperated, "but how do I deal with the situation? I've got some real enemy ships out there capable of harming us and getting away with it. Do I simply charge in and fire only when fired upon? Will that do it?"

"No, no," Tregonsee said. "Keep your distance. There's something worse that's developing, and you'll soon know what it is. I'm sending Cloudd to you with further information and advice. Nadreck! Keep sweeping the enemy sector. If you spot anything unusual, put it on Kinnison's net. I'll be busy for some time on a certain planet, but I'll be monitoring the net.

"Anything to say worth delaying me, Kinnison? No? Then I'm clearing ether."

"Tregonsee!" That was Nadreck, breaking off his scanning to call. "Tregonsee!"

"He just cleared ether, Nadreck," Kinnison said.

"It's Cloudd I really wanted. I've some important news, but it'll await his arrival. And I want you to identify where Tregonsee is going; I sense that there's something I should know."

"I'll brief you and Worsel shortly on narrow beam. But what's the important news?"

"Cloudd should know there's a huge massing of datadrones behind the Spawn fleet. They are zooming in from as far away as the First Galaxy. I deduce the scale of this conflict is drawing all of them to this battlefield. Maybe they anticipate Armageddon.

"More to the point, I have scanned the sector of enemy space out to the edge of the galaxy. Most enemy spaceships are imitations made from abnormal matter, nothing more. I have also found controlled vortices in the area with the same configurations as hyperspatial tubes. They are invisible, probably lying just on the other side of Nth space, and probably artificial. Also I find that the super spaceships, unlike the earlier conventional ones, are impenetrable by my sense of perception. I therefore cannot tell what they contain."

"Thorny!" Kinnison called to LaVerne Thorndyke, agitated by Nadreck's findings. "Did you hear? What do you make of Nadreck's report?"

The expert on hyperspace was slow to reply. "I don't know. I think I should transfer to one of our scout ships, with all my portable equipment, and make personal inspection as close as possible. I also want to take along the crystal Nadreck is carrying as possible bait. May I respectfully request authorization?"

"Sounds too dangerous," Kinnison began, but was interrupted by Thorndyke with, "Let me judge that. Laf feels responsible for my protection, tell him you approve."

"What do you think, Nadreck?"

"It sounds interesting. I will go and take Thorndyke and the crystal with me."

"QX. Got that, Laf? Good luck, both of you!"

Within minutes Nadreck and Thorndyke had left the flagship in Nadreck's undetectable speedster, each with their own equipment, and with the special crystal.

As they began their huge circle of the Spawn fleet, Kinnison, finishing his tightly beamed confidential report to Worsel on Tregonsee's complete disclosures, narrow beamed Nadreck in turn.

Nadreck learned what he intuitively expected to learn. It was not the name of Helmuth that surprised him, as Worsel had been. It was the name of Ish-Ingvors. That name perturbed him, shocking him as much as that strange nonchalant Palainian was capable of being shocked. "Shingvors!" Nadreck reminded Kinnison that such was the name of the planet where, in the past, an important Boskonian link with the Eich had been broken. "Shingvors! There is a smell of the Dregs about this whole affair!"

Nadreck cut off without further explanation, beginning to sense that there was an inimical, shadowy yet potent entity personally confronting him. He did not know that this foe, to be his implacable, hidden enemy for many years, was the monstrous Kandron, fugitive from Onlo, the world Nadreck had destroyed. Nor did Kinnison suspect this; in fact, Kinnison did not realize Kandron still lived, now ripening into one of the worst malignancies to confront Civilization in the following decade. If Kinnnison had known, he would have exploded with dismay.

Ten minutes passed with no further communication with Nadreck. The two great fleets slowly circled in silent confrontation, the Patrol almost imperceptibly slipping backward, the Spawn almost immeasurably nudging forward. Nadreck's ship had vanished into the blackness, its cloak of invisibility denying by any means a reading on its location.

The huge Spawn maulers, although each one five times larger than the Patrol's and numbering in the tens of thousands, began to withdraw! From the circling formation they had assumed, they split their ring and in a trailing single file accelerated away in a twisting S-curve, blinking out of sight one by one as they went inert. Simultaneously, one by one new spaceships took their places, reversing the maneuver. There were only a tenth as many—but they were each ten times larger than those they replaced! They were incredibly monstrous!

No one on the Patrol flagship believed that they really existed. But every instrument, every perception said they did!

The sense of an open communication channel with Nadreck and Thorndyke, which had been up to this point firm within the minds of the Lensmen, was gone now. It had been snuffed out like the midnight noises in a forest when disturbed by evil omens.

"Nadreck!" Worsel called. "Give us a sign you're all right! Thorndyke! What's happening?"

The silence in the war room of the flagship, with those monster ships floating on the wall screens, was oppressive.

Then Thorndyke's mechanically projected terror-filled thoughts shot into the waiting Lensmen's minds:

"...a black hole disappearing into another black hole...the mass of a galactic cluster...!"

And at that moment, each monster warship jerked backward into accelerating flight and, bursting into view for all of the Patrol to see, so large and so close as to block out the view of all of the Spawn's titanic super-super-maulers, was an even larger *single* Spawn warship! There had been a tenfold increase of the tenfold increase! The thing was beyond comprehension. By itself it seemed to equal the entire Spawn fleet!

Admiral LaForge shifted his gaze from his glowing tank, in which the image of the thing was suspended like a metal egg confronted by tiny Patrol dots of light, to the electronic viewing screen, where the enormity of the ultra-super-ship could be really grasped, so many thousands of miles away, and he whispered in awe, "A—Doomsday—Machine!"

The link with Kinnison went dead.

15

A Galaxy Faces Death

"It is your decision," Tregonsee told Cloudd. "I will not make it for you."

Benson Cloudd's face was inches away from the hard, sharp bristles and the pliant, fleshy hairs of the pulpy head of the Qu'orr. They undulated across his skin, not touching, but stirring the air to make him feel they did touch. His eyes were tightly closed, as much a natural reflex from the nearness of the living whiskers to his eyeballs as it was to shut out the horrible sight. Was he himself to become a semi-zombie like that burned-out Kalonian?

"It may be painful," Tregonsee whispered in his brain, "but I believe they will stop such pain when they realize you suffer it. If anything goes wrong, I know I can save you, and if your arm is mutilated, I know it can be healed."

Cloudd thought, "QX. QX. I'm on your side, Qu'orr."

"They are just looking for the truth," Tregonsee repeated, calmly soothingly. "They have read me and treated me honorably."

Cloudd raised his right hand and blindly reached out, slowly and carefully, toward the inevitable contact.

"Remember, when it takes your arm, don't draw back. Relax."

Relax? I have courage, but I can't simply turn off my nerve ends and throttle my imagination. His hand encountered the waving stalks. He felt the writhing, snake-smooth things wrapping around his entire arm. There was no pain, except in his imagination. *Take a good look at one of the good guys, me. The Galactic Patrol is on your side.* As Tregonsee had coached him, Cloudd asserted, *The Galactic Patrol is not your enemy. We do not enslave. We fight evil. We are your friends, and we will destroy your real enemies.*"

Cloudd felt his arm going numb. Were they dissolving it? Would he have only a stump left? Would they feel cheated because two of his fingers were already gone?

Will Civilization destroy the Qu'orr? Is the Galactic Patrol its terror weapon? These questions scratched at Cloudd's brain. Thoughts from the Qu'orr!

Like the spinning blades of a fan, where solid pieces moved so rapidly as to be invisible, the thoughts of Tregonsee and the Qu'orr whisked through his head. Time stretched, so that a tenth of a second existed for a minute, and every Qu'orr on the moon seemed to pass in and out of his mind. Cloudd's mood underwent a change. Like a modulating knot twisted within him, he had peace instead of anxiety, harmony instead of conflict.

The Qu'orr were good people. The Qu'orr had listened and had been convinced. The Qu'orr were now the friends of Civilization and the enemy of the Boskonians and their Spawn.

The Qu'orr knew a part of the secret of the black hole weapon. And what they told Tregonsee could save the Galactic Patrol and Civilization.

With care and patience, the Lensman from Rigel transferred that knowledge into the brain of Technician Benson Cloudd.

In a daze, Cloudd was led away from the encounter by the mental grip of Tregonsee. The circulation in his arm was returning; he looked down, half-fearful, and saw the arm was still there, unharmed. Into his brain there was being stuffed all kinds of explanations and information by the Rigellian Lensman, but at the moment he didn't understand and didn't care.

"Listen, Cloudd!" Tregonsee was repeating over and over. "Listen to me!"

The human being sat down on the coffin ship and made a determined effort to listen.

"Cloudd! I am sending you back to the fleet in this Tanse spaceship. I'll drag it into free flight with my flitter. The fleet will have instructions to intercept you. When you recover there from your stupor, you'll recall all I've said."

Cloudd felt himself climb into the coffin, close the lid and fasten it from the inside. Tregonsee was no longer in his head. After some immeasurable time, he sensed his trip begin and, as he slipped past the speed of light, he lost what little awareness he had to unconsciousness.

When Tregonsee had launched Cloudd's ship, he returned to the no longer hostile Qu'orr. No awful mental winds buffeted his mind now. The armistice was in effect. But full trust did not yet exist. In the same manner that the Qu'orr were on the alert, cautious and not completely convinced, so was Tregonsee prepared to defend himself from the unexpected.

"This is Tregonsee. I am your rescuer. I have promised you salvation, conservation, and protection, all in the name of Civilization and the Galactic Patrol. As agreed, my helper has left to begin to keep my promise.

"I understand why you must persist in the creation of warships for your enemies. I understand that to stop now would draw attention to us and cause more torture. So, to free you all, I must destroy the leaders on Kresh-kree, as I have told you. I will carry the body of the Kalonian leader imprisoned here to Kresh-kree. And I will use him to destroy your enemies. You approve of my plan. I expect your help. Do not fail me."

Tregonsee listened. There was no opposition to his words. Neither was there agreement. But there came upon him a *feeling* that what he was doing was right, and that support would come at the climax of his need.

"As I go to Kresh-kree to bring about our victory, the Qu'orr must try to stop the black hole weapon. You cannot? Then, at least, discover for me how to stop it. You were asked to create a black hole, but you wouldn't or couldn't. You were asked to make vortices or hyperspatial tubes, but you again wouldn't or couldn't. But you did examine these things. How are they used? How can they be stopped? You and I together will destroy your enemies on Kresh-kree. But unless the Galactic Patrol survives, far worse can enslave us all."

Again came that *feeling* that he was understood and that he had approval from a consciousness separate from his own.

"I have a helper on Tanse who made it possible for me to come here. This person, who suffered for our cause, awaits news from this moon. Allow me to contact her."

He sensed no opposition, so he called to Ulie and, through her bursts of jubilation, reported his success. "I go to Kresh-kree," he guardedly told her by narrow beam. "I must leave you on Tanse. It's best that you remain to monitor the watchers on Tanse Moon Two. Anything new?"

"Yes," Ulie said. "The Kalonian Spawn are about to wipe out the GP fleet. Seena says they have a new weapon, utterly devasting, using hyperspace and black holes. She has been desperately trying to warn you."

"Thank her," Tregonsee said, "and tell her I will see her there in a matter of hours. Tell her I will contact her when I can, so she must be ready for my call. Tell her the revolution must begin. She will soon take over the planet. She will be Number One, the Overseer. Got that? Nothing else pressing? T out."

There was no interference. The Qu'orr sent not a single vibration across either his or Kinnison's frequencies.

"Before I go, I must communicate with the leader of the force which will protect you, the Galactic Patrol. He is a very great human being, Kimball Kinnison. I will contact him at a very great distance by an indetectable narrow beam of thought which you can monitor."

Without waiting for another feeling, Tregonsee proceeded.

"Tregonsee calling Kinnison." At first, Tregonsee felt some resistance, and then he felt it drop away.

"Kinnison here! Hello, Trig! Are you QX? How did things go?"

"Things are going well, but keep this off the net and confidential for a while. I have found a new race ready to join Civilization and in need of the protection of the Patrol. They are called the Qu'orr. I have promised them our brotherhood. Will you confirm this? They have heard of you, Kimball Kinnison. They were told you were a terrible foe. They wish you to be their friend. They will be impressed by what you say, for they now can sense what is honest and true."

191

Kinnison, solemnly and simply, spoke of the ideals of Civilization, of freedom and equality, of the rule of reason, of the guardianship by the Galactic Patrol of one hundred thousand million planets. He invited membership application to the Galactic Council, and pledged protection in the meantime. When he finished, he paused, but there was no response from the Qu'orr.

"Coordinator Kinnison," Tregonsee said, thinking in precise images for the benefit of the Qu'orr. "I am sending Cloudd to Worsel with facts I have learned. Worsel will send you what details are safe to transmit. Don't let LaForge engage the enemy. Have him keep the fleet far back. The black hole weapon may be in place, ready to demolish us. I'm wearing my Lens, about to go to Kresh-kree to confront and destroy a son of Helmuth, and an Onlonian called Ish-Ingvors. Put me on the mind link after you bring me up to date."

Kinnison brought Tregonsee into the net, after a review by mental wave recorder. Within moments of his briefing, hearing the discussion on the flagship, he reassured the Lensmen with a few words about the deceptive size of the Spawn fleet, although personally cautioning LaForge.

"Anything to say worth delaying me, Kinnison? No? Then I'm clearing ether." Until he had eliminated all Qu'orr suspicions about the Patrol, he would not abuse his communications privilege, charily granted to him by the Qu'orr. That was when he missed Nadreck's call.

The Qu'orr, he learned, were now making spaceships differently, according to plan. Larger ship sizes were formed by grouping five minds to an image, rather than one for one. It was just a matter of time, Tregonsee knew, before the ships would be doubling and redoubling in size, an attempt to demoralize the GP fleet which might even succeed despite his reassurances. He contemplated using the link again and decided he could trust Worsel and the rest not to panic and to figure it out for themselves. The Qu'orr would follow their masters' plan until Tregonsee demonstrated he could keep his promises. He made them repeat their agreement with him, reaffirming that they would act as he had suggested when the time came.

Having held his long-range thoughts to a minimum with Ulie and Seena and Kinnison, Tregonsee departed for Kresh-kree under strict silence, his mental screens firmly up. He did not know the Kinnison link was dead. Next to him, in his cockpit, lay his Trojan horse, the mad Kalonian who was Helmuthyounger-the-Son.

Cloudd's eyes opened and his head cleared. He was half-reclining on the bunk in the Officer of the Deck's cubbyhole. His trip, in the manner of a shipment of frozen livestock, had been painfully fast, and the revival efforts after his retrieval had been akin to a rescue effort. He could see part of the pilot house stuffed with bulky figures of Valerians and Rigellians overshadowing humanoid Patrolmen identifiable as admirals, generals, captains, colonels, and Lensmen. He was imperfectly aware of what had been happening.

On the far wall he saw a close-up projection of a Spawn mauler. Slowly he realized that it was not a close-up picture. It was one ship whose bulk filled thousands and thousands of cubic miles of space! The description "Doomsday Machine" came to his mind.

In a rush the information with which Tregonsee had stuffed him flooded into his consciousness and rushed out like a tide to LaForge and Worsel and Kallatra and Maitland and all the others in the control rooms.

"Don't believe what you see!" was his message. "The Spawn fleet is not of normal space, not of normal matter! Stay away from those ships now; to give battle is to battle ourselves! Be patient! Normality will return! Be ready, for then the real conflict, worse even than this seems, will begin!"

Worsel was the first to recognize the potential catastrophe, and he immediately visualized it for all telepaths to see. If the vanguard of the Patrol moved too close, or the monster-ship jumped nearer, the Patrol ships would be caught as if in an overwhelming tractor beam and sucked toward the enemy. They would pass through the side of the monster-ship—and disappear. The forward elements of the fleet would go first. Then the line of cruisers. The entire battle ring of the GP fleet would be pulled centerward, to condense, then to elongate at the eye of the center. The circle would be an uncoiling spiral, twisting forward into annihilation. The walls of the Spawn monster-ship would dissolve to reveal, within the depths of the ship, the horrifying shell of a revolving globe of smokiness, the sinister event horizon of a black hole! Not only would the Galactic Patrol then be swallowed into nothingness, but planetoids and planets joining the flow, a stream of galactic molasses, funneling down into oblivion! With the nearby stars pulled from their courses, plumes of gases marking their paths to destruction! That section of the Second Galaxy would collapse into nihility, the beginning of the end of the universe itself!

"Look!" Worsel said. "Everyone! Send this picture to everyone. This is the real force we must overcome. This is Tregonsee's warning. This is what Thorndyke went out to discover. We cannot fight. We must not fight. We need collective wisdom. All Lensmen of the fleet! Concentrate with me! Reestablish the link with Coordinator Kinnison!"

A mental thunderbolt of thousands of Lensmen's minds was formed and hurled back toward Klovia, through the interfering cosmic fields. There, in Ultra Prime, Kinnison was staggered by the power which struck his groping mind. The network snapped on again.

Kinnison heard the bad news. His thoughts were icy calm in the face of calamity and he said, "Tregonsee is working on the solution. But he is out of touch and has offered us no guarantee. We, on the entire network, must ponder the problem, find a solution. Where are Nadreck and Thorndyke? Kinnison calling!"

At first there was no answer. Then, through heavy interference, there came the answer, "Behind the Spawn. Near the datadrones."

Cloudd, for the first time, was aware of the concentration of datadrones and received the skimpy details from Worsel.

There was a long silence on the network filled with etheric static.

Thorndyke's thought suddenly burst in upon them. "Nadreck is fighting the interference. Etheric space is being disrupted by gravitons out of Nth space. They're being used to manipulate a cluster of black holes out here! This is the secret weapon we've been worrying about! A terrible combination of things!" Thorndyke tried to continue, "...gone wild! ...out of control!" but more static broke up his thought waves.

"I'm getting to you through another dimension," Nadreck

said. "I agree with Thorndyke; the black hole has gone wild and is out of control. The Spawn fleet seems unconcerned. They may not realize the danger. They want it to grow, but I doubt if they can stop it. Our whole galaxy faces death, Thorndyke is convinced. However, I believe it will only affect the three dimensions of space-time and it will take a couple of hundred thousand years, even over light speed. There's a lifetime for me to figure out a solution. The cost can be held down to a few million planets. No need to panic."

"Be serious! We need a solution now, Nadreck!" Kinnison seemed to shout. "Don't be so damned casual!"

"I am serious," Nadreck said. "I'm being optimistic. You humans get so pessimistic."

"Thorny! Do I understand that there are a number of black holes falling in on themselves?" Kinnison said, trying to filter out Nadreck's provocative laziness. "How do we fight that?"

"We can't." Thorndyke's thoughts came, boosted by Nadreck. "They'll soon be one big mass." The static was still disruptive. "Our primary concern is how to stop the Spawn manipulation. Maybe we can even use it to send the hole out into deep space, away from our own galaxy." The static crashed heavily and then was gone. "Nadreck says you should hear me better now. Do you?"

"Yes, yes. Go ahead, Thorny," Kinnison said. "The network is functioning. GOMEAC and the scientists are connected. What do you recommend?"

Thorndyke launched into a mathematical explanation which even Kinnison wasn't sure he understood. Thorndyke's point was that the black holes, soon to be one, were being steered by Nth-space gravitons controlled by a small fleet of 10,000 Spawn ships within the area of the monster-ship. "So!" Kinnison interjected. "That's the true size of the enemy!" But Thorndyke pointed out to him that the true magnitude of the enemy power, using the black hole weapon, was the equivalent of the size of the monster-ship. That fact turned Kinnison from being momentarily happy into being glum. "Ten thousand Spawn ships are knit into a complex graviton generator-projector, englobing the hole," Thorndyke explained. "Ten thousand hyperspatial tubes are pointed in ten thousand directions at right angles to the axis of the core hole. The ten thousand ships are thus balanced between the two forces, and, by drawing upon the gravitons of hyperspace, can move the hole in any direction."

"This is Cardynge, Thorndyke. I think you're wrong. The control must be electromagnetic—gravitational force doesn't produce enough power, unless it was coming from the other direction, the hole itself. Besides, no tube terminus can be established within such proximity to the mass of the hole. Your theory's impossible."

"There are no tube termini, Cardynge. Each tube is continuous, U-shaped, with each ship at a bend. The termini pass through hyperspace, where they pump gravitons around the bend. The ships siphon off at the elbow the amounts they need. Not one needle of the vortex-detectors has stirred from their zero pins, which demonstrates this truth."

For minutes the two men argued the probabilities of the situation. They rattled off esoteric arguments and complicated mathematical formulas as though they were wired to computers. Every once in a while the arrogant Cardynge would shout out some slanderous insult or make some rude remark. Kinnison tried to be referee, but gave up, not so much because Cardynge referred to him as a "lame brain" and a "gorilla who jumps to the wrong conclusions," but because he thought Cardynge might be right.

"This is Nadreck, and I have something to say," came a calm thought, but so forceful that both of the cantankerous scientists were silenced. "I suggest I blast the Ordovik crystal I have been guarding into the black hole at light speed. A hyperspatial tube should, under the space-warping stresses of the hole, be spontaneously generated. Then, by the mass tractor beams of our half-million ships, we can pump out through the tube enough mass from the interior of the hole to reduce its critical density. After a sufficient drop, the collapsing will be halted and reversed, and the unbound energy within the black hole will flow outward. The black hole will turn white. And we'll have another star cluster. The threat will be gone."

Cardynge, Thorndyke, the rest of the scientists and even GOMEAC became a cauldron of thoughts and counter-thoughts. There was not the slightest doubt that Nadreck's idea was being enthusiastically worked out. The sticking point seemed to be that the GP ships had nothing firm to anchor to, and that the likely result, instead, would be the whole Galactic Patrol Grand Fleet getting sucked down the tube.

The most discouraging opinions came from an almost unanimous judgment by all Ordoviks who were hooked in, including the wounded P'Keen. The Ordovik crystal simply wasn't large enough. Perhaps, in the future, when a hundred thousand crystals could be collected . . .

"Bad news, guys," Kinnison reported. "GOMEAC confirms that the crystal has too little mass. It also suggests that we could definitely run the risk of having the plan backfire— the whole Grand Fleet could be swallowed, even without a push from the Spawn."

Cloudd had been excited by the prospect of his Ordovik crystal saving the Patrol and Civilization. Now he was disappointed. If his crystal had worked, they could also have thrown into the black hole the entire force of datadrones, carrying as they did more potential energy in their antimatter than a fleet of freighters loaded with duodec. That was a way he could get rid of all his headaches in one sweep.

16

Death for the Spawn

"Stand aside! I am Helmuthyounger-the-Son!"

The words were uttered by the half-dead body of the reanimated Kalonian, but the power behind them came from Tregonsee of Rigel. The guard at the golden double doors to the chamber of the Council of Six recognized the royal robes and the handsome, if haggard, face. He knew this was most certainly the eldest son of Helmuth-the-Younger, Number One of the Chosen Six, Overseer of Kresh-kree, so, therefore, he asked for no other identification, nor for the customary written authority to gain admittance. Nevertheless, from his disciplined training in the palace guard, he did not immediately move.

"Stand aside!" Tregonsee commanded. "I will go into the council chambers!" With the palm of the son's right hand, Tregonsee struck the guard a powerful blow across his cheek. The guard obsequiously cringed aside, and Tregonsee arrogantly pushed open the doors and strode within. He immediately slammed the double doors shut, not just to act out his imperiousness, but to shut off observance from the bloody scene he was about to cause.

Under the sculptured crystal pendants stood three purple-clothed Kalonians, their backs to him. Three others lounged on the silken cushions on the floor.

As the heavy doors banged shut, all of them turned their heads to look at the newcomer.

"Son!" exclaimed the one with the two gold ornamental chains around his neck. "Son!" All six were frozen stiff with surprise.

"Father!" Tregonsee said, taking his cue from the reaction. "I am returned from the death you condemned me to." He observed the shaking hands and the darting blue eyes of one whose ruthlessness expects no mercy.

"You are not the man that grandfather was," Tregonsee said, making the voice of the son boom. "Helmuth had a right to speak for Boskone! You have not earned the right to speak for the Bosko-Spawn! I am here for vengeance for myself and justice for the Qu'orr. You sentenced me to a slow death. I now sentence you to a fast death!"

With this ominous pronouncement, each Kalonian instinctively reached for his long knife in the scabbard on his belt. As they were drawing them, five small bursts of energy, with five soft, plopping sounds, came from the organo-mental killer-ring on the left hand of the son, and five Kalonians collapsed to the black marble, dead. The sixth, the Helmuth-father, had, with a blindingly swift motion, thrown from the palm of his hand his weighted knife, and it plunged to the hilt into the breast of his son.

Tregonsee did not allow his body to fall. Even with the heart now permanently stopped, he could keep the organism functioning for several minutes.

Helmuth's son, the first and last of the Chosen Six, fell to his knees in terror, clasping his blue hands together, pleading silently for his life.

"I will give you a final chance, father. Tell me how the black hole weapon works. Speak!"

"Oh, my son, my son! The weapon is not mine. It is the work of Ish-Ingvors! Only he can tell you! One of the chains around my neck is a transmitter which can link you with him!"

"Then tell me how I can end the slavery of the Qu'orr. Speak!"

"The other chain! It is my absolute control over every Tanse slavemaster on The Moon of Lost Souls! Now, son of mine, spare my life!"

The gold double doors banged open, and a purple-tinted-skinned woman in the straps and buckles of a palace guard jumped into the room, followed by another ten men and women in mixed dress. Tregonsee, his Kalonian figure still tall and regal-looking, with the blood running down his chest and dripping on the floor, nodded to the woman. This was S.I.S. agent KK-45. She did not hesitate. Her long knife came out of its scabbard, and, with a slash, she decapitated Helmuth's son.

Tregonsee tried to speak, but his lungs had collapsed. No air was being pushed through his vocal cords. Instead, he said telepathically, "Welcome, Seena. Thank you all." He allowed the body he had possessed to crumple to the bloody floor. "Listen, Seena—

"I am now completely back in my own body, lying in my speedster in the military van. The driver has not moved it from the entranceway where he let you out. Send someone from the room immediately with the two gold chains which Helmuth had. Slip them off his neck and warn the deliverer not to unclasp them. Otherwise the mechanisms will be deactivated. I must fly as soon as possible from this spot, while all attention is focused on the ships in the sky.

"Seena, you are now Overseer of Kresh-kree, and as a woman the shock to all will be great. Follow the plan. Quickly. Form your Council. Proclaim yourself Number One. Later, Lanion will reunite Kresh-kree with the rest of the Civilized Kalonians of the old Thrale-Onlonian Empire.

"The Qu'orr have kept their promise. The great fleet of warships overhead will remain for the next few days while you consolidate your rule. The entire planet will believe they are yours. Their presence alone will insure by intimidation that your revolution will succeed, and when they go you must claim you did it for the sake of peace and harmony and good will."

While Tregonsee's voice was in her head, Seena was wasting no time to complete the take-over, but she stopped to hear the final thought from her S.I.S. boss. "I have the two chains. The Onlonian one is worthless. I will leave the other behind for Ulie to operate. Her work is almost done. Ulie will soon be with you. May you both prosper."

En route to join the Grand Fleet, Tregonsee called to Kinnison, preparatory to linking up again on Kinnison's re-established network. "I've a confidential report to make first to HQ-S.I.S.-Klovia, Kim. Listen in for the up-dated details." With Captain Garner tuned in and Kinnison discreetly in the background, Tregonsee reported everything, ordered more agents to Kresh-kree as help, checked out the placid aftermath of the Meppy unit-cluster situation, directed Ulie to join Seena, and finally: "Notify Chaplain General Chon's office that there are three serious dislocations of the religious frameworks of the planets Kresh-kree, Tanse, and Tanse Moon One. I'm particularly concerned about Tanse Moon One. There's a dangerous lack of sophistication in the Qu'orr, which leaves them vulnerable to unscrupulous exploitation as well as racketeering by zwilniks.

"Everything clear, Garner? Any questions, Kim, before I go on line? Then plug me in."

Tregonsee rejoined the link and immediately asked about the "Doomsday Machine," the description he had overheard just before his landing at Kresh-kree. Had the Qu'orr wiped out the appearance of the monster-ship?

"Yes, Treg," Worsel said. "One moment it was there, blotting out the stars, and the next moment it was gone. Personally, I would have been happier looking at it if I'd known the greater horror it was masking. When it faded away, it uncovered the globe of ten thousand Spawn ships, fixed there like an enormous, porous cocoon cradling a black gateway to hell. Laf dubbed that preposterous space leviathan created by the Qu'orr 'a Doomsday Machine.' The real Doomsday Machine was not the mask, but that hideous, hungry, black beast at its heart. We're hoping you know how to stop it. Do you?"

"Maybe. I heard Nadreck's suggestion about using the crystal for autogeneration of a hyperspatial tube to pump out matter, a good idea. But I also heard the Cardynge and Thorndyke arguments and the Ordovik doubts. I thought I had the solution. The Qu'orr could make a massive Ordovik crystal, just like they made the monster-warship. The radiating matter we withdraw by our tractors is directed against the Spawn ships, annihilating them. But . . ."

"But? What's the glitch?" Worsel asked.

"The Qu'orr balked, believing it too tricky for them.

They create matter out of mental energy from Nth or hyperspace as a direct extension of themselves. A black hole warping might suck the life right out of them."

"You don't think it's too dangerous for them?"

"No, I don't," Tregonsee said. "They're a very timid race, and they're just plain scared. To them their new freedom means they can stop being used and vegetate for a while. They need some time to stabilize themselves. Maybe later they'll help."

"Too bad," Worsel said. "But we've come up with our own idea. If we can throw enough tractors around the Spawn sphere of ships we can drag the sphere together with the black hole into the outlaw sector of the galaxy out there. We'd turn their own plan into a counterweapon. That ought to shake up that Ish-Ingvors, or whoever is running the Spawn show. Cardynge and Thorndyke are working out the mathematics while Nadreck and I figure out our formation. Both Nadreck and Thorny will be back on board, after their scouting mission, about the time you arrive. Nadreck is in danger of building up steam in his refrigerated suit, he's so hot over this Ish-Ingvors, Shingvors revelation, with his hints of some kind of Onlonian Dregs gang."

The impossible picture of Nadreck giving off steam in his almost absolute zero cold atmosuit was too much exaggeration for Tregonsee to take from Worsel. "That's an outrageous exaggeration, Worsel. Nadreck wouldn't raise his temperature by one degree because of unconfirmed facts and rumors. However, he is certainly agitated. Something personal, I feel," he shrewdly theorized. "Probably about the so-called Dregs of Onlo he's been mentioning lately."

Nadreck himself answered. "We will discuss this when you get back to the flagship, my Rigellian friend. Not all Onlonians were destroyed by me, of course, when we overthrew those bandits who ruled the Thrale-Onlonian Empire. There are clues suggesting that my obliteration of Kandron's base on Thrallis IX has produced a band of survivors seeking vengeance against me. They seem more bloodthirsty than their vicious relatives, the Eich. Undoubtedly they're Onlonians. This Ish-Ingvors must be one of them. I am wasting my time talking like this. Ish-Ingvors seems to be as mad as he is evil, so I will simply find him, interrogate him—and then kill him."

"QX, fellows," Kinnison said. "Let's get back to thinking. GOMEAC has been churning out some stats and a few encouraging conclusions. Let's see what we can come up with by the time Tregonsee gets there. And don't overlook the possibility that if you need me I can get there faster than a blistered cat coming out of a bucket of itchygreen."

By the time Tregonsee had reached the fleet and boarded the flagship, the plans had been made and the execution had begun. The Patrol ships had encircled the Spawn and had tried to change its steady course toward the center of the galaxy. The black hole proved to be an unshakable anchor. So a new tactic was being undertaken. The Patrol ships were equally divided against the small number of enemy ships and were to concentrate maximum firepower simultaneously, at Admiral LaForge's signal. The pinpointed target in each case was the weak bend in each hyperspatial tube. The tubes would be fractured—the prediction was that it would be easy, because the tubes themselves were under stress to straighten out from their abnormal shape. Instead of one U-shaped tube, there would be created two straight hyperspatial tubes passing through the ships. The graviton web would be destroyed, and the ships would be doubly hurled from one direction and doubly sucked from the other direction, down into the maw of the hole. Although Tregonsee had formulated his own plan, he agreed this other plan should be tried.

The signal was given, and the ray beams flashed out to slice into each of the Spawn. There were ten thousand sparkling balls of coruscant energy, spitting back only a fraction of the deadly concentrated energy of the entire Grand Fleet of the Galactic Patrol. The result was nearly instantaneous. The Spawn ships imploded in a beautifully precise geometric pattern, into the surface of the hole's event horizon. Their images stayed there, making the black hole a spectacular Christmas tree ball speckled with a perfect design.

There was some wishful speculation that the black hole might be somehow unbalanced and thus destroyed. Admiral LaForge was ready to order his fleet into a full Bergenholm-drive retreat, should the black hole inexplicably shed its increased energy so fast as to reverse itself into a supernova. No such order was necessary, as there was no explosion.

"The enemy fleet is gone, completely destroyed!" LaForge said.

"But the black hole isn't," Worsel said. "The ending of Spawn control over it simply leaves it moving inward toward the center of the galaxy. The mass/energy of those ships has, as expected, added more fuel to the gravitational collapse, producing more geons. Geometric law in quantum mechanics may postulate geons, but it doesn't give us a solution as to how to change the charge of such geons. It's really too bad those Spawn ships weren't made of anti-geons."

"The datadrones are still there," Cloudd pointed out politely. "They contain countless tons of anti-matter. If there were some way by which we could throw them into the sub-surface or heart of the hole..."

"That's it!" Tregonsee exclaimed. "That's what a giant Ordovik-generated hyperspatial tube should be used for! The irreducible gravitational energy stored on the surface of the one-way membrane can be driven into oscillation by the opposing energy particles released in matter-anti-matter reactions. The whole black hole entropy, or degree of disorder, might be exploded into a reversal effect. That's not making anti-geons, but the result should be the same!"

Cloudd was surprised, and pleased, at the commotion his offhand suggestion created. All the high-powered brains in linkage seized on the idea as the best available hope and quickly discussed and organized a plan. Then, together, spearheaded by Tregonsee, they managed to convince a grateful race of Qu'orr to make the giant crystal needed to execute the plan.

"Each one of us," Tregonsee said to all, and especially to Worsel and Nadreck, "has an assignment to handle last moment improvisations. The final decision remains. Who takes charge of capturing the drones and planting the crystal?"

"I'll do it," Cloudd said immediately, previously silent, but now emphatic without being presumptuous. "The datadrones are my babies. I know how to corral them."

"Excellent!" Tregonsee said. "The crystal must be planted deep. Then the Patrol will pressor the drones down the tube. You can use my speedster."

"You're volunteering for a one-way trip, Cloudd," Worsel said, "and I admire you for that..."

"That's hardly something to be admired for," Nadreck said. "Suicide, no matter what the reason, is not admirable. Anyhow, there's no reason why Cloudd can't get back safely."

"Impossible!" Thorndyke said. "I know Cloudd thinks he can approach the surface, fire the crystal down, and pull away before he's trapped. But the small tube that forms will have to be followed immediately by the Qu'orr crystal and the entire mass of datadrones. There's no way that Cloudd can get back through a tube plugged solid with the drones. You must see that, too, Nadreck."

"There is a way," Nadreck said, "by using my speedster," and when he explained to them, they all agreed it was feasible. Cloudd, however, did not feel that the Patrol would be able to pressor the drones into the tube. "I have my own method," he said, and, just as in the case of Nadreck, when he told them they agreed that Cloudd's alternative was better.

So Benson Cloudd found himself alone in Nadreck's speedster, plunging straight into the bloating surface of the black hole. His Ordovik crystal, instead of being loaded for firing from the front missile projector, was held by a tractor field on the nose of the ship. The almost infinite power of the hole made for an almost infinite tensor, and the "mechanism of energization" needed only the tuned crystal for autogeneration; the super-Bergenholm engine of the ship warped, then negated, space, and the hyperspatial field, so naturally created, became the deliberately created hyperspatial tube. The whole concept and execution, in Cardynge's hyperbole, was "child's play." And so Nadreck's ship plunged down the tube. Behind it, following Cloudd in a strung-out line like some titan's pearl necklace, was the front end of the chain of all types of datadrones. They were spinning out from their assemblage, one after another, as fast as the Patrol ships could throw tractor hooks on them and link them together, hook to hook. The technique which Cloudd had developed worked perfectly on the obviously disoriented drones.

Cloudd had his face pressed up close against the chronodometer trying to read the numbers. It was dark in Nadreck's cockpit, built for a Palainian who did not use normal sight. Cloudd was using two slender flashlights, one taped to his temple and another to the back of his right hand, both permanently lighted, to check the instruments and dials. He had only one job to do: monitor the measuring devices. The depth of penetration had been determined and pre-set, but the automated equipment could not be assumed to be impervious to the forces of the fields they would be subjected to, in particular the gravitational and electromagnetic fields. The great fear was that the tube would be carried too deep in its formation and that the datadrones with their anti-matter would emerge beyond the center of the interior, be ejected into space, and the hoped-for result completely lost.

The determinative number, 7849184, was approaching its final display on six separate, synchronized readouts. If the number flashed by, he would manually start the final process. The numbers were turning over erratically, without rhythm, and they blinked past 7849184 before he jabbed the button. The numbers held at 7849199. Was this within the desired range, within the margin for error?

Nadreck had explained how the crystal should be inserted in the black hole and the tactic which would permit Cloudd to escape. "Cloudd doesn't fire the crystal," Nadreck had said, "he takes it inside the hole almost to the core. When the tube is activated, Cloudd stays inside the tube, completely protected, and rides it in as it is forming. The large tube, preceded by the Qu'orr crystal, follows close behind him. He turns my speedster inside out, so that he is facing backward, the crystal still in place in front of him, but now on a reverse course. He races out through the same kind of tube he had been creating. The old tube, on his way in, had been replaced by the newer and bigger one. Now, on his way out, he creates another small tube right up through the big one. A tube within a tube now shields him from collisions with the drones. When the drones reach the center of the hole, emerging from the large tube, the Qu'orr are told to collapse their tube. They aren't a part of the cataclysmic explosion of energy as the black hole turns white, so they're protected. That's why they'll agree to this, Tregonsee. Cloudd will be parsecs away, traveling free, as we all will be. What could be simpler?"

Indeed, what could have been simpler?, Cloudd told himself, the numbers on the chronodometer beginning slowly to reverse as Nadreck's little ship began its fantastically impossible maneuver. Inside out. Front to back. Peeling the solid ship into another direction as he had so often peeled his laboratory rubber gloves inside out off his hand. Reversing it through the fourth dimension! That's how Nadreck described it so matter-of-factly, insinuating that Cloudd was rather stupid to think it couldn't be done. Would he end up left handed? Would his heart pump on his right side instead of on his left?

The time came and he pushed the button. 7849199.

For one long horrifying moment he was outside his body looking at some distant lenticular lights in space. Distant galaxies from another universe! And then he was back in his body, far away from the exploding black star as it mimicked the first days of Creation.

He never saw the great event. It had not even been recorded by any of the fleet, so rapid was the departure from the impending holocaust.

But he was told that it had happened.

He and the Galactic Patrol and its Lensmen had saved the Civilized universe. He felt as if he had been reborn.

Epilogue

~~~~~~

"What we haven't agreed on," Kinnison said, "is just
who the real villain has been in this whole affair."

"Don't be a dolt, Kinnison," Nadreck said, utterly serious, but without malice. "Every sign points to an Onlonian,
not Ish-Ingvors, but someone over him."

Kinnison was tilted back, sunk deep into his leather
chair, his muscular legs stretched out before him, keeping his
knife-creased trousers wrinkle-free. On the soft patch of
gow-bear fur he kept specially for the purpose on the corner
of his massive desk, he rested the heels of his polished gray
boots. This fairly large room, the Office of the Coordinator,
was furnished in an eccentric but remarkably harmonious
manner, which managed to blend the informality of a sports-
man's den with no-nonsense military efficiency. Scattered
around the room, in a semi-circle in front of their leader,
were nearly a dozen assorted entities in nearly a dozen
different kinds of Patrol uniforms, each one typifying race or
special status. The heroes, the special band from the flagship,
had just returned to Klovia to the enthusiastic welcome of
Kimball Kinnison. The other three Second Stage Lensmen
were there, in Rigellian and Velantian harness and in Palainian
atmosuit, a couple of top fleet officers, a couple of scientists, a
female robotoid, and a lowly technician. This was a moment
of triumph for them all.

"I disagree with your conclusions, Nadreck," Worsel
said, splitting his massive jaw with one of his rather sardonic,
tooth-flashing grins, "if only because of their rigidity. You are
too obsessed with pinning the blame on your special villains,

208

the Dregs of Onlo, with whom nobody but you seems to have had any trouble."

"The planet Kalonia seems to be the key," Kinnison said. "I feel the culprit comes directly from there, and hasn't been identified by us. The very fact that nothing is known about Kalonia, as verified by GOMEAC, is exceedingly suspicious. Does the S.I.S. know what GOMEAC doesn't, Trig?"

"Nothing has been held back from you, Kim," Tregonsee said. "GOMEAC has all our information. My biggest disappointment was the deaths of Eramista and the other two Manarkan renegades from Tanse Moon Two. The Council of Six would never have disclosed anything, but Eramista, a mercenary, could have. Pardon me, some of you don't know what happened—that crystal we used, Cloudd's, had been tuned for Eramista to use in an attack. When Cloudd came back out of the hole with it intact, the hyperspacial tube targeted itself on the three Manarkans, and zipped them right into the black hole. A most ironic fate, well deserved, but a sad loss for S.I.S."

"Kalonians have consistently been at the center of the Boskonian conspiracy," Worsel said. "But it seems to me, Nadreck, that if you really want to pick on one of your Z-type cousins, don't pick on an Onlonian, pick on an Eich. There's a whole nest of them some place, if we can just kick over the right stone. Kallatra and I know they're our worse threat. We keep warning about them."

"Not to mention the Eichwoor," Lalla Kallatra said, banging a metal hand accidentally on Worsel's resting pole in her perturbation. Benson Cloudd, across the room, was surprised at how much feminine emotionalism could show through a robotoid body and a mechanical voice. He was still smarting from their conversation just fifteen minutes before, which had made him feel stupid. She had asked if it concerned him that some datadrones had escaped toward Pinwheel DW433 of the rotating jets. "What's that?" he had said, pretending indifference. She told him. "Material shooting off in two cyclic rhythms, making it seem like a star sometimes approaching, sometimes receding." "Oh, *that* star," was his supercilious reply. Then she rattled off in a high speed voice, "Star? Maybe two stars. More likely a ring of matter orbiting a neutron star or black hole at very high velocity, in the red shift, at twenty to thirty thousand miles a second, every half GP year, smack in the center of a wide source of radio emissions from an expanding cloud of a supernova." He said sarcastically, "Thanks for the astronomy lesson. I'll start tracking those drones right away." Then she said, "But that's the point, the tracking rays will be distorted, or completely jammed, and with the drones traveling inert into a system that's gobbling up gas from its companion stars at a prodigious rate, your drones will soon be wiped out." "Well, then," he had said, "I won't have anything to worry about," and moved to the other side of the room.

Cloudd came back to the present. "Eichwoor?" he said, rather loudly. "That's just ghost talk." He bit his tongue; why pick another argument, in front of the greatest Lensmen, too?

Worsel quickly replied, his grin losing some of its humor. "Yes, they're ghosts. But there's nothing illogical about the supernatural. It's just that one can't apply the logic of our physical world to the other plane of existence. Ghosts are a continuation of life-essences, forces existing which ordinarily aren't mixed into our worlds and the lives we live. The Eichwoor are dislocated reality. Ghosts are a manifestation of another universe of the spirit. Believe me, Cloudd—and all you other doubters, like Nadreck—the Eichwoor phenomenon is logical, scientific and explicable."

"I must admit that S.I.S. has no hard evidence of the existence of the Eichwoor," Tregonsee said. "But then we have very little evidence of the existence of the real Eich, and yet I know they exist and are interfering with my agents frequently. I might mention to you, Cloudd, that your very distant relative—if you wish to claim him as such—Dr. Neal Cloud is involved in some kind of mystical experience. He's a recluse somewhere awaiting another Call."

"A brilliant man," Kinnison said, "a Master of Thought, Type Six mind. And no Lensman is higher than a Five."

"What's he doing now?" Cloudd asked, intrigued by this genius who could be a distant relative.

"Studying, pondering, meditating, probably awaiting his Second Call. But happy once more, I understand, with a new companion to share his new life."

Benson Cloudd thought to himself guardedly, aware of the danger of self-pity: Cloud and Cloudd, such tragic lives, there's hope for me.

"Poor man," Kallatra said. "He sounds something like my father, 24of6."

"Well," Nadreck said, ending the digressions, "I want to know what's happened to Ish-Ingvors, and I want to know if the datadrones went with him, and so, Kinnison, let's be done with reminiscences about Eichwoor and Doctor Cloud and get on with your little surprise for Benson Cloudd, here, because I have plans for him."

"Oh? Plans for him, Nadreck?" Kinnison said. "You have his first assignment picked out for him already, you who have always worked alone? Then I'd better delay no longer." Kinnison took his feet off the desk, picked up an imposing scroll with a ribbon, and, in a ceremony so fast and so unexpected as to leave Cloudd bewildered, swore in the new Patrol officer.

"Congratulations, Lieutenant Cloudd," Kinnison said, passing him along to the others for handshakes and salutes and pats on the back. "The next step is Lensman, mark my words."

"Thank you again, sir." Cloudd was genuinely flustered. His new insignia was pinned on by Admiral LaForge. "I will be a good officer. But that's enough. I'll never measure up as a Lensman. And if you choose me, I will decline. I don't like myself well enough for that because, frankly, I'm just not personally worthy."

"QX, then, we'll wait and see." Kinnison laughed. "Should Mentor call, though, you won't back away so easily."

"Actually, I've failed," Cloudd said. "I never found the source of the datadrones. Now I may never do so. However, Kallatra tells me something I didn't know, that they are traveling inert, so I have a chance to catch some more before they're destroyed in Pinwheel DW433. I want to try."

"Now that is what I have in mind," Nadreck said. "Some of us are wasting time. As for me, I'm going to Kresh-kree and uncover the trail of Ish-Ingvors, which may lead to the masterminds. Perhaps, as reported, Ish-Ingvors did go beserk and destroy himself, but that can just be another Dregs ruse. I want Lieutenant Cloudd to come with me. I'll persuade

211

Seena-KK-45, with Tregonsee's approval, to outfit him for a research party. I think the drones are another Ish-Ingvors project which needs clearing up. Cloudd will work one trail, and I will work another. If there's no objection from you, Kinnison, my friend, we will leave. I sense no objection. Come, Cloudd...Yes, Cloudd! Good bye, friends."

Cloudd went around the room, shaking hands with everyone, including the cool, hard hand of Lalla Kallatra. Then he and Nadreck left.

"This is my cue to state my own plans," Worsel said. "I'm going back to Velantia. Bluebelt tells me work has piled up for me at the Institute." He stretched out to his full thirty-foot length and then coiled himself around his resting pole. "But first I deserve some shuteye, which for me," Worsel said, chortling grotesquely within his slim throat, "is very expressive." One by one by one by one by—he retracted his eyestalks and closed his eyelids and went noisily to sleep.

The rest of the Lensmen and Patromen—LaForge and Maitland and Cardynge and Thorndyke, all of whom were human, and even Kallatra who really was, too—lapsed into a babel of trivial, human small talk. Kinnison concentrated on his bureaucratic chores, quietly dictating, as first priority, a report of this meeting for the Galactic Council.

Tregonsee's huge barrel body remained planted in the center of the room, motionless and silent, disconnected from everything around him. His great mind, however, was as thoughtfully profound as it was serenely placid. His minor uneasiness over Nadreck's strange obsession with a new menace named the Dregs of Onlo was briefly considered and put aside for future investigation. Now his mind was ticking over like a precise machine to consider and solve the next great security problem for himself, as head of the Secret Intelligence Services. "So, let me see, for human beings it's nine months. How many more days do I have before Cris and Kim's big event...?"

ABOUT THE AUTHOR

DAVID A. KYLE's experience in writing science fiction goes back to the "Golden Age" of the late 1930s, when "Doc" Smith's works were setting the style for all others. For some years he confined himself to radio broadcasting (owning one New York State station and associated with several others), and then lived abroad. He is now returning to full-time writing. His most recent books are *Science Fiction and the World* (a nonfiction title) and *Worsel the Dragon Lensman* (Bantam). He was a close personal friend of "Doc" Smith's, and discussed future stories with him during his lifetime; some of the concepts discussed are embodied in this novel.

A powerful new novel by one of the most brilliant
and evocative writers of our time.

NEVERYÓNA
by Samuel R. Delany

For Pryn, a young girl who flees the village of Ellamon
on the back of a dragon, Neveryóna is a shining symbol, just out of reach. Her search leads her to the
exotic port city of Kolhari, where she walks with
Gorgik the Liberator as he schemes against the Court
of Eagles. It brings her to the house of Madame
Keyne, a wealthy merchant woman trapped by her
own desires. And it sends Pryn on a journey with a
circle of strange stars, seeking a mad queen's golden
treasure and an answer to the riddle of a city beyond
the edges of imagination.

(#01434-X • A large format book • $7.95)